Larbalestier

Title Withdrawn

OCT '07

ED

Praise for the first two books in
Justine Larbalestier's Magic or Madness trilogy

Magic or Madness

★ "In this fierce, hypnotic novel, character, story, and the thrumming forces of magic strike a rare, memorable balance."
—*Booklist*, starred review

★ "Radiant gem."—*School Library Journal*, starred review

"Justine Larbalestier writes books that stay in your hands like they were coated with Krazy Glue, until you've turned the very last page."—Green Man Review

2006 ALA Best Book for Young Adults
2005 Best Book of the Year, *School Library Journal*
2005 Best Book of the Year, TAYSHAS
2005 *Locus* Recommended Reading

Magic Lessons

"This fast-paced tale delivers plenty of surprises, shadings and shocks."—*The Washington Post*

"[Readers will] race through this second one and wait anxiously for the . . . end of the trilogy."—*Kirkus Reviews*

"*Magic Lessons* does what only the best sequels do: it takes what we thought we knew and turns that on its head."
—Holly Black, best-selling author of
Tithe, Valiant, and *The Spiderwick Chronicles*

The Magic or Madness trilogy
by Justine Larbalestier

Magic or Madness
Magic Lessons
Magic's Child

Magic's
Child

by
Justine Larbalestier

razOr
bill

Magic's Child

RAZORBILL

Published by the Penguin Group
Penguin Young Readers Group
345 Hudson Street, New York, New York 10014, U.S.A.
Penguin Group (USA) Inc., 375 Hudson Street, New York, New York 10014, U.S.A.
Penguin Group (Canada), 90 Eglinton Avenue East, Suite 700, Toronto, Ontario, Canada M4P 2Y3
(a division of Pearson Penguin Canada Inc.)
Penguin Books Ltd, 80 Strand, London WC2R 0RL, England
Penguin Ireland, 25 St Stephen's Green, Dublin 2, Ireland (a division of Penguin Books Ltd)
Penguin Group (Australia), 250 Camberwell Road, Camberwell, Victoria 3124,
Australia (a division of Pearson Australia Group Pty Ltd)
Penguin Books India Pvt Ltd, 11 Community Centre, Panchsheel Park,
New Delhi – 110 017, India
Penguin Group (NZ), Cnr Airborne and Rosedale Roads, Albany, Auckland 1310,
New Zealand (a division of Pearson New Zealand Ltd)
Penguin Books (South Africa) (Pty) Ltd, 24 Sturdee Avenue, Rosebank,
Johannesburg 2196, South Africa

Penguin Books Ltd, Registered Offices: 80 Strand, London WC2R 0RL, England

10 9 8 7 6 5 4 3 2 1

Interior design by Christopher Grassi

Library of Congress Cataloging-in-Publication Data is available

Printed in the United States of America

In memory of Jenna Felice (1976–2001)

and

Marie Wilkinson (1952–2003).

One from New York, the other from Sydney.

I miss them.

Note to Readers

Like the first two books in this trilogy, *Magic's Child* contains both Australian and American spelling, vocabulary, and grammar. Chapters from the viewpoint of the Australians, Reason and Tom, are written in Australian English, and those from Jay-Tee's point of view are written American style. (I was tempted to switch that in this, the final book, so that Jay-Tee talked Aussie and Tom and Reason Yankee, but my editors didn't think that was as funny as I did. Sigh.) To help you out, there's a glossary at the back of the book, which is almost a hundred-per-cent true. Enjoy!

1
Reason Cansino

My name is Reason Cansino. I'm fifteen years old, pregnant, and magic.

I could fly if I wanted. Or turn lead into gold. Or my enemies into frogs. Or anything, really.

I think.

No one knows the extent of my magic. Least of all me.

❋

When I was little, magic was the sensation of water sliding past my skin as I dove into the Roper River and burst back through the surface with a crayfish in my hands. I had no idea how it had gotten there.

Magic.

Sarafina stood on the bank and applauded. "Yes! Yes!" And I felt dizzy and proud.

Or the taste of that crayfish later, cooked in coals, sweet and clean and fresh as dawn, its juices dribbling down our chins.

Magic was long, steady rain after years of drought.

My first taste of ice cream.

Stories of ancestors told around the fire.

Fibonaccis cascading through my body, opening up in a spiral dance into infinity. A spiral I could trace on my ammonite, unwinding from the tiniest point and stretching out into forever.

❀

Before I came to Esmeralda's house, I hadn't known magic was real. Now I know that a magic person can get from Sydney to New York City by stepping through a door, can make light just by thinking about it, or money appear out of thin air, or clothes that are almost alive.

I know the cost of that magic too. Use too much and you die. Use too little and you go insane. That's the choice: magic or madness. Which will it be?

My mother, Sarafina, chose madness.

My grandmother, Esmeralda, chose magic.

So did my grandfather, Jason Blake, and my friends Tom and Jay-Tee.

Each of them with a finite amount of magic, winding down their lives every time they used it. *Tick-tock. Tick-tock.*

Magic-wielders don't live long. Use a little, no more or less than once a week, and you can make it to forty; use a lot, recklessly, and never see your twenties.

That was me and Jay-Tee: reckless with our magic. Me, because I didn't know; Jay-Tee, because she didn't care.

Tom was sparing and careful, because my grandmother taught him how, and because he had tasted madness like an unripe lemon. Better to live short and sane, he decided, than long and mad, like his mother, like mine.

And, of course, you can always cheat. Find someone with magic who doesn't know the rules, ask them for some of theirs. (They needn't understand the question, just so long as they say yes.) Trick them, drink them, live longer. Take a little (or a lot) of their life; add it to yours.

Just like my grandparents did. That's why my mother chose madness.

If you're magic, you can't trust other magic people. They want to drink you dry, steal all your magic, so that you die in seconds and they live forever. Or to fifty even.

Magic is a disease.

2
Bruises

Even Though my belly was full of bacon, eggs, fried onions, and mushrooms, I still reached for my fourth rambutan. I pushed my thumbnail into the thick, hairy, reddish skin, slit it open, and peeled off the jacket, revealing the translucent fruit beneath. I bit in, let the sweet juice explode in my mouth. Doing something as normal as eating kept me from panicking.

Jay-Tee pushed her plate away. She'd eaten the bacon but not her eggs. "What?" she asked.

"Nothing." I blinked. I didn't turn my head away quick enough to avoid seeing how faint her magic was. How close she was to dying.

It was less than twenty-four hours since my should've-been-dead ancestor, Raul Emilio Jesús Cansino, changed me. Every time I closed my eyes—every time I blinked—I saw magic. Light of varying intensity dotting the darkness. Each time my eyes closed, the magic world of light had gotten bigger, stretched further.

I was afraid it wasn't going to go away. I was afraid of what it meant. I hadn't been able to sleep last night and didn't know if I'd ever be able to sleep again.

Most of all, I hated barely seeing Jay-Tee. Tom's light was strong and clear; Esmeralda's was dazzling, but Jay-Tee's was a smudge, fainter than the Milky Way.

"Really nothing?" Tom asked, peering at me. "You don't look like it's nothing." He took another bite of his chocolate muffin. Tom didn't like fruit.

"Yeah," Jay-Tee said. "You look weird. Why do you keep staring like that?"

I was trying not to blink. My record so far was three minutes. Any more than that and my eyes burned and watered until my lids shut. And there were the magic lights again, waiting for me.

"Reason? You're doing it again." Jay-Tee got up and walked towards the back door. She leaned against it, looking back at me.

"Sorry," I said. "You're not thinking of going through the door, are you?"

Jay-Tee snorted. "No, of course not. Esmeralda made it very clear that it's out of bounds. Besides, I don't know where the key is."

"Well, even if you did know, you can't go through. It would use up too much magic. You don't have enough."

"You're saying I can't even—"

The doorbell rang. Jay-Tee pushed off from the door. "I'll get it," she said, heading down the hall, "but you have to tell us what's going on."

"Yeah," Tom said. "You can't hold out on us when something

this big is happening to you. It sucks for us too, you know."
The front door groaned open. "Probably just Mormons or
something."

I closed my eyes and Tom became nothing but shining
magic as bright as the door that led to New York City. I could
recognise his magic now, feel the Tomness of it. He had years
of it left. Jay-Tee had more like minutes. I wondered how much
I had. Did this new magic run out the same way the old did?
Jason Blake seemed to think so, at least about the Cansino
magic he and Esmeralda had. I was something different. Raul
Emilio Jesús Cansino had chosen me. I wished I could see
inside myself the way I could see them.

"What?" Tom asked. "What's *up*, Reason?"

"Nothing. *Really*. What are Mormons?" I asked. From the
front hall I could hear Jay-Tee talking to someone, but not
what they were saying.

"No way," Tom said. "No way do you not know what
Mormons are!"

I hadn't the foggiest. I let Tom go on about how I didn't
know anything, even though he should be used to it by now. I
reached for another rambutan, wishing Jay-Tee's brother were
here. He wouldn't muck me about; he'd just tell me what a
Mormon was. I wondered if Danny would still like me with my
eyes all red and watery and my belly pregnant with our child.
How was I going to tell him about that?

"You really never heard of Mormons?"

"Nope."

"Reason!" Jay-Tee yelled from the front of the house. "It's for you!"

I put the fruit down, wiped my mouth, and headed out of the kitchen and along the hall. In the doorway stood a woman dressed in jeans and a T-shirt, with shortish, feathery hair, and a backpack slung over one shoulder. She was smiling—or rather, beaming—at me.

When I blinked there was only darkness where she was standing.

"*You* must be Reason, then. I thought Jay-Tee was, but that's been cleared up. Not that you look alike. Well, except for the bruises. Were you two in a fight?"

Jay-Tee touched her cheek and I touched my eye at the same time. Jay-Tee's bruise was all garish purples, reds, and blues, a souvenir of Esmeralda's attempt to give her Raul Cansino's magic. She wasn't a Cansino; it hadn't taken.

"Two different fights, looks like. Your bruise is older, isn't it?" she asked, looking closely at my face. I'd almost forgotten about it, days old and faded into pale yellows and browns. I'd gotten it shifting the heavy box buried in the cellar. It had smashed into my face as I prised it free. Inside I'd found the dried-up corpse of Le Roi, my mother's cat.

The woman stuck out her hand.

I shook it, wondering who on earth she was. She caught my expression and laughed.

"I'm your social worker. Jennifer Ishii."

"Hi," I said, thinking, *My social worker?* Then I remembered.

A million years ago, when my mother, Sarafina, had gone mad and been sent to Kalder Park and I'd been sent to live with my grandmother, Esmeralda, they'd said a social worker would be along to check on me once a fortnight. They'd said lots of other things too. I'd been in such a daze I hadn't heard half of it. Yet it hadn't been a million years ago: it had been twelve days.

Two weeks ago I hadn't had a friend in the world; now I had Tom, Jay-Tee, and, back in New York City, Danny. Two weeks ago I hadn't been pregnant. Or known I was a magic-wielder.

"Did you forget I was coming today?"

"Er . . . " I didn't think Esmeralda had told me the exact day the social worker was supposed to visit.

"Can I come in?"

"Oh," I said. Tom came and stood behind me. Jennifer Ishii took a step into Esmeralda's house and offered her hand to Tom.

"And you are?"

"Tom. I'm Tom Yarbro."

"And you were in the same fight as Reason and Jay-Tee?" She leaned forward, peering at his cheek.

Tom looked confused. "Oh, you mean this?" He touched the bandage that covered the long scratch that had come courtesy of my grandfather, Jason Blake.

"She's my social worker," I whispered to him, which was silly, because she was right there.

Way back when, before I'd known about magic, all I'd wanted to do was escape my grandmother and rescue my mother. Back then, I'd planned on persuading the social worker that I was being mistreated, so they'd move me away from Esmeralda. And here I was with an incriminating bruise on my face. All I had to say was, *She belted me! She belts us all!* and Jennifer Ishii would snatch me out of there faster than a croc taking its prey. But I didn't want to go. I wanted to stay in Esmeralda's house. I still didn't trust her. Not entirely. But I felt safe there, with my friends and out of my grandfather's clutches.

"Social worker? Huh," Tom said.

"That's right. It's my job to report on Reason's well-being. How things are going, whether she's well looked after. Is she being fed? You certainly don't seem malnourished, Reason. How's your accommodation?" She looked around. "Seems quite fabulous to me."

"You don't look like a social worker," Tom said. "Shouldn't you be wearing a suit or something?"

Jennifer Ishii laughed again. "We're supposed to look pre-sentable. I don't like suits and I find that most of my clients don't either."

"Clients?" Jay-Tee asked.

She shrugged. "That's what we call the people I check on. So how about these injuries you all have?"

"We were just . . . " I trailed off.

"Messing around," Jay-Tee finished.

"Reason fell in the cellar," Tom said at the same time.

I nodded. "I tripped."

"In the cellar?"

"Uh-huh."

"You were all mucking around in the cellar?"

"Oh, no," said Jay-Tee. "Not Tom and me. We were wrestling and it got a bit out of control. I won, though, 'cause Tom was cut, but I just got bruised."

"No way. You *so* didn't win! My cut's tiny! That bruise is huge. Practically your whole face. You can't call—"

"I see," Jennifer Ishii said, with a smaller smile. "Do you want to show me your bedroom, Reason? Give me a tour of the house? Or do you want to sit down first and have a chat? I think we need to chat, don't you?"

I blinked. Saw the faint light of Jay-Tee, the brighter one of Tom, and the nothing of Jennifer Ishii. She wasn't magic. Like Danny, she was entirely magic-free. No running out of magic for her. No dying young for Ms Ishii. "I guess. We were just finishing breakfast."

I led her into the kitchen and pulled up a stool at the table. She sat down, looking out the windows at the backyard and the huge Moreton Bay fig that, for some reason, Tom and Esmeralda called Filomena.

"Great kitchen. Nice backyard. Do you climb that tree?"

I nodded and then wondered if I shouldn't have. Was climbing trees a bad thing? Would it get Esmeralda in trouble? "I mean, only a little bit. Carefully."

"Do you want something to eat, Mrs Ishii?" Jay-Tee asked, saving me.

"Just call me Jennifer."

"Jennifer," Jay-Tee said, obediently. "There's fruit. Though some of it's kind of weird." She slid the fruit bowl even closer to the social worker.

"Or something to drink?" I asked.

"That would be lovely. Is that orange juice?"

Jay-Tee jumped up, got a glass, and poured her some.

"Thank you," she said, taking a sip. "So you both live here too?" she asked Jay-Tee and Tom.

Jay-Tee nodded. Tom shook his head.

"She's a friend," I blurted. "From America."

"I live next door," Tom said at the same time.

Jennifer Ishii smiled. "That's interesting. I didn't realise you'd ever been to America, Reason. How did you two meet?"

"Her parents are friends of Esmeralda's," I said, quickly, hoping she wouldn't ask to see Jay-Tee's passport or anything. I didn't think Jay-Tee had a passport. Or if she did, it was probably back in New York City, on the other side of the door.

"Do you always call your grandmother by her first name?"

I nodded, blinking again, and found myself surprised once more by Jennifer Ishii's total absence of magic. With my eyes closed, it was like she wasn't there. I dreaded the moment when Jay-Tee would disappear like that.

"We all call her that," Jay-Tee said. "I think she wants to seem younger or something." Jay-Tee held her hands out palms up as if to say, *I dunno.* "At first I thought it was an Australian thing. Reason never calls her mom 'Mom.' But then Tom does. Well,

'Mum' anyways. My parents said I could come visit. Seeing as how Esmeralda's never looked after a teenager before."

"Your parents thought it would be easier for her to look after two?" Jennifer Ishii didn't raise her eyebrow or change her tone, but she was definitely teasing Jay-Tee. I didn't know if that was a good thing or a bad thing.

"I think Mom and Dad were anxious and wanted Reason to have company."

"And how long will you be staying?"

"Dunno."

"How long have you been here?"

"Not long. Just a week or so. I really like it. Back home it's freezing right now. Plus we don't have flying foxes. I really like flying foxes."

"And where is home?"

"New York City."

"That must be wonderful. I've always wanted to visit."

Jay-Tee shrugged. "Yeah, it's pretty cool. Great . . ." She trailed off. I wondered what she'd been going to say.

"Great what, Jay-Tee?"

"Pizza. The pizza in New York's much better than the pizza here. The pizza here has all this weird stuff on it. And it's way too thin. There's even pizza without cheese. It's not pizza unless it has cheese on it."

"How do you get along with Reason's grandmother?"

"I really like her," Jay-Tee said. "It's much more fun living with her than with my parents."

Jay-Tee lied so effortlessly. Her parents were dead. Her mother had died not long after she was born, and her father she'd just found out about. She'd run away from him, hadn't lived with him for at least a year. Neither of her parents had known Esmeralda. I turned away from Jay-Tee before my next blink. I didn't want to see her smudge of magic again.

Jennifer Ishii sipped at her orange juice. "And what do you think of Esmeralda, Reason?"

"She's okay," I said cautiously. She'd have to know that I'd spent most of my life running away from my grandmother, that I'd begged not to have to live with her. I could barely remember feeling like that. It wasn't as if I trusted Esmeralda now. Not entirely. But there was nowhere I wanted to be other than here in her house. "It's not as bad as I thought."

"Esmeralda's ace," Tom said. "She's been great to me. Been teaching me, er, stuff, and—"

"Stuff?"

"Clothes," Jay-Tee said. "Esmeralda taught Tom how to make clothes. He's really good at it." She pointed at my pants. "See those? Tom made them. He's gotten better than Esmeralda."

Jennifer Ishii looked at my pants. "Wow, they're fab, Tom. You wouldn't want to make me a pair, would you?"

Tom opened his mouth and she laughed. It seemed genuine. "Just kidding. So, where's Esmeralda now?"

"At work," I said.

"Does she work long hours?"

"No," I said, but Tom said, "Yes," at the same time.

"Not really," Jay-Tee said. "Tom's just comparing with his dad. He works at the university."

I saw a smile flicker at the edges of Jennifer Ishii's mouth.

"But he's never there," Jay-Tee continued. "He's home practically all the time."

"It's summer," Tom protested. "Da's on holiday. I mean, he's not teaching, but he's working. He's writing a book."

Jay-Tee rolled her eyes. "How long's he been writing his book, Tom?"

"A while."

"Years and years," Jay-Tee told the social worker.

"So?" Tom said. "It's not like writing a shopping list, you know."

"Esmeralda will be back at lunchtime," I said just to shut them up. "She almost always has lunch with us."

"And brings us home yummy stuff to eat like chocolate—"

"And healthy things too," Jay-Tee interrupted. "You saw all the fruit, right?"

Jennifer Ishii suppressed another smile. "So what have the three of you been doing with yourselves over the holidays?" she asked.

We exchanged glances. *Let's see*, I thought, *I fell in love for the first time, with Jay-Tee's brother, Danny. Had sex for the first time, got pregnant, discovered magic was real, ran away to New York City, though back then I didn't know it was on the other side of Esmeralda's back door. What else? Discovered that my mother lied to me my entire life, met my evil grandfather, Jason Blake, also known as Alexander. Had my long-dead ancestor change me into I-don't-know-what. For all I know, he could be living inside me, turning me into—*

"Studying," Jay-Tee said.

"That's commendable. What have you been studying?"

Magic, I thought. *All about magic.*

"Just about everything," Jay-Tee answered. "Well, mostly Reason's been helping me and Tom with math 'cause we're hopeless."

"Speak for yourself," Tom interjected. "My geometry is stellar!"

"And," Jay-Tee continued, ignoring him, "we've been helping her with everything else. Honestly, Ree doesn't know anything about anything."

"Yes, I do!"

"What's a Mormon, Ree?" Tom asked.

I blushed.

Jennifer Ishii grinned. "Ree? Is that your nickname, Reason?"

"Yes," I said, though before I'd met Tom and Jay-Tee no one had ever called me that.

"Do you prefer being called Ree or Reason?"

"They're both fine, I guess." I wasn't sure I wanted anyone but Tom and Jay-Tee to call me Ree. It felt kind of private.

"And when you three aren't studying, what do you do?"

Tom shrugged. "We hang out. I've been showing them around Newtown. They don't know Sydney hardly at all."

Out of nowhere my stomach somersaulted and my mouth filled with bile. I dashed to the downstairs bathroom just off the kitchen. I made it in time—barely—filling the toilet bowl with breakfast. Why was I vomiting? I didn't feel bad or anything.

"Are you okay?" Jennifer Ishii asked from the bathroom door.

I grunted, waiting a moment before looking up just in case there was more.

"Are you sick?" She came and felt my forehead. "You're not hot."

I shook my head. *Just pregnant*, I realised. That's what it had to be. Didn't being pregnant make you chunder?

"She's nervous," I heard Tom say. "She chunders when she's nervous."

I looked up, wiped my mouth with the back of my hand. "No, I don't." I rose unsteadily and flushed the toilet.

"Here, let me help you." Jennifer Ishii guided me to the sink. "Are you dizzy? Does your stomach hurt? Could it be something you ate?"

I wished she'd go away. I rinsed out my mouth, then washed my face and hands. My eyes stung so I closed them. Magic lights everywhere. I opened them again. "Must've been something I ate. But my stomach doesn't feel so bad now." Which was true. The horrible nauseous feeling had completely vanished. I stood up and wiped my hands on the towel.

"Do you want to sit down?"

"No, I'm okay. Really. I feel much better now."

"Are you sure?"

"Yes. Whatever it was, it's gone. I feel fine."

"So it was nervousness?"

I opened my mouth to deny it and then decided that agreeing was better than admitting the real reason. Me being pregnant after less than two weeks under Esmeralda's roof definitely wouldn't look good. "Well, maybe a little bit. I'm not used to social workers."

She smiled again. "I imagine not." I wondered if all social workers were told to smile and laugh as much as possible. They probably thought it relaxed the clients. "But if it happens again, you should see a doctor. Vomiting like that is not normal."

"I will."

"Are you well enough to show me your bedroom now?"

"Okay."

"You're sure you're all right?"

How did I answer that question? "I think so," I said.

"Have you always been a nervous vomiter?"

I glared at Tom. "I guess."

3
Not Alone

Jennifer Ishii walked around my room slowly. I watched her and tried not to seem nervous, though after vomiting like that, I didn't know why I bothered. I'd made Tom and Jay-Tee stay downstairs so they wouldn't inadvertently say anything else wrong.

She ran a finger along the top of the bookcase, opened the glass doors to step onto the balcony. "Nice view," she said, though all you could see was the street and parked cars and other houses, but only tiny bits of green, stunted trees growing out of the footpath with their roots covered over with asphalt.

She peered into the wardrobe. Pushed the winter coat that Danny'd bought me on its hanger. "Don't think you'll get much wear out of that here. You don't have many clothes, do you?"

"No. Esmeralda says she'll buy me some more."

"Do you always call her Esmeralda?"

"Yes. That's her name. We don't really know each other very well yet."

"No," Jennifer Ishii said, smiling. "I imagine not."

She stepped into the bathroom. "This is lovely. Must be nice having your own bathroom."

"Yup. I never have before. It's grouse."

"Are you happy, Reason?"

I blinked, saw dots of magic light and the dark gap where Jennifer Ishii must be standing. Shivered again. Her not being there was spooky. It was as if she were dead.

"Are you okay?"

I nodded.

"Really? You don't seem okay. Or happy."

"I miss my mother." It was true. I missed our life together. I missed her being sane, or at least not scary mad, like she was now. Sarafina had always been odd. Even the little I'd seen of other people had taught me *that*. I missed the time when I hadn't known about magic.

And even though it had only been one night, I missed being able to close my eyes without seeing it everywhere. I missed how I was before Raul Cansino had done whatever it was he'd done to me. I missed being able to sleep. And Danny. I missed Danny, even though we'd only been apart for a day. Jay-Tee had called him, but I hadn't. I didn't want Tom and Jay-Tee overhearing.

"You've been to visit your mother?"

"Yes, twice, but she's . . . she's not how she was." I sat down on the bed.

"Are you getting enough sleep?"

I opened my mouth, then shut it again.

"Those are very dark shadows. And your eyes are so red. Like you've been crying. All the time."

Not like I've been crying—like I've been trying not to blink, not to see the world the way Raul Cansino saw it: a world of magic. "I don't sleep very well." That wasn't true. Usually I slept fine, but yesterday the old man had given me his magic and taken sleep away. I wondered what I'd look like in a week.

"Does she treat you well? Your grandmother?" Jennifer Ishii was peering at my face, at the fading bruises around my eye.

I touched it. "Oh, no, that wasn't Esmeralda. Truly. I tripped."

"In the cellar?"

"I really did. Esmeralda would never hit me." *Drink my magic, maybe, but hit me? No.*

"But she leaves you alone a lot?"

"Oh, no," I said. "I've hardly been alone since I got here. First Tom, then Jay-Tee." And Danny. "The three of us hang out all the time. Like I said, Esmeralda's almost always here for lunch. And Tom's dad keeps an eye on us. You can talk to him if you want." Then I remembered that Tom had said he was spending the morning at the library.

"I'll be doing that after I've talked to your grandmother."

"Also, I mean, we're fifteen, so it's not like we're babies that can't be left alone. My mum had me when *she* was fifteen."

"Which is not recommended. But Reason, I'd be worried about an adult who'd been through what you've been through."

I didn't know what to say. She didn't mean magic. I tried to think what she did mean.

"It must have been awful for you, finding her like that, having to call the ambulance. . . ."

I flashed to my mother, covered in blood. She'd tried to kill herself. I blinked, wanting to push the image away, and saw only magic: Tom's, Jay-Tee's, all the magic objects in this house and next door, and a little way out Sarafina, and, I supposed, Tom's mother too, stuck together in the loony bin, and beyond that countless other magic lights, belonging to who-knew-what or who. I wobbled. Jennifer Ishii steadied me.

"Are you all right, Reason?"

I nodded, though my eyes had filled with tears. They stung but at the same time felt good against my eyeballs. None of them spilled out.

"Here," she said, handing me a tissue. "It's good to cry, Reason. You're allowed to if you want to."

I blinked, saw magic. The tears were already gone.

"Have you had a chance to talk to anyone about what you've been through? Your grandmother? Your friends?"

I shook my head. "Not really." There had been too many other things to talk about: magic and the choice between using it and dying young, or not using it and going mad, the new Cansino magic, the baby growing inside me . . .

"It might do you good, Reason. To talk to someone." She handed me a card. "It's the name of a counsellor. She's a friend of mine. Isabella's very good at listening and at suggesting ways to look after yourself. I'll tell your grandmother about her. It will help you, Reason." Jennifer Ishii looked at me as if she'd asked me a question.

I looked away so I could spare myself the sight of her not being there when I blinked.

"Reason, you've been through so much. It makes sense that you would feel sad, or angry, or nervous, or any of the ways you've been feeling. You need to let yourself feel those things. You need to let yourself rest, take care of yourself. It's still early days. In a very short amount of time, you've been through a lot, including moving into a new house in a whole new city. Just that alone would be overwhelming for most people."

"You won't send me away from Esmeralda, will you?"

Jennifer Ishii smiled again, but it was a smaller smile—realer—sadder too. "Of course not. My job is to make sure you're okay. The last thing you need right now is to be moved again. I wouldn't recommend it unless it was absolutely necessary. You're lucky, Reason. Most kids in your situation don't end up in such a lovely house. Your grandmother has a lot of money, but I have to keep in mind that just because a household is rich doesn't mean it's healthy. Children can be neglected anywhere.

"I'm trying not to be distracted by how gorgeous this place is. It seems to me you need more attention than your grandmother has been giving you. No one should be left alone with the kind of experiences you've been through. You're only fifteen, Reason. You've had to look after yourself and your mother for a very long time. You don't have to continue taking on everything all alone."

She was staring at me. I nodded, not knowing what to say. I hadn't been prepared for her to say something like that. Had I really been looking after Sarafina?

"Promise me you'll go and see Isabella."

"Isabella?"

"The counsellor."

I looked down at the card in my hand. ISABELLA SANDITON, SPECIALISING IN CHILD PSYCHOLOGY. I couldn't imagine taking the time to sit with some stranger and tell them the tiniest portion of my troubles, when I had so many bigger and scarier problems, like what to do about this scary Cansino way of seeing, and how to keep Jay-Tee from dying and bring my mother back to sanity. Not to mention seeing Danny again, telling him about our baby.

I grunted.

"I'll tell your grandmother the same."

I nodded.

"Are you ready for your tests? I was pleased to hear that you've been preparing. It's great that you've decided to go to school even though you don't have to anymore."

"I always wanted to go to school," I said, feeling confused. "Test?"

"This Saturday. Your scholastic abilities test."

"Scholastic abilities?" I had no idea what she was talking about.

"Isn't that what you've been studying for?"

"Um."

"You don't know? You were supposed to be told about this. All the information has been sent to this address. Your grandmother hasn't mentioned it?"

Too late to lie. "Not that I remember."

"She really should have told you." Jennifer Ishii's forehead crinkled and her lips turned down before she remembered to smile.

Another black mark against my grandmother.

It wasn't as if she'd had time to fill me in. The first day I'd stayed locked in my room not talking to her, and then I'd gone through the door to New York City. There hadn't ever been a quiet, let's-talk-about-your-future moment. Well, there had, but it was the more pressing immediate future: *Don't use magic or you'll die; your mother is a liar, your grandfather a very bad man*. Not a single mention of my scholastic abilities test.

"You have no school records, Reason. You have to be tested so we can work out what class to put you in. Obviously, it would be great if you could be placed in year ten, so you'll be the same age as your classmates, but you've had a very unusual upbringing. We can't be sure you'll be able to cope with year ten."

I nodded. "That makes sense."

She opened her backpack, pulling out a sheaf of papers. "Your grandmother should already have these, but just in case. The test is on Saturday. I'll come and pick you up a half hour beforehand. Is that okay?"

I nodded again.

"My contact numbers are here." She pointed to the top of one of the pages and handed me a card. "And this is my card. Same information. Smaller format. Call me anytime. I'm serious, Reason. Even if you need help at four in the morning, I want you to call me, okay?" Jennifer Ishii lost her smile again and stared at me as if . . . I wasn't sure what. She seemed to pity me.

"I will," I said, taking the papers from her. They felt slippery in my hands.

"And if you keep vomiting like that, you must see a doctor. Yes?"

I nodded.

"I think I've seen everything I need to see. You've been very helpful, Reason. I know how strange this must be for you."

There are stranger things, I thought.

4
Pots and Pans

"So, is she putting you in a foster home?" Jay-Tee asked, which made Tom want to smack her. Couldn't she see Reason was upset? He elbowed her instead.

"What?" Jay-Tee turned to glare at him. "She knows I'm joking, Tom!"

Tom didn't know any such thing. Reason had been acting strange ever since she got back from the cemetery. She kept staring off into space like she could see stuff they couldn't. It was creepy. He wasn't surprised she was freaked: after all, that weird monster had done unspeakable things to her in the cemetery.

Well, okay, not exactly unspeakable. Tom could say what had happened: that Cansino ancestor-thing had made Reason pregnant using magic. He wasn't sure he was capable of taking it in without his head exploding. What kind of baby was it going to be? If he were Reason, he'd have been doing a lot more than staring into space.

"I'm okay," Reason said. "It wasn't that bad. Jennifer Ishii seems okay. You know, for a social—"

"For someone whose job is to pry into other people's lives," Jay-Tee said. "She smiles too much."

Tom couldn't help agreeing. She'd definitely been trying too hard.

"She was being nice," Reason said flatly, as if talking was just too exhausting. "You probably have to smile a lot in her job. Show that you don't mean any harm. Something like that."

Tom wondered if being pregnant was making her so tired. Was it extra tiring because there was a weirdo magic baby growing inside her? Or was it too early for it to have any effect? Even without the pregnancy thing, yesterday had been knackering. Reason could be worn out from fighting her grandfather, from all the magic she'd used, from all of it. He touched the bandage on his cheek. He knew he was still reeling.

"I guess," Tom said. "As long as she doesn't take you away."

"She won't."

Tom wished he could be sure of that. He didn't think they'd made a very good impression. "Do you wanna sit down?" he asked. "You look knackered."

"Yeah," Jay-Tee said. "Maybe you should lie down."

"You know, I am kind of tired."

They trooped up the stairs to Reason's bedroom. She lay down on top of the covers and closed her eyes. Tom couldn't help thinking how gorgeous she looked. She opened her eyes and he blushed.

"You okay?" he asked.

"Yes. No." She let out a long breath. "I dunno, Tom. I'm confused, knackered, dizzy."

"Me too," Tom said. "Well, not dizzy, but I'm definitely confused. Did—" He closed his mouth.

"Did what?" Jay-Tee asked, sitting down on the end of the
bed.

"Nothing," Tom said, pulling up a chair and sitting down.
He'd been going to ask if Reason knew that Esmeralda had
stolen some of his magic. But he wasn't sure it mattered anymore, plus it was selfish of him to be still thinking about that
when there was a monster growing in Reason's belly.

They'd spent all morning acting normal. Tom wasn't sure
he wanted to be the one to break the spell. At breakfast none
of them'd mentioned anything that'd happened: not the weird
old monster man making Reason pregnant; not the brand-new,
souped-up, scary magic he'd given Reason, Esmeralda, and
toad-face Jason Blake; not the fact that Jay-Tee had almost
died. Jay-Tee was only alive now because Tom had given her
some of his magic.

Tom could feel all the things they weren't talking about
hovering in the room around them. If he closed his eyes, he'd
probably be able to see them as hexagons and trapezoids and
rhombuses. Not that he was going to use his magic again. Not
for another week.

In the past week he'd used more magic than ever before:
he'd given some to Jay-Tee, then used even more losing his
temper with Esmeralda, and he'd followed that up with helping her way too much in her fight against Jason Blake. How
much magic had he gone through? Was he as close to dying as

Jay-Tee? He didn't feel any different. But he'd never used that much before. Tom had no idea how many days or weeks or possibly years he'd burned up.

And who knew what was going to happen to Reason? What did that new magic do to you exactly? Could she explode from magic overload? Another thought he didn't want to think about.

Seemed like none of them wanted to be thinking about this stuff; they still weren't talking about it. Reason was staring at the ceiling, Jay-Tee at her hands, and Tom at the two of them. "Do you want some water, Ree?" Tom asked at last.

"Yep," Jay-Tee said. "Water: well-known cure for confusion."

"I *am* thirsty."

Tom gave Jay-Tee an I-told-you-so look and went into the bathroom to fill the glass. He handed it to Reason and she gave him a fraction of a smile.

"Do you need anything else?" he asked Reason. He wanted to do *something*.

"I could make you a sandwich," Jay-Tee offered. "My specialty."

Reason shook her head. "Nah, I'm okay. I think I just need to rest for a bit."

"I can imagine," Tom said. "It's tiring just thinking about what happened."

Jay-Tee let out a long sigh. "Yup."

"Um, yeah," Reason said. "I kind of meant on my own. Resting, I mean."

"Oh, sure." Tom jumped up, pushed the chair back.

"Sorry," Jay-Tee said, standing up. "We're gone already."

❁

"She'll fix things," Jay-Tee told Tom in the kitchen. The two
of them were cleaning up slowly, as if the previous week's
events were piled up so heavy on them they could barely move.
It took Tom many attempts to get the butter, three different
jams, and Vegemite into the fridge. He'd lost his ability to
stack. Jay-Tee was just as slow loading the dishwasher.

"That doesn't go in there," he told her, channeling
Esmeralda and resenting it. "No wooden things. No pots or
pans and not the good knives either." Esmeralda was a bit thing
about her kitchen and everything in it. Why wasn't she that way
about her clothes? He thought again about how insanely messy
her bedroom was. How could anyone care more about kitchen
stuff than clothes? At his place they put everything in the dishwasher—but then, they didn't have any "good" knives.

"Hand wash 'em, then?"

Tom nodded, though he couldn't really see that it mattered.
He could feel himself on the verge of a massive attack of the
whatevers. Jay-Tee put the plug in the sink and turned on the
hot water. She squirted dishwashing liquid in. The sink filled
with bubbles.

"You want gloves?"

"Gloves?"

"You know, 'cause the water's so hot."

"Er, okay."

Tom bent down and opened the doors under the sink. *Why had Esmeralda lied to him? Why had she taken his magic without asking?*

"Wow," Jay-Tee said. "It's even tidy under the sink."

"Rita," Tom said. "She's Esmeralda's cleaner."

He handed her the gloves. She put them on and started to wash one of the good knives. Tom grabbed a tea towel, ready to wipe. Good knives had to be dried straight away. Stupid good knives.

"Reason's going to find the fix," Jay-Tee said again.

"The fix?" Tom asked, wondering what was up with Jay-Tee. She hadn't even protested when he said they should clean up. Very un-Jay-Tee.

Jay-Tee stared at Tom like he was bonkers. "To *this*! Reason'll find a way to stop us from going mad. Stop us dying young."

"She what?"

Jay-Tee nodded, looking absolutely certain. "He dreamed about it." Her voice sounded strange. Oddly tight.

"Who dreamed about it?"

"You know. *Him*." She waved a hand, splashing water and suds around. "In New York City."

"Your brother?"

"No! Reason's grandfather."

"Oh, sorry. Jason Blake. What did he dream about?"

Jay-Tee groaned. "He dreamed about Reason finding the fix for magic, for what it does to us."

"Okay," Tom said, pretending Jay-Tee was making sense. "That'd be grouse."

"I'm not using my magic again till then," Jay-Tee said, her voice rising. She handed Tom the knife to dry, her hands trembling, and started work on the frying pan. "I put my magic objects away. I'm not wearing my mama's leather bracelet anymore."

"Are you—"

"I'll probably go nuts in the meantime, but Reason'll bring me back. I'm not going to die young. I'm not."

"Okay," Tom said. "If that's—"

Jay-Tee burst into tears.

For the first time, that phrase made sense to Tom. A shuddering, torn sound burst from Jay-Tee's chest, as if the tears were being ripped from her body. She shook with it. Water ran down her face, soaking into her (Esmeralda's, actually) T-shirt.

Jay-Tee slid to the floor, leaning against the kitchen counter, washing-up gloves still on, soapy frying pan still in her hands. She pulled her knees up to her chest, so the pan was caught between chest and thighs, and continued howling.

Tom stared at Jay-Tee, tea towel in one hand, good knife in the other, with no idea what to do. He hadn't realised Jay-Tee was capable of crying. She always seemed so . . . so not cry-ey. He should do something.

Jay-Tee howled louder, tears and snot mixing as they poured over her chin. Tom put the knife and tea towel down, grabbed a tissue, and started to hand it to her, but she still had wet rubber gloves on; instead, he wiped at her face with it. Within seconds it was soggy. He slid the pan out of her grasp and put it back in the soapy water, then grabbed more tissues and mopped at her face and chin, being careful not to press too hard on her bruise. She didn't stop shaking or howling.

"It's going to be okay," he told her, even though it was a spectacularly lame thing to say. Things were not going to be okay. Jay-Tee would go crazy and join his and Reason's mums in Kalder Park. If they'd even admit her, what with her being American and everything. Once they found out she wasn't Australian, she'd wind up in a detention centre as an illegal immigrant, and then she'd use magic to try and escape, and she'd die.

Now *he* felt like crying.

He wiped at Jay-Tee's tears some more, avoiding the red, blue, green, and purple monster bruise on her cheek, wondering if he should get another box of tissues. He patted her knee, told her not to cry, and several other lameries in as soothing a voice as he could manage.

Jay-Tee's tears began to slow, as if she were a balloon with a tiny hole letting all the air out. He patted her shoulder, slid his arm behind her back. She let her head rest on his shoulder. She sighed and then hiccupped.

"Sorry," Jay-Tee said, then hiccupped again. Tears were still leaking out. Tom could feel his shoulder getting wet, but at least she wasn't shaking anymore.

"No worries," he told her. "It sucks."

She nodded against his shoulder. "Does. Big time."

Tom brought his hand up to stroke her hair. "No point *not* crying, really."

Jay-Tee made an odd sound. It took Tom a few seconds to realise she was giggling.

"Yup," she said, sitting up and wiping her eyes. "Nothing left to do but weep and wail and give our lives up to God. Time to join a convent."

"Speak for yourself!"

Jay-Tee laughed again. "Or a monastery."

"Again, speak for yourself! I'm not religious."

"You're not?" Jay-Tee seemed amazed.

"Course not. Don't believe in God."

"You don't? How could you not? I mean, you're magic! Of all people, you know God is real."

"Excuse me?" It was Tom's turn to be amazed. "How do you make that out?"

"Magic," Jay-Tee said. "You know it's true. Everything in the Bible: water into wine, the fishes and loaves, raising the dead. You *know* it's all possible. More than possible."

"Raising the dead?"

Jay-Tee nodded. "My daddy told me about it. It can be done. It's just not a very good idea. He wanted to bring my mom back—"

"Ewww."

"Yeah. But not when the son of God does it. That's different."

"You're saying Jesus was a magic-wielder like us? You're saying I'm just like Jesus? Isn't that kind of blasphemous, given that he was the son of God and everything?"

Jay-Tee crossed herself. "Of course not! Jesus wasn't just

some magic-wielder! His miracles were a whole other thing.
I'm saying that we've seen—hell, we've *done*—things that most
people would think were miracles. We know miracles are real.
We *know* water into wine can totally be done, so why is it a
stretch for you to believe that Jesus did all the things he did?
Why don't you think there's a God?"

Tom opened his mouth, closed it again. She had a point. A
really good point. His dad was an atheist, and his sister. As far
as he knew, his mum was too. Though seeing as how she was
insane, her opinions on the subject might've shifted. He
couldn't imagine his dad marrying someone who wasn't an
atheist. Da was as likely to marry someone who voted for the
Libs.

The idea of there being a God had always seemed lame to
Tom—fairytales. Why did people need some supernatural
bloke in the sky to believe in? Wasn't the world cool and complicated and amazing on its own? It had never occurred to him
that there might really be a God, yet he had accepted magic
immediately.

Well, of course he had—it was there—in his bones. He had
evidence—bloody hell, he *was* evidence. What was the evidence
for God? Why did magic existing mean that God did? He tried
to think about it the way Jay-Tee did. All right, then: who'd
made the magic in the first place? But wasn't that the same
question as who made life? Couldn't magic have evolved in the
same way as life? Little by little, over millions of years?

But Jesus being a magic-wielder, and Mohammed, and

Buddha, maybe even L. Ron Hubbard—now that explained *a lot*.

Jay-Tee laughed. "You should see your face! You never thought of that before, did you?"

Tom shook his head slowly. The set of thoughts Jay-Tee had opened up were cascading through his mind. He felt dizzy.

Jay-Tee stroked his cheek just below his bandage. "It's not that bad, honest." Then she gave him a quick kiss on the lips. Tom was sure she didn't mean anything by it. Her lips were only against his for a fraction of a second, but he could still feel them there. He'd caught a whiff of her breath. It smelled good. He blushed.

She stood up. "Really, Tom. You should find it comforting. There being a God? That's a *good* thing."

Tom nodded, but he wasn't thinking about God.

5
Feeling That Way

Jay-Tee wasn't thinking about God either. She was wondering why she hadn't kissed Tom properly.

She'd given up magic, which meant that she couldn't run anymore—not the way she wanted to. Worse, it meant dancing was out of the question. She wasn't sure she could live without dancing. No more unraveling into the dance maelstrom, no more being consumed by the beat pulsing through her body, no more drawing energy from the crowd. Thinking about it made her want to cry. And she'd already done enough of *that*. What did Tom think of her now he'd seen her bawling like a baby?

Okay, so she wasn't going to be able to dance or run decently until Reason found the fix. At least there was one thing she could do just fine with or without magic: hooking up.

She liked Tom. He could be annoying—very annoying—but he'd grown on her, and even though he was pale and skinny, he was nice looking. She liked his gold eyebrows and his blue eyes. She even liked his freckles. They were almost as gold as his eyebrows. He smelled good. He had a gorgeous smile. His hands through her hair had made her shiver. Plus, well, it wasn't like there was anyone else. Tom was a good person, and not in a gooey way. He'd saved her life!

Jay-Tee trusted him.

Tom stood up and looked at her oddly. She bet he was still freaked by God existing. His face had looked like something else, which was another reason she'd kissed him. He looked so cute when he was confused, his eyebrows pulled together, his forehead scrunched up, and his nose kind of wrinkled. She contemplated kissing him again, but with more oomph.

It'd've been a lot easier if he'd kissed her back, but he hadn't. Not even a little bit. She sighed. Maybe later, when he wasn't so God-bothered. Or maybe never. She kind of suspected he was into Reason, not her. What a waste. Reason definitely wasn't into him at all, or anyone else for that matter. She was a very young fifteen, which made it so weird that *Reason* had wound up pregnant. But then, she hadn't exactly gotten that way normally. Jay-Tee's skin tightened at the thought of Raul Cansino putting his skinny hands into Reason's belly.

Tom's cell rang. He looked at his pocket, his forehead wrinkling even more, as if he was trying to figure out what the sound could possibly be.

"Your phone," Jay-Tee said, trying not to laugh.

"Oh." He blushed and dug it out. "Hello? Oh, hi, Cathy. Sure. Can you hold a sec?" He turned to Jay-Tee. "It's my sister. I really have to talk to her. I'll come back straight after, okay?"

Jay-Tee nodded. "No worries," she said in her best imitation

Tom Australian accent. He didn't notice her mockage, just gave her a quick wave and disappeared down the hall.

She looked at the frying pan in the sink. But without Tom policing her, no way was she going to do any more washing up. She sat down again, all energy gone. The old man's magic had wrecked her pretty bad. She still ached from it, was still exhausted. If only she could go dancing, then she could absorb the crowd's magic. The net gain was tiny, but it was the only magic thing she did where she didn't *lose* magic. But she didn't have enough left even to get started. It'd kill her.

The rest of her life was going to be dance-free.

Jay-Tee felt her eyes water again. She wiped at them. Nope. She was not going to turn all waterworky again. Enough of that. Not using any more magic meant that she had a future— a bat-shit crazy future, but still, *a future*. All she had to do was sit back and wait for the loopiness to begin. Yay, Jay-Tee. Yay, future. Yay, insanity.

If only she'd kissed Tom properly, not just a peck. Making out would've taken the edge off her hopeless mood. Would've steered her clear of despair. Would've been fun!

Her timing sucked. She shouldn't have tried to mix God and kissing. How dumb was that? She wondered if Tom had ever kissed a girl before. Probably not. From what she'd seen so far, Australians seemed kind of backward.

6
Light and Dark

As i lay in bed, Jennifer Ishii's sadness settled over me, heavy and cloying. She thought I was someone who had to be looked after, felt sorry for. I shivered. I wasn't going to lie around waiting for the Jennifer Ishiis of the world to set things to rights. I could do that myself.

I jumped out of bed, went to the walk-in wardrobe, pulled on the blue jumper Danny had bought me over my T-shirt, slipped on the blue-and-silver shoes, and grabbed the rest of the winter clothes I'd need. All of them from Danny, which felt right: I was going to New York City to see Danny and tell him about our baby. Jennifer Ishii said I didn't have to do everything myself, look after everyone. Danny would help me with the baby.

I slid my ammonite into my pocket, and the pants Tom had made for me shimmered around the stone as it made contact with the soft fabric. Magic reaching to magic. I blinked and the ammonite glittered, a tiny speck of glowing dust amidst the hazy glow of Tom's pants.

Magic everywhere, but none of it as strong as mine.

✹

The kitchen was empty. No Tom, no Jay-Tee. I put my hand on the door to New York City. It moved under my hand, rippling like water, but not angrily as it had when Raul Cansino had tried to force his way through; the door didn't mind my touch.

With my eyes closed, the door became 610 tiny smudges of light woven together with near-microscopic filaments. The sixteenth Fibonacci. Sarafina would like that.

I turned the handle and it swung open to reveal New York City, gray and dim and claustrophobic. I paused between the two cities. Behind me was the intense summer light making the metal coffeepot on the stove gleam: in front, two women walked by, so swamped in clothing that I couldn't tell if they were skinny or fat, black or white.

I pulled on the coat Danny had given me, buttoning it up high, pulled the hat down low, and wriggled into the gloves before shutting the door behind me. My door now, not just Esmeralda's. I could open it without the key too.

When I blinked, my vision was crowded with thousands of lights. New York City glittered with magic. So much more beautiful than the drab New York my open eyes saw.

The snow that remained on the street was dirty, grey, and broken up. Its smooth whiteness was gone, making the city uglier than it had been. At least Sydney had flashes of colour from the flame trees in bloom and the rainbow lorikeets flittering by. New York City looked barren. I watched my breath turn into puffs of condensation; the air tasted metallic.

A yellow car approached. A taxi, I remembered. I held my arm up the way I'd seen Jay-Tee and Danny do. Like magic, the taxi stopped. I opened the door and slid inside.

"Where to?" the cab driver asked. He had lots of matted hair piled up under a yellow, red, and green hat.

"The West Village," I said. "The West Side Highway."

"Any particular place on the highway?"

"I'll know it when I see it."

He looked back at me in the rear-view mirror, like he was going to say something else, but then he nodded and drove off.

There were lots of cars out on the street, most, but not all of them, yellow. There were buses too, and small trucks, people on the footpaths. The last time I had been in a cab had been with Danny. Before we'd had sex, before we'd made the baby growing inside me. How many cells would it have this soon after conception? Sixteen? Thirty-two?

When I saw Danny's building, I told the driver to stop. I paid him with the thought of money in my hand. He thanked me.

❀

I pressed the buzzer. The doorman, Naz, let me in. He sat behind his shiny desk with the high counter, a large grin on his face.

"Hey, Reason. How you doing?" He tilted his head and screwed up his eyes. "Are you wearing new make-up? You look kind of different."

"Thanks," I said, wondering if he could tell that I was pregnant. I could see the tiny traces of magic coiled through Naz's darkness. Not enough to be pretty. "How are you going?"

"Can't complain. Night shift again, which kind of blows. Hey, but it's better than not working, right?"

I nodded.

"So I thought you went back to Australia already."

"Not yet."

"New York too cool to leave, yeah?"

I nodded, opened my mouth to ask about Danny, blushed, and closed it.

"You here to see Danny boy?"

I nodded, feeling very stupid. "Is he home?" I asked in a much smaller voice than I wanted.

"Yup. And he's alone too, which can be kind of rare." Naz winked as if he knew about Danny and me. I didn't know what to say. We'd only been together once. Did Naz mean that Danny had other girls he liked? *Lots* of other girls? What was he going to say when I told him I was pregnant? Would he not want to be with me anymore?

"He just got in. I'll buzz him."

"That would be great. Thank you."

He pressed something out of my sight behind the desk. "There you go. Danny's sending the elevator down."

On the word *down*, the elevator chimed and its doors opened. I walked across, turned back to wave at Naz, and then got in. The lift lurched into life without me pressing any buttons.

"Hi, Reason," Danny said, when the doors opened. His hair was damp. He was wearing a T-shirt and jeans. I could smell his cleanness.

"Hi," I said.

"Your eye looks a lot better than last time I saw you."

I touched it. I'd forgotten I'd ever hurt it.

"Good timing. I just got back from a game and I'm about to take off again." He nodded at a suitcase sitting near the door.

"Huh," I said. I'd forgotten how beautiful Danny was. His eyelashes were long, thick, and curved up towards his eyebrows. "You're going away?"

"Yup. I'm going to see Julieta."

"You're going to *Sydney?*"

Danny nodded. "I fly out tonight. I'm all packed and ready to go. I figured I'd surprise her." He paused to look at me. "You think that's a good idea?"

"You're going all the way to Sydney?" I tried to imagine Danny in Esmeralda's house. I failed.

He smiled and the smile got into his eyes. It made him even more beautiful. "Well, that door of yours doesn't work for me, remember? So you think Julieta will like the surprise?"

"I guess," I said. I was wondering what would happen if Danny got there and she was already dead. How long did it take to fly to Sydney from New York? "I'm sure she'd love it. She misses you."

He smiled wider. "Good. I'm glad. So how come you're back in the city?"

"I, um . . ." I said, not ready to just blurt it out. "It's sort of complicated."

"Do you need somewhere to stay? If you want, you can stay here while I'm gone. Are you okay?" he asked, and I couldn't help watching the way his lips moved. I blushed. I'd kissed that mouth. "Julieta said you got home fine. And that old guy is dead and won't bother you anymore. That's true, right?"

"Yes, he's dead," I said. "And I'm fine." I wasn't sure if either statement was true.

"So, ah, why are you back in the city? Things haven't gone wrong with your grandmother, have they?"

"No, no. Esmeralda's been great. Not so evil after all." But still not entirely good either.

"Well, that's good. Should I give you the keys? You really can stay if you need to. Thing is, though, I gotta shoot pretty soon. Plane to catch."

"Right, uh, thanks." In my Cansino vision he was invisible. It was like he didn't exist. I almost told him how lucky he was . . . *not* to be magic.

"You want something to drink? I got soda. You like Coke?"

"No, thanks."

"Huh. Jay-Tee said you've got a lot more magic now. That you're some kind of superhero? What's that like? You don't look any different."

"Um."

"You do know what a superhero is, right?"

"Um."

Danny laughed. "Superman? Batman? Flying, fighting bad guys. Stuff like that."

"I can't fly," I said. Though I had no idea if I could or not. I hadn't tried.

"Well, that's something. That shit would be too weird." He smiled at me, waiting for me to say something. I couldn't imagine us doing any of the things we'd done. I blushed to think of going into his bedroom, touching him. How had I been able to do that? I blushed again.

"So, uh, what was that complicated thing you wanted to talk about?"

"Er." I shook my head, wondering how to go about telling him. It was so strange. This was a person I'd touched. My skin had been naked against his. He had been inside me. Why couldn't I talk to him without blushing?

"You sure you're not thirsty?"

"*Positive.*"

"Well, I am. D'you mind?"

"No. I mean, do you have time? How long before your plane leaves?"

"I got fifteen minutes before the car gets here," he said, walking across to the kitchen area. "Time enough for a beer."

I sat down on one of the stools and watched him take one out of the fridge. I could see the muscles in his arms. Strong and beautiful. He smelt good, too. I wondered what our child

would be like. As dark as me, or a shade lighter, like Danny? I
hoped it would have Danny's eyelashes. His mouth too. If our
child was human, that was. If it didn't come out looking like
old man Cansino.

Neither of us said anything for a while. He sat sipping
his beer and drumming his fingers against the table, like
the basketball game hadn't gotten rid of enough nervous
energy.

My nervousness multiplied. Danny wasn't going to be
happy to hear about the baby. Especially when I told him I
couldn't be sure it would be human.

"So, uh, Reason? There's some stuff I have to talk to you
about too. Other than Julieta, I mean. Well, it's sort of got
some to do with Julieta, of course."

"Yes?"

"But you can tell me your thing first if you want."

I blushed. "I don't mind."

He took another sip of his beer. "Well, you know I like you,
right?"

I nodded, suddenly afraid of what he was going to say. He
wasn't looking at me.

"So it's my fault. Totally my fault. I accept that and I feel
really, really bad, 'cause you're a nice kid and, ah, it was, you
know, ah . . . You sure you don't want something to drink?
Soda? Water?"

"I'm sure." What did he think was his fault?

"You got any thoughts?"

"Thoughts?" I had lots of them. But mostly I just wished I knew what he was talking about.

"About what I'm saying?"

"Well, um, I like you too?"

Danny looked down. "Well, that's good, seeing as how you and Julieta are getting real close. Like sisters, she said. Um, is that how you feel about her? Like a sister?"

"I guess." I'd never had a sister before, but then I'd never had a friend either. It had always been just me and Sarafina. Other people were there to work for; or buy water, food, and supplies from; or tell us if the flood levels had dropped and we could cross the bar up ahead. Money, food, and information, but not friendship. "It would be nice to have a sister."

"It's great that you and Julieta are friends. She's been through a lot, you know? Our dad was real rough on her. And, well, you're the first friend she's had in a long time, so that's great and I'm really happy. I don't want her to lose a friend. I need to know that you're going to stay friends with her."

"Of course, Danny. Why wouldn't I?" My stomach felt weird. I wondered if I was going to chunder again.

"Well, right, yeah. See, that's the thing. I do, you know, I do like you. You're a great kid. But you're young. Really young. You're only fifteen! I'm eighteen, Reason."

"That's only three years—"

"It's a big difference. Trust me. And . . . " He took another long sip of his beer, finished it, and then crumpled the can in his left hand, flattening it into a metal disc. He wasn't acting as though he liked me, more like he wished I'd go away. "What happened was nice, but it was a mistake. It shouldn't have happened. I'm going to be starting college and you're still in high school—"

"No, I'm not. I've never been to high school."

"Right. I forgot. Well, you know, you *should* be in high school. So should Julieta. It's what I want for her. It's what Dad wanted: for her to be educated, make a life for herself—"

"She's dying," I said. "She doesn't have much of a life left."

Danny stood up abruptly, opened the fridge, pulled out another beer can, but instead of opening it, he held the can against his cheek. He looked like he might cry.

"She has hardly any magic left. Esmeralda tried to save her, but . . . " The Cansino magic hadn't worked for her because she wasn't a Cansino. She had only the normal kind of magic, and it was almost gone.

"And she's there," Danny said, "and I'm here." He glanced at his watch. "But not for much longer. Soon I'll be on the plane. I'm even gladder I'm going now. If she doesn't have much time, I *have* to be there. She's my sister."

I nodded. I felt the same about being separated from Sarafina.

He looked across at me, met my eyes. "I keep thinking that it's not true, you know? When I talk to her on the phone she's Julieta: full of spunk, buzzing. Not dead girl walking at all . . . " He rolled the can across his forehead then back again. "You're

sure she won't get mad at me for coming to visit? I really need
to be with her, you know?"

"She'll be happy. You can stay at Esmeralda's. It's a really
big house."

"Right," he said. "Shit. I totally forgot about that. What's
the address? Hang on a second." He dashed into his bedroom
and returned with paper and a pen.

I told him and he wrote it down. "Great," he said. "Glad I
got that sorted out. Coulda been awkward on the other end.
And you understand about us, then? That's cool with you?"

I blinked. Danny wasn't there. And then he was, looking at
me, waiting for me to say yes. "What's cool?" I asked. The
small voice had come back, was pretending it was mine. "You
coming to stay with us?"

"Well, yeah, that, but also, you know, the other thing, the
you-and-me thing."

I stared at him, trying to make sense of what he was saying,
but he was as elliptical as Raul Cansino. I hadn't told him
about the baby yet; he couldn't be saying what it sounded like
he was saying.

"It's too awkward, Reason, what with you being Julieta's
best friend, you so young and all. We can still be friends, you
know? You can think of me as a big brother." He winced. "Well,
maybe not. But forget about the other thing, okay?"

"The other thing? You mean sex?" I stared at him, open-
mouthed, then closed it in case he thought I wanted to kiss
him.

"Anyway, I'm not really into the girlfriend thing, Reason."

The girlfriend thing? Danny was saying he didn't want to kiss me again, or touch me, or have sex with me. I blushed. Furious with myself for not being able to control the blood underneath my skin.

Had he ever wanted me? How could I have kissed him in the first place when he didn't want me to? But he had kissed me. He had touched me all over! He had helped make the baby inside me. I hadn't even told him about the baby and he was rejecting me.

Danny's big brown eyes were staring back at mine. He was a very handsome man. A very handsome man who didn't want me or our baby.

Was that what had happened to Sarafina? She'd slept with a man once and then he'd told her to go away? She always said that she hadn't told him about getting pregnant, that it had been her choice to never see him again. But what if she had? And he said no and *that* was why I didn't have a father? My dad hadn't wanted my mother; why would he have wanted me? I didn't have a father, and now my child wouldn't have one either.

There was a buzzing sound. Danny picked up the phone next to the lift. "Car's here," he told me. "Can I give you a ride somewhere?"

I nodded and gripped the ammonite in my pocket to keep my voice steady. "Back to the door would be good."

"Sure," he said, picking up his suitcase.

He didn't want me.

The pain inside me was sharp, but it burned too. My eyes stung.

I closed them, let Cansino's world surround me. The pain went away. Everywhere was the light of magic. It was beautiful here, and safe. I could hear Danny talking to me from the other world, but his voice didn't hurt me at all.

I could see the sixteenth Fibonacci that was the door to Sydney. I saw other sets of magic light wound together with filaments. I wondered if they were doors too. And if they were, where they would go.

I would stay in Cansino's world, I decided. But first I would endure the short ride with Danny, and then I would finally rescue Sarafina and bring her into Cansino's safe haven of mathematics and lights. She was a Cansino, after all.

All I had to do was give her some of the old man's magic.

7
Telling the Truth

Tom listened calmly to Cathy reaming him out for not returning her call earlier or answering her emails. Da had finally said he could tell Cathy about magic, and he was wondering how to break it to her. What could he say? "Um, yes, Cathy, sorry 'bout that. So, you know how me and Da have kind of been holding out on you? Well, that's because it turns out I'm magic! How 'bout that?"

Nope, that wouldn't work.

He wondered again if Jay-Tee had meant anything by that kiss. She'd stroked his cheek. That wasn't really a friend thing, was it? Reason would never stroke his cheek. He was amazed at how much he wished she'd meant something by it. It was *Jay-Tee*, after all, cranky Jay-Tee who never missed an opportunity to hassle him. Why would he want to kiss her?

Because she smelled good. Because when he remembered that kiss his lips tingled.

But he liked *Reason*, not Jay-Tee. He wondered how he'd be feeling now if Reason had kissed him.

"Tom? Tom? Are you listening?"

"Yes, Cath, I'm listening. I'm really, really sorry and it

won't happen again. But, you know, there's something I have to tell you. Something big."

"I'm waiting."

Tom paused. How the hell do you tell someone that you're magic?

"Well?"

"Where are you, Cath?"

"What do you mean where am I? I'm at home. You think I'm going to rack up this kind of phone bill on someone else's phone?"

"Esmeralda'll pay for it."

"You know, Tom, you're going to have to stop relying so much on her generosity. It won't last forever, and, as it happens, Tom Yarbro, Esmeralda does *not* pay my phone bills."

"Sorry."

"You were about to tell me something momentous."

"Um, yeah. Look, can you do me a favour, Cath? Can you stay at home? I have to do something, but I'll call you back within an hour."

"'Ken oath! No way, Tom, you tell me now! Right now! And why do I have to stay here? You know my mobile number."

"It's much better talking on a landline. Please, Cathy? Just an hour?"

"Okay, but if you don't ring I'll kill you. Got that?"

"Got it. No call equals death. It won't be an hour. More like twenty minutes, okay?"

"Okay. Talk to you then."

"'Bye."

"'Bye."

He put the phone down, swapped his shorts and T-shirt for jeans, polo neck, woolly jumper, thick socks, boots, and coat, and stuffed a hat and gloves into his pocket.

Tom closed the door behind him. Night time. He'd forgotten it would be dark. Well, not exactly dark, with all the streetlights blazing. He pocketed his sunglasses and shivered. He'd never get used to the cold. What time was it? He looked at his watch: 11:15 AM, so, what time here? Was it six or seven or eight? He could never remember. Reason would know.

It was winter, that was for sure, so whatever the time, the sun had been down for hours. Over here when it was winter the sun set practically seconds after it rose. He imagined going to school in New York City: leaving in the dark, coming home in the dark. Majorly sucky.

No Jason Blake in sight. Tom hadn't really expected him to be there. He touched the bandage on his cheek where the bastard had scratched him. He'd be lucky if it didn't get infected. That man was toxic.

He had to be quick, better to get back before anyone missed him. Esmeralda hadn't explicitly told them *not* to go through the door. At least, she hadn't said anything about it for a few days now, but he doubted she'd be thrilled with him going through on his own. Esmeralda was the boss of who went through the door and when. But it was the only way to tell Cathy: face to face.

How else would she believe him?

Tom still had the keys to Cath's flat from his last visit. Come to think of it, she still had his backpack. He paused in front of the door to her flat, only partly because there were so many locks he'd forgotten in what order to unlock them. It would probably be a better idea to knock. Surely him being here in New York City mere minutes after he'd been on the phone to her from Sydney would be enough to convince her. Tom raised his hand to the doorbell and then put it back in his pocket.

He was nervous.

What was he going to say when Cath opened the door? "Surprise"? What if she fainted? What if she had a heart attack and died? He'd read somewhere that way more women have them than you'd think. He imagined explaining that one to Da and shuddered. *He* was the one who was supposed to die young, not her.

Don't be retarded, Tom, he told himself. The sooner he got this over and done with, the sooner there'd be no secrets in the family. Whatever remained to him of his life would be a whole lot better because he'd be able to tell Cath everything. No more lies. No more quoting Esmeralda to himself: *That's just part of being magic: sometimes you have to lie.* Not anymore!

He pressed the doorbell.

After a few long seconds, during which Tom decided she'd racked off despite her promise, he heard the sounds of scrabbling at the thousand locks. The door opened. Cathy's mean, don't-touch-my-bathroom-products, crooked-seam, dropkick wanker of a flatmate let out a scream. "No, no! Absolutely not! No way! You are *not* staying here." He slammed the door.

"Wait!"

Tom pressed the doorbell again. Then again. Then he just leaned on it, watched the tip of his finger go white. He heard shouting. Then at last the door opened and Cathy was there.

"'Ken hell. I don't believe it," she said, staring at him. "No way. We were just on the—"

"Yep, it's me. This is what I came to tell you about."

"He's not staying here," Dropkick interjected. "Over my dead body is he staying here."

"No," Tom said, swallowing the language he really wanted to use—he'd be *very* happy to see Dropkick's dead body. "I'm not staying here. I just came to take my sister out to dinner. Not that it's any of your business."

"Not a single night," Dropkick said, turning to Cathy. "I'm warning you."

"Oh, piss off, Andrew," Cath said, not even looking at him. "I'll grab my coat."

"Could you get my backpack too?"

"No worries. You just wait there. Don't want to set the poxy wanker off again."

Cath led Tom along the dark, wintry streets. The only snow left was grey and miserable. Everyone outside was rugged up and in a hurry. They passed a man selling roasted chestnuts. The smell was so good Tom's stomach rumbled, even though breakfast hadn't been that long ago.

Every step of the way to the restaurant Cath pestered him to tell her what was going on, but Tom stayed firm.

"It's not something I can blurt out on the street," he said, watching his words turn into puffs of condensation. "It's going to be a serious conversation. Your mouth's going to drop wide open a lot and it's too cold for that out here."

"Ooooh, Tom! So intriguing."

"It's too cold, Cath. Save it—"

"Here we are," she said, opening the door and leading him into a posh-looking restaurant, all pale green, maroon, wood, and metal, with a curved bar in front and a tree of wine bottles lit up like it was still Christmas. It looked like the kind of place his Da liked to eat at, but said he couldn't afford.

"Pretty flash," Tom said as Cath chose a low table with lounge chairs. He sank into his. It was lower and less comfortable than it looked. The tables and chairs at the back of the restaurant seemed much better, but he didn't fault Cath's choice: these were more private. He didn't fancy telling his sister within anyone else's earshot.

"It is, isn't it? You'd never know it was vegetarian, would you?"

Tom bit his bottom lip. She was about to hear some

unbelievable news. She should at least be somewhere she felt comfortable. He figured he could stomach budgie food this once. "Nope, you wouldn't."

A waiter brought them menus. Tom scanned it quickly, seeing lots of stuff he'd never heard of, like cauliflower risotto and strata and who-knew-what-else. Eww. Bloody vegos. Fortunately they had burgers, even if they were fake. At least they came with chips.

"You know that's not meat, right?"

"Yup, I do know what vegetarian means, Cath."

She ordered them two coconut waters. Tom hadn't known they had such a thing in New York City. These weren't as good as at home. It was winter after all; he wondered where they were imported from.

A waiter came and reeled off a stack of weird-sounding specials. Tom ordered his burger and Cath one of the specials, which was when he realised he'd forgotten to bring any American money.

"Um, Cath?"

"Yeah?"

"You know how I said this was on me?"

She groaned. "Don't worry about it, Tom, I can cover it. I think."

"You know, I could pop back and get the money. It's in my sock drawer. I just don't wanna get busted. Esmeralda doesn't exactly know I came through."

"Came through?"

A waiter refilled their waterglasses. Tom said thank you, wishing he would go away. He resolved to drink slowly.

"Through the door. Esmeralda's back door. That's how I got here so fast."

"Well, of course," Cath said, as if he'd gone mad.

Another waiter went by. Cath beckoned him over. "Could I have a glass of the Malbec, please?" She turned back to Tom, who was wondering what Malbec was—probably wine. "I need it, okay? You were talking about a door?"

"Esmeralda's door. Yeah."

"I know," Cath said. "You didn't go home, did you? You've just been pretending to be back in Sydney, but you've been here the whole time."

"Cath, *you* called me."

"That was some kind of phone number routing thing. To make me think you were at home when really—"

"I'm magic. So's Mum."

"Magic," Cath said, as if she had no idea what that word meant.

Their food arrived, along with Cath's wine. Tom was pleased that his burger looked like a real burger. He had a bite. Not bad at all. Pretty good even. Cath started hoeing into her food, which came in a big bowl and wobbled. Only the fancy lettuce on the sides was recognisable. Rather her than him.

"I came here by opening the back door in Esmeralda's kitchen. When you step through, you're in New York City."

"Just like that?"

"Just like that."

Tom told her about meeting Esmeralda, about madness. He told her about dying. He told her everything. She said she didn't believe him, but he could see that she did.

"Show me," she said, after she'd ordered a third glass of wine. Her cheeks were pink.

"Didn't you hear the part about not using too much magic? The part about me dying?"

"Just a little, then."

Tom sighed. "Just this once, right?"

She nodded, her cheeks flushed.

"See the candle?"

"Yup, I might not be magically abled, but I ain't blind." She took a long gulp of her wine. "Yet."

Tom thought about the candle going out. It went out. He thought about it being lit. It came back to life.

"Oh," Cath said. "Right, then."

"Yeah. It's like that. You should've seen Da after Esmeralda told him. Not happy. He's still not happy. He's not wild about talking about it. Ever."

"I can see why not. It's not exactly comfortable, is it?"

"Comfortable? No, not really."

"What about Mum, then?"

"She's mad because she won't use her magic. I mean, she doesn't know she's magic and so she doesn't use it. Same thing in the end."

"Didn't you tell her?"

Tom nodded. "She's nuts, Cath. She didn't believe me. And when I tried to show her, she totally lost it."

"Lost it?"

"She lunged at me. They had to—"

"That's okay. I get it." Their mother had once cut Cath with a knife, screaming that she was going to kill her. They'd never talked about it. Tom had been there, but he was too young to remember. "So you're . . ." She trailed off, but Tom could see her struggling with what he was telling her. "Why aren't I magic, then?"

Tom shrugged. "Dunno? Why am I an albino?"

"You're not an albino, you're just pigment-challenged."

"Cheers, sis."

"No worries."

"Is it really real?" She looked straight at him, a softer version of her high-voltage interrogation stare.

Tom nodded sadly. "Wish it weren't."

"'Ken oath," Cath said fiercely. "My daggy little brother is going to die young." She reached her hand across the table and squeezed his. Tom felt his eyes getting wet. "Don't think that means you're forgiven, right? You're still a bloody, buggery little bastard for holding out on me for so long." A tear trickled down her face. "Complete and utter, utter, utter bastard."

8
Glowing

Jay-Tee tried the handle of the door to New York. It turned, but the door didn't open. Locked solid, of course. She didn't know where the key was, and even if she did she wouldn't have used it, on account of how opening the door was still using magic, even if it was only the tiniest, tiniest bit. She'd sworn she wasn't going to use magic anymore. Looniness before death!

Jay-Tee just wanted to see home. She bent down and peeked through the keyhole and could barely make out the bottom of a rickety fire escape. New York didn't seem to have any colors. It was blurry, like she was looking through Vaseline. It made Jay-Tee feel weird inside, as though fleas were crawling under her skin, like magic was leaving her. She shivered and slid to the floor and, knowing she shouldn't, pulled herself up to the keyhole for one last blurry glance of a higher-up section of the fire escape and the bricks behind.

How was she going to keep from using magic?

Jay-Tee wished she could squeeze through the keyhole. Go stay with her brother. She missed Danny more than she ever had now that he was her only family in the world. Now that she was stuck in Sydney with no way to get home. She couldn't go through the door, so how else was she going to get back? On a magic carpet? Nope, that used magic too. She didn't have enough magic, and she didn't have a passport either.

Suddenly Jay-Tee was so tired she felt like crying again. She was trapped with no passport, no clothes of her own, no money, no family, no magic, no nothing.

She went upstairs, collapsed onto the bed that wasn't hers, and shut her eyes. She didn't care if Tom never came back from talking to his sister, or if Esmeralda never took her shopping for clothes, or if Reason turned into a monster elf man like that Raul Cansino guy. What did it matter? Jay-Tee wasn't going to be around to see any of it.

Jay-Tee dreamed *he* was chasing her through the streets of Manhattan. Only they were covered in mist and all the buildings were tall. No matter how fast she ran, the man who'd drained away most of her magic was always just a few feet behind her. But then he wasn't him anymore, he was her father.

She sat bolt upright in bed. Where was she? For a moment Jay-Tee thought she was in *his* apartment. But this room was so big, so light. White curtains, shiny wooden floorboards. That wasn't right.

Then she remembered: she was in Sydney. In Esmeralda's house. With Esmeralda, the wicked witch, who hadn't turned out to be anything like as bad as *he*'d said, which figured. Why

had she ever believed a word he said? Except that sometimes
he did tell the truth . . . when it was useful to him.

Jay-Tee was so glad she'd escaped him, that Reason had rescued her. She had been too afraid to run away on her own.
Reason wasn't afraid of anything. Right now Jay-Tee was afraid
of pretty much everything.

She was in Sydney, where the best she could do was peek
through the keyhole at New York City. Where . . .

Tom hadn't come back. Or maybe he had seen that she was
asleep and gone away again.

She went into the bathroom, splashed her face with water,
looked at her clothes. The T-shirt she was wearing (one of
Esmeralda's) was all wrinkly. Figured, given that she'd just slept
in it, but there wasn't anything else to wear. Not anything clean.

Jay-Tee headed downstairs, thinking about finding Tom. He
was probably at his house, next door. She could resume teaching him about God, and about kissing too. First she checked
out the fridge, but it was just as full of all sorts of scary junk as
the last time she looked. Certainly nothing edible. She reluctantly took a green apple from the fruit bowl, the only normal-
looking fruit in it.

She heard the back door open behind her.

Jay-Tee swung around, crossed herself with the apple still in
her hand, and backed away. But the person who stepped
through was Reason, not *him*.

"Reason!"

"Jay-Tee?"

She nodded. "You were in New York?"

"Yes," Reason said. She pulled off her winter coat and dropped it on the kitchen table, then added her sweater, gloves, and hat to the pile.

"Why were you there?"

"To see if I could get through without a key," Reason answered, taking a few strides past her. She misstepped in the hallway, and Jay-Tee dashed to grab her before she fell.

"Are you okay?"

"Fine," Reason said, shaking Jay-Tee off and continuing toward the front door. But she wobbled like a baby horse learning to walk. Her eyes were only half open.

"Are you drunk?"

"No," Reason said, pulling the front door open.

"Stoned?"

Reason ignored her and stepped into the tiny front yard, where the sun hit her. Jay-Tee blinked. Reason's skin wasn't the same color it had been. Except that it was—it was still caramel colored, a shade or two darker than her own, but the depth had changed. Or something.

Reason collided with the front gate, or rather, didn't. Somehow she was now on the sidewalk, seemingly undamaged. Jay-Tee wasn't sure what she'd just seen. One second she was on this side of the gate, next second she was over there. Reason continued down the street.

"Where are you going? Are you sure you should be going anyplace when you're like this?"

"Yes," Reason said. "It takes practice. It's harder when you make me talk too."

"Walking takes practice?" Jay-Tee knew Reason wasn't the most coordinated girl in the world, but she wasn't usually this bad.

Reason kept walking, her steps becoming more even and certain. Jay-Tee jogged after her. "Reason! Where are we going?"

"To my mother."

"Your mother." *Okay.* "In the loony hospital?"

"Kalder Park."

"Why?"

Reason started walking even faster. The sidewalk was narrow and uneven and crowded by trees and weeds. Jay-Tee had to weave around them, sometimes onto the road to keep up with her. The almost-running made her feel the tingle of her magic. She slowed a little, shook her arms out, willed the magic to just STOP. She refused to drop dead here on the street.

What was up with Reason? Her arms didn't look right. Actually, none of her did.

"Is there something you need from your mother?" Jay-Tee ducked under a low-hanging tree branch and almost tripped over a root that made the pavement buckle.

"No."

"Are you okay, Reason?" Jay-Tee asked, even though she obviously wasn't.

"I'm fine."

"Shouldn't we tell your grandmother where we're going?"

Reason didn't say anything. They reached the end of Esmeralda's quiet street and, without looking, she walked across the road crowded with zooming cars.

Jay-Tee crossed herself again. "Reason!" she screamed, but Reason was already on the other sidewalk. It had to be her new magic. No way could the old Reason do that. She could barely run without falling over.

Reason disappeared around the corner. "Ree! Wait up!" Jay-Tee screamed, even though there was no way Reason could hear her over the traffic. She waited for a gap, but it was like trying to cross the FDR. If she'd had enough magic, she could have used it, but she didn't. The lights finally changed and she dashed across the street and around the corner. Reason was a block ahead. "Wait up!"

She picked up her pace, feeling the magic tingle grow, and slowed again. In two blocks she was behind Reason. "Can you stop for a second, Ree? Tell me why you're acting so weird?"

Reason stopped dead in her tracks and Jay-Tee ran into her. A woman in black track pants and a pink T-shirt walked by. Jay-Tee realized how few people she'd seen since they left the house. Ones that weren't in cars, that was. It was hard to believe Sydney was a city at all. There were so few people around.

"Sorry," she said, even though it was Reason's fault. Reason didn't look out of breath, even though she should have.

"What's going on?"

"I want to give Sarafina some Cansino magic. So she doesn't have to be insane anymore."

"Okay. And Tom's mom too?"

"She's not a Cansino. There's nothing I can do for her."

Jay-Tee had learned that truth herself, but it didn't make it any less painful. Reason and her family, even *him*, her vile grandfather, were going to live with all the magic they needed, but Jay-Tee was going to be dead soon and Tom probably wouldn't see thirty. It wasn't fair.

"Whatever, but what's wrong with you? Why are you acting so weird? Is it what Raul Cansino did to you?" Standing in the bright sunlight Reason looked like someone had made her up with bronzer, but not just her cheeks: her hands, her face and neck, her everywhere. Maybe it was just the light.

Jay-Tee looked at her own hands. It wasn't the light. Reason was somehow shinier.

"I'm fine. Why do you keep asking?"

"Because you're walking like you're crazy drunk. Okay, you *were* walking like that. Now you're all Amazon-y or something. And you're glowing, Ree. You're glowing like a statue."

9
Disappearing Magic

Staying in Cansino's world while walking in the other world was hard. And managing to hear what Jay-Tee was saying and answer her was even harder, but I was learning. Every step I took, every word I spoke, I got better at it: I saw more, I heard more, I felt more. It was as though the world I'd spent most of my life in was black and white and now, seeing it through Cansino's eyes, it had sprouted colour. Except that there wasn't any colour, just magic everywhere I looked, making everything richer, deeper. More.

But I needed to see what Jay-Tee was talking about. I stopped walking and opened my eyes completely, losing the richness and complexity, and landing with a thunk in the world of colours. Some of it resolved into Jay-Tee: instead of being a wisp of magic, trailing behind me, she became someone who looked a lot like Danny.

Danny. My head exploded with everything he'd said to me. Tears oozed out of my eyes, trickled down my face.

"Reason? You're crying. What's wrong?"

"Nothing," I said, though the tears came even quicker. I took a deep breath and it hurt so much I was ready to climb back into Cansino's world. Why had Danny rejected me and my baby? Though I hadn't told him about the baby. Well, of course not—he hadn't let me.

"Aaargh!" If Danny had been standing there, I would have kicked him as hard as I could.

"Reason? What's wrong?"

"Nothing."

"You're crying over nothing?"

"Yes!"

"Sure you are. You going to tell me what's up? I can help. Or Esmeralda can. Why don't we call her?"

"You can call her if you like. I'm going to Sarafina." I wiped the tears away, but more just joined them. I wished Jay-Tee didn't look so much like her brother.

"Like there are any phones around here. I wish my cell worked in your country."

"Can we keep walking? I want to get to Sarafina."

"Sure thing. We can walk and talk. So, Ree, how come you've changed again? I mean gone back to normal? You're talking and moving like you used to. Not that crying is normal. I mean—"

"Because I opened my eyes."

"You what now?"

"It's because of the new magic. I'm not sure how to describe it. You're slowing up, Jay-Tee."

"Sorry," she said, and shrugged the same way Danny did.

"You know, you could go back to the house and call Esmeralda, then meet me at Kalder Park."

"I don't think so. It's not like—"

"Glowing, you said?"

Jay-Tee nodded and made the strange gesture across her forehead, chest, and shoulder that she made whenever she was nervous or scared. "Look at your arms."

I looked down. "Bugger." My skin was shining. It looked almost like Raul Cansino's: smooth, hairless. Were my pores disappearing? I looked closer. Not yet: there was still fine, downy hair on my arms, but I was definitely glowing as if I were made of gold or bronze. "It's beautiful," I said, finally able to stop crying.

"You think?" Jay-Tee said. "Looks freaky to me."

"No, it's beautiful." But what was Sarafina going to think? She hated magic. One look at me and she'd go even madder than she already was.

I led Jay-Tee past gum trees, and grassy slopes spilling down to water that shone bright with sunlight. I wondered how it would look from Cansino world, started to imagine the added depth of the mathematical patterns that made up the movement of the waves, of the boats through the air currents.

I noticed that Jay-Tee and her brother even walked the same: an almost loping stride, like a big cat, which made sense in Danny because he was so tall, but Jay-Tee was even shorter than me. I shook my head. I wasn't going to think about him.

"It really is a park, huh?" Jay-Tee said. "I didn't expect that. Thought it would be all hospital-y."

"This is the art school." We walked past a sandstone building overrun with ivy. In front of it students sat on the grass sketching. It was like they hadn't moved since last time I'd been here. All of them still dressed in black.

"Isn't it summer? How come they're still in school?"

"Dunno," I said. "Maybe art students don't get holidays."

"Huh. So what did you do in New York? I mean once you saw the door worked without a key and everything. Did you see Danny? Or, you know, *him?*"

Her saying Danny's name made my eyes well up again, which made me mad at myself. What was I supposed to say? *Your stupid brother told me to rack off?* I was relieved to see the first of the buildings that made up Kalder Park.

"Sarafina's somewhere in there. You wait here."

"What do you mean, 'wait here'?!"

"I'm going to use Cansino magic, Jay-Tee, lots of it, okay? You can't help me with it. I have to sneak in there to fix her. I can't have you tagging along."

"I could be a decoy or something."

"I don't want to attract any attention, Jay-Tee. I won't be long," I said, walking away from her. "Honest."

I turned a corner, went through the first ten Fibonaccis, and when Jay-Tee didn't follow, I ducked into the shrubbery between two buildings: bottlebrush and a stunted gum tree. Then, checking that no one could see me, I sat down with my back against the weatherboard slats of the closest building.

The truth was, I needed to be away from Jay-Tee reminding me of Danny every time I looked at her.

I closed my eyes. The pain of Danny not wanting me vanished and Cansino's world unfolded; the bushes and trees beside me became a dusty scattering of the tiniest magic imaginable, completely drowned by all the brilliant lights around them, more than I'd seen before, more even than New York City, and so many of them close by. Magic-wielders. They had to be.

Were they all like my mother? Mad because they didn't use their magic? Had all the magic at Kalder Park over the years started rubbing off on everything? Made the couches, the windows, the doors magic as well? This place exploded with magic.

I saw Sarafina's light. I knew it was her; I could feel it. I zoomed closer, the feel of her got stronger, but then the texture wasn't right. The light flew apart, exploded into dusty particles, into nothing. Not Sarafina.

It wasn't her. Hadn't been her. Hadn't been anything— which didn't make any sense. I saw something familiar, a faint trace of magic. I recognised it but couldn't place it. I searched through the lights that were farther away. Still no Sarafina.

I stood up, feeling the thickness around me giving way slowly, more resistant than before. I concentrated, trying to find the real world. I heard what could have been a myna bird calling; somewhere, not far, cicadas buzzed in chorus. I saw the barest edges of a path and pushed my limbs along it, as though I were moving in low gravity.

I wondered what the gravity of pure magic was.

"Ray gun." I heard someone call. "Raise them. Read arse. Rea-son!"

"Jay-Tee," I said. Through the wavering texture that surrounded me I could see the faint dust of Jay-Tee's magic.

"Sarafina's not here," I said. The words moved out of me slowly, glittering in a spiral pattern that wove round and round until it disappeared out of sight. So beautiful. Before they'd gone, Jay-Tee overlaid them with more words of her own. There was no spiral or glitter to them. I heard nothing.

I continued searching for Sarafina, striving to listen for more words from Jay-Tee, but they reached me only in tiny fragments. "Mer." "Ont." "Elp." "Ezon." I could feel vibrations, like a butterfly's wings beating against a soft cloth. They weren't from this world: they had to be from where Jay-Tee was.

I wasn't strong enough to search for my mother in Cansino's world and stay aware of the real world. I focussed on Sarafina. And found her. I recognised the movement of her magic, the undulating Fibonacci waves. She was away from here. And in motion. Not alone. Another magic tumbled around her, stronger than that of my mother. An entirely different flavour. I said its name.

I forced myself to open my eyes completely, to reclaim daylight.

"What did you say?" Jay-Tee screamed, hurting my head.

"Jason Blake," I said. "My mother is with Jason Blake."

10
Following Magic

"No! How? Where?" Jay-Tee spluttered. She couldn't believe it. Not him. Not here. "Why would he be here? What would he want with—"

Reason took off at a run for the main road. Jay-Tee easily kept pace, without even remotely needing to use magic. Reason was moving like Reason again, not like she was under a spell. Jay-Tee grabbed her arm. "Reason? How do you know he's got your mom? What's going on?"

Reason shook Jay-Tee off, jumped the low stone fence, and stuck her arm out for a taxi. Two women walking by in office clothes turned to stare at them. Jay-Tee ignored them. "Reason! Tell me what's happening!"

"I have to get to Sarafina!"

Several cars drove by, none of them yellow. Jay-Tee wondered if they even had taxis in Sydney. Maybe they had gypsy cabs, but she didn't see any black limos drive by either.

Reason moved a little farther out onto the road, waved her arm some more.

"Reason, where are we going?"

"I'm not sure."

"What do you mean you're not sure? What do you mean you saw *him*?"

A taxi pulled up, painted red, blue, and white. Only the small light on top made it look remotely like a cab. What was the point of a taxi that didn't look like a taxi? Why wasn't it yellow? Reason climbed in and Jay-Tee scooted after her.

"Where to, girls?"

"Ah," Reason said. "Er." She paused, turned to Jay-Tee, like Jay-Tee had some idea of what was going on. "This is going to sound weird, but I'm not sure exactly where to. Can I just give you directions?"

Jay-Tee thought it sounded very weird, but the driver turned around and grinned at them. "What? You're not going to tell me, 'Follow that car'?" One of his teeth was metal. Jay-Tee shuddered. Metal in her mouth made her want to barf. She didn't even like accidentally touching a fork or spoon to her tongue. "Can you at least give me a general direction," he continued, "or do you want a scenic tour of the inner west?"

Reason stuck her head out the window, then her shoulders, and then started easing more of herself out of the cab, until Jay-Tee worried she was going to fall. She was just about to grab her when she slid back in. "South," Reason said, "and a little bit east. You need to do a U-ie."

"Consider it done."

The cab turned to the right violently. Jay-Tee clutched her seat belt and winced, expecting to be wiped out by oncoming traffic. It took her a second to remember about everyone driving on the wrong side of the road here.

Jay-Tee didn't much like cars, especially being in back. It made her carsick. Walking was better. Running was best. Not that she could run properly anymore, not without killing herself. She glanced at Reason. Well, Jay-Tee might never run or dance again, and she was about to go barking mad, but at least she wasn't glowing or moving like an alien or seeing stuff that wasn't there. She wished Tom were with them. He'd be bummed, missing all the excitement.

"So where are we going?" she whispered to Reason.

"We're following my mother. She's headed southeast."

"What's southeast of here?" Jay-Tee asked.

"I don't know. The ocean, I guess."

"You think she's going to get on a boat?"

"You got some kind of tracker on your mum?" the driver asked, and Jay-Tee wondered how he could hear them from the front seat.

"Yes," Reason said. Jay-Tee hoped the driver wouldn't ask to see it. "She's, um . . . she gets confused."

The driver nodded. "I saw where youse were coming from. Kalder Park. Must be hard."

Reason agreed that it was. Jay-Tee suppressed a laugh. The driver didn't know even the half of it.

"You know, the airport's south of here," he said. "Do you reckon your mum could have it together enough to catch a plane someplace?"

Reason looked at Jay-Tee. "The airport," she said. "Jason Blake couldn't have come through the you-know-what, could he?"

Jay-Tee shook her head. There was no way he'd come through the door. They'd been at Esmeralda's practically the whole time. But he could have come by plane.

"So you want me to head to the airport?" the driver asked.

"Yes, thank you."

"No worries."

"We should call Esmeralda. Tell her what's happening."

"There'll be a phone at the airport."

"That might be too late. What if we have to catch a plane or something?"

"Do you have a mobile phone?" Reason asked the driver. Jay-Tee was so embarrassed, she didn't know where to look. Reason didn't know anything! Only someone bone ignorant or bat-shit crazy would ask to borrow a taxi driver's phone.

"Sure," the driver said, as if Reason had asked the most normal question in the world. He handed it to her. "No calling overseas, mind."

"Thank you," Reason said, passing it to Jay-Tee.

"Okay," Jay-Tee said, wondering if this was just another thing they did differently in Australia. "What's Esmeralda's number, math girl?"

✷

Esmeralda didn't pick up on her work number, so Jay-Tee tried her cell. She answered first ring.

"Cansino. Who's speaking?"

"Hey, Mere, Jay-Tee. Wha—"

"Where are you?" Esmeralda said, sounding angry. "I came home for lunch and there's no Reason, no you, no Tom. I checked Tom's place and the other house. Why didn't you call me?"

"Sorry," Jay-Tee began. "We—"

"What happened with the social worker? She's left me messages at work and on the mobile. What did you three say to her?"

"Nothing. I mean—"

"Whatever it was, she wasn't very impressed. Where are you now? Is Reason with you?"

Jay-Tee told her as much as she could with the driver listening. Esmeralda said she would meet them at the international terminal in front of the departure gates. She was convinced that Jason Blake and her daughter would be flying back to New York.

Jay-Tee hoped she and Reason would be able to find their meeting place. She'd never been to an airport before. She also hoped that Mere wouldn't be so mad at them by then.

Reason paid with money she pulled from the air, and the driver wished them luck. She jumped out of the cab and dashed through the sliding glass doors, skidding along the tiled floor, around people laden with suitcases or enormous backpacks—there were so many of them, and a ridiculous number had small children clutching their hands, or worse, attempting escape and getting in the way of everyone else. Reason headed up escalators, then into a maze of overcrowded shops and restaurants. Past hundreds of confusing signs. If Jay-Tee hadn't been chasing after her, she could've gotten lost pretty damn quick. So many different airlines, different exits. So many doors with big signs, all in red, screaming that only authorized people were permitted.

It was as crowded as midtown. All of the people not out walking the streets of Sydney, Jay-Tee decided, had found their way here. She finally believed that Sydney was a city. She wondered how big JFK airport was. It had to be at least ten times the size of this one, given that New York was at least that much bigger than Sydney.

Reason moved faster than Jay-Tee'd ever seen her move before. Jay-Tee weaved her way through the crowd, her skin prickling with magic. She could feel it pulling at her and started to move faster, easier, her legs becoming oiled and limber.

No! She couldn't do this.

She slowed, biting her lip, forcing herself to resist the crowd magic. But that magic was so easy—it felt so good.

A cute guy smiled at her, did a turn to keep looking, half held his arms out, like he was asking her to dance. So many people in between them, and yet the path to him was so clear, she tingled with it.

Jay-Tee pinched her palm, let go of what she'd been feeling, said no to the pull of crowd magic, and followed Reason without giving in to her own speed, her own rhythm. She had so little magic left.

By the time Jay-Tee caught up, Reason was standing with

Esmeralda at a big entranceway littered with discarded luggage carts. A big sign said, PASSPORT CONTROL, PASSENGERS ONLY BEYOND THIS POINT; smaller ones instructed passengers to leave their carts behind. Jay-Tee bent over to catch her breath.

"Through there?" she asked.

Reason nodded, looking like she was going to cry again.

"That sucks," Jay-Tee observed, when her heartbeat was almost back to normal.

"Sarafina doesn't have as much magic. I think he's draining her."

Jay-Tee didn't know what to say. She wasn't surprised. It was what he'd done to her too. Over and over. And to Reason, that once. He was greedy and evil. He didn't care about anyone but himself.

"I'll just get us tickets. Doesn't matter to where," Esmeralda said. "We'll go through there and rescue her." She took a step away, then stopped. "Passports. Mine's at home."

"I don't have one," Reason said.

"Me neither," Jay-Tee said. "Never have had one. This is my first time anywhere foreign." And Jay-Tee's first time at an airport, though she wasn't going to admit that. She'd never been outside New York (well, except for Hoboken and Jersey City, which hardly counted). If you're born in the coolest city in the world, Jay-Tee figured, you didn't need to travel. "Can't you just magic your way past them? Can't be that hard. I've been getting into clubs for years."

Mere looked at Jay-Tee, considering. Jay-Tee didn't like the look.

"Getting past all that security, passport checks, immigration," she said, "would take serious magic, Jay-Tee. A lot of it. And if just one of them is a dead spot . . . Well, I'd be buggered, wouldn't I?"

"How many dead spots are there, really?" Jay-Tee asked. "I mean, I've only—"

"I'll do it," Mere said firmly.

"You will?" Jay-Tee hadn't expected that turn.

"Oh, no! She's moving *really* fast now." Reason turned and ran to the huge glass window, pressed her face up against it.

In-a-plane fast, Jay-Tee thought, joining Reason at the window. "It's okay. We'll find her."

Reason nodded, a tear trickled down her face. She wiped it away. "Why did she go with him?"

"Maybe he drugged her? Or . . ."

Reason turned to her, looking bleak. Jay-Tee shut up.

"Come on," Mere said. "Let's check departing flights."

Reason walked along beside them, but her movements had changed. She'd gone alien again. Jay-Tee suppressed a shudder.

"They're flying west," Reason said as they came to a large board thick with flights to all parts of the world. A whole bunch Jay-Tee'd never heard of before. Where were Auckland, Bahrain, and Guangzhou? Or Incheon, Nadi, and Nouméa?

"West?" Esmeralda asked. "You're sure? If they're heading to the U.S. they'd be flying east."

"Of course he's going to New York," Jay-Tee said. "Where else would he want to take her?"

"None of the recent departures are to America," Esmeralda said. "Look: the flights at the right time are to Auckland, Bangkok, Nouméa, Shanghai, and Singapore."

"And Kuala Lumpur," Jay-Tee said, reading it off the board. "Why would he go to any of those places?"

"There are other doors," Reason said in her new, creepy way. This time Jay-Tee failed to suppress the shudder.

❁

In the car on the way home, Jay-Tee felt dizzy again. She leaned her head against the window, closed her eyes. She remembered once driving out to Coney Island with her uncle and aunt and five little cousins. It had been August, and the car was so crowded that her littlest cousin, Tia, had to sit on her lap. Tia'd thrown up before they'd even hit Brooklyn.

There was no air conditioning. They had all the windows rolled down, letting them breathe in hot, fumey air. Even after cleaning up, all Jay-Tee could smell was Tia's vomit.

The traffic was bumper-to-bumper, like everyone in the whole city had decided to go driving. Jay-Tee remembered wishing that they'd just taken the train, because then her dad could've come too and it would've been quicker and more comfortable. Though nothing would've gotten Danny to go—he was always too busy playing basketball.

When they'd gotten there, she'd been stuck looking after Tia and Angela and only going on the lamest rides, but she'd ended up enjoying it. They both looked up to her so much. She was only eleven, but from their six- and four-year-old vantage points, she might as well have been a movie star, they were so in awe of her.

The more annoyed she was by them, the cooler they thought she was. They trusted her to look after them, see them through the crowds, buy them cotton candy, get them on the lame-ass rides they wanted to go on. They wanted her to put their hair in ponytails like hers. They both wanted red shirts, because that was what she was wearing. They were so cute, they mellowed her down to only snapping at them a little. Anyway, no matter how mean she was, they just giggled.

They were both going to live longer, better lives than Jay-Tee. Last she heard, Tia was doing great in school and had already declared that she was going to be a doctor. Angela was playing basketball with the boys and was better than most of them. She was going to play for a WNBA team when she grew up. She worshipped Danny.

Jay-Tee had never had ambitions, never had any plans. She just did stuff, when she felt like it, and not when she didn't. School was a chore. Looking after her cousins, likewise. She never wanted to hang with kids her own age, but until she'd run away, Danny'd always scared away the older boys.

She could have been a dancer or a runner. But she hated adults telling her what to do. She hated the way they broke her favorite things down and turned them into boring work. They made her roll her eyes and goof off.

Her head felt heavy, yet light at the same time.

Jay-Tee recognized the feeling. It didn't scare her this time, now that she knew what was happening. It was gentle. Like floating on water. How she imagined it would be if she could glide through the air, or drop through it like a feather.

She felt exactly like a feather. Soft, small, dissolving . . .

11

Broken Pattern

"Why are you so sure he's going back to New York?" Esmeralda asked.

Jay-Tee didn't answer.

I was back in their world, experiencing the full force of the competing pains of my mother disappearing with Jason Blake and of Danny rejecting me. Sarafina's absence was worse, but it didn't turn the other pain off, especially when I caught sight of Jay-Tee smiling just like Danny did. Stupid rear-view mirror.

Esmeralda repeated her question. Jay-Tee said nothing. I looked in the mirror again. Jay-Tee was asleep. I blinked. Jay-Tee disappeared.

I turned around. And there she was, leaning against the side of the car, her mouth a little way open. When I blinked again, she vanished again.

She wasn't sleeping; she was dying.

Ignoring Esmeralda's protests, I undid my seatbelt, climbed over into the back seat, stretched out my arms, made my fingers thin and wiry like medical instruments. Just as Raul had shown me. They felt good that way.

I pushed them inside Jay-Tee, closed my eyes, felt my tension

and panic disappearing. Here there was only calm. I could see
the cells that made Jay-Tee, the strings of her DNA. I was
searching for something, but I wasn't sure what.

Then I found it: a long stretch of frayed particles. Her
magic. What was left of it. Like broken dust. I threaded it
together with my needle fingers, noticing what the pattern
had been—fours: 4, 8, 12, 16, 18, 24, . . . 356, . . . 1,424, . . .
22,784, and on, and on.

Of course. All her music—even when the beats per minute
multiplied out of control, each minute so crowded that only
Jay-Tee could keep pace—all of it was 4/4. The solid dancing
number.

But Jay-Tee's fours were crumbling, losing their pounding
beat, losing their shimmer. There was too little left to put back
how it had been: fours were eroding into threes, twos, ones,
into nothing. I had to break the sequence, make a whole out of
broken pieces. I had to make it random. I had to kill that pattern. As I worked, the faint glint of the numbers faded under
my sharpened fingers.

I patched and threaded, pulled what was left together,
watched the fours disappearing, becoming part of the darkness. I could still see them, but not in the same way. They were
textured, like a blue heeler's coat, a soft roughness. Dark
against dark.

Was I killing Jay-Tee's dancing? Breaking her 4/4 rhythm
forever?

I finished the last one, pulled my hands out of her; I could no longer see the boundary of where Jay-Tee ended and space began.

From outside, Esmeralda's voice was calling. Reluctantly, I opened my eyes, made my fingers normal.

The panic returned. Was Jay-Tee alive? Had I killed her?

Her eyes were still closed. Esmeralda had stopped the car. We were somewhere out of the sunlight. She'd opened the back door and was crouched beside Jay-Tee, feeling for a pulse. Esmeralda looked up at me, her mouth open. "Reason," she said. "Oh my God, Reason."

"Is she—"

Jay-Tee coughed; her eyelids fluttered. Then she smiled. "Did I fall asleep?"

When I blinked, she still wasn't there.

Esmeralda insisted that we eat. "I already bought sandwiches." She put them on plates and poured me and Jay-Tee water and herself wine. She kept looking at both of us, staring most intently at me.

"Can I have some wine too?" Jay-Tee asked.

"No."

"I almost died."

"You're still fifteen. Death didn't bring you any closer to being allowed to drink legally."

Jay-Tee screwed up her nose. "Whatever," she said.

I couldn't stop looking at Jay-Tee. She hadn't *almost* died; she'd been all the way dead. I saw her magic go, every last bit of it. Yet here she was, sitting in front of me, breathing, without the faintest trace of magic. What I'd done had kept her alive *without* it.

"I'm all right, Ree," Jay-Tee said. "Stop looking at me like that. I'm fine. Whatever you did, it worked. Death's door is miles away."

I looked away and mumbled, "Sorry." Would Jay-Tee stay like that and live a normal life? Or had I just delayed her dying for a day or two? If it *was* permanent, could I do the same thing again? Could I free Sarafina of magic? It was what she had always wanted—so much that she had lied to me, told me magic wasn't real.

If I could find Sarafina again before Jason Blake took *all* her magic and killed her. What would I be without my mother? I felt as if the main tether of my existence had been severed. I hadn't even had a chance to tell her about her grandchild.

I put the half a sandwich I was holding back on my plate. "Do we really have time for lunch?"

"There's time," Esmeralda said. "If he's gone to Auckland, it's still another hour and a half before he gets there. If there's a door there to New York, we can still get there before him."

"*If* he's gone to New York City," I said. I tried to picture them going through a door in Auckland and coming out in New York City. Or would the door go to somewhere else? Where he had yet another that took him to New York City? How had he found these doors? Not to mention their keys. Even Raul Cansino hadn't been able to get to Sydney without the key. How many doors were there in the world?

"He's definitely heading home," Jay-Tee said. "Why would he go anywhere else?"

Esmeralda started asking Jay-Tee questions about where my grandfather lived, what he did, where they were likely to find him. It was almost impossible not to look at Jay-Tee, to examine what I'd done.

"Reason," Jay-Tee said, rolling her eyes at me. "Quit it. I'm fine, okay? You did great. But stop blinking at me. It's creepy."

"Sorry."

"And stop saying sorry."

"Sorr—"

"Reason!" Jay-Tee laughed. She certainly didn't seem like she was dying. "I wonder where Tom is. You said he wasn't at home, Mere? Shouldn't he be told what's going on?"

"Well, he's probably gone out with his father. You can't expect him to be around all the time. Why don't you call him?" My grandmother pulled her cell phone out and clicked at it. "Just hit the green button. It'll call his mobile." She handed it to Jay-Tee.

"Hey, Tom? It's Jay-Tee. What's up? Everything's gone crazy here and we're wondering where you are. Come on back!" She handed the phone back to Esmeralda.

"Not there?"

It occurred to me that if I could turn Jay-Tee's magic off and she stayed alive, then I could do the same for Tom too. He wouldn't have to die young either. And his mother. She was mad. If I turned her magic off, wouldn't that make her sane again? But first I had to find Sarafina. "We have to find her," I said. "We can't just *talk* about it."

"Reason, that's how we *are* going to find her. By figuring out where Alexander's likely to go, by making educated guesses. How many doors did you see in New York?"

I didn't answer, because my stomach had contracted horribly. I barely made it to the sink before I chundered again. The fourth time in as many days, which was about as many times as I'd vomited in my entire life up till then.

Morning sickness was horrible. I could see why Esmeralda and Sarafina only had one baby. But, I realised, I didn't have to be sick again. I didn't have to experience any pain at all. If I shifted into perceiving the world the way Cansino did and stayed there, I wouldn't ever be sick again. Nothing would touch me.

I ran the water, washing the mess down the sink.

"Are you okay?" Esmeralda asked.

I nodded, then rinsed my mouth out with water, splashed my face. I squirted some detergent into the sink and a little on my hands to wash them.

"Morning sickness," I heard Jay-Tee say. She sounded proud of knowing it.

"How can it be morning sickness?" Esmeralda replied. "She can't have morning sickness already. She's only been pregnant a day or two."

"Less than a day, you mean."

Esmeralda knew Danny was the father, but Jay-Tee still thought Raul Cansino had made me pregnant with magic.

Esmeralda was looking at her. "Yes, of course, one day. It can't be morning sickness."

"How do you mean, it's not morning sickness?" I asked before Jay-Tee started thinking about it too hard. I wasn't ready for Jay-Tee to find out that her brother, Danny, was the father of my baby and that he didn't want it or me.

"It's too soon."

"Too soon?"

"It usually takes about four weeks for morning sickness to set in."

But Danny and I slept together only two days ago. I blushed; it turned into a flush of anger. *You can think of me as a big brother*, he'd said. *Forget about the other thing.* His words burned me in a whole other way. How could he reject me?

"Then why's she been barfing like crazy?"

"She has? When?"

"This morning, when the social worker was here. Tom told her Reason's a nervous vomiter." Jay-Tee laughed and scowled. "He thought he was being helpful, Ree."

"Fabulouser and fabulouser," Esmeralda said. "I am going to have fun talking to her, aren't I? How do you feel now?"

"Pretty good, actually," I lied. I was burning from the memory of Danny's words. And aching with the need to find Sarafina, rescue her. "Once the vomiting stops, I feel fine. So if it's not morning sickness, then what's causing it?"

She put down her wineglass. "I can't be sure, of course."

"But you have an idea?"

Esmeralda nodded. "Your hair . . ."

"What about her hair?" Jay-Tee asked.

I brought my hand to the top of my head. I couldn't feel anything there, just my scalp.

"What?" Jay-Tee repeated.

"You can see magic in a way I've never heard of before," Esmeralda said. "Don't you think the vomiting could be part of those changes?"

"Like the glowing?" Jay-Tee asked. "Hey, she isn't glowing anymore."

Esmeralda stared at Jay-Tee and then at me.

I looked down at my hands: they were glowing. Like Esmeralda had said. I was bald too, but Jay-Tee just couldn't see it, because all her magic was gone. I waited for Esmeralda to tell her.

"Since Raul Cansino gave you his magic," she said to me, "you've changed. You're becoming more like him."

"Yes."

"I don't think he ate. I don't think he needed food."

Jay-Tee made a face. "Or if he did eat, it wasn't food."

I sat down. My body so changed it didn't need food? I *loved* food. What would it be like never eating again?

But would I even miss it if I were like Cansino all the time? Seeing magic and numbers everywhere? The world he lived in was so beautiful. And if I found Sarafina in time, she could join me there.

But could my baby grow without food? Without nutrients? What would my baby *be*?

Esmeralda was staring at me, an expression I couldn't identify on her face.

"What . . . ?" I began.

"He gave you everything. That's what Alexander meant when he said that Raul chose you."

"Well, duh," Jay-Tee said. "He gave you a baby too."

Esmeralda coughed. "What Raul gave you is very different from the magic he gave me and Alexander. You're changing so fast."

"Yes," I said, not looking at her.

"Alexander said this new magic wouldn't last. But yours will, won't it?"

"I don't know. But I don't think my grandfather was lying."

"How long?" she asked, leaning towards me. Too close. "How long do I have?"

I shifted away. "I don't know. You look bright, strong. Jason Blake, Alexander, whatever my grandfather's name is—he does too. I think it doesn't last compared to what Raul's done to me. He lived centuries. I think what you have now is a normal life. Thirty or forty more years."

"That's great!" Jay-Tee said. "You're already forty-five. Another thirty years means you get to live practically forever."

Esmeralda smiled, but I didn't think she was amused. The look she cast at me was so greedy I almost flinched. My grandmother was like a child who'd just tried chocolate for the first time and now, more than anything, wanted more.

Lots more. I didn't want to be in the same room with her, the same world with her. I had to find Sarafina and get away from Jason Blake and Esmeralda.

"If there is a door directly from Auckland to New York City, I want to find it before Jason Blake gets there."

"How do you propose to do that?" Esmeralda asked.

"I told you—I can see them."

"Are there lots of them?" Jay-Tee asked. "How will you know which one is Jason Blake's?"

"I'll see him come through it." I shook my head. "Look, you can stay here and talk as much as you like. I'm going to New York."

I closed my eyes and the world became points of magic light, mathematical patterns swirling around me. Jay-Tee disappeared; Esmeralda shone brightly. I looked closely and found her pattern. I'd half been expecting Fibonaccis but found instead primes. That made sense—Esmeralda being only divisible by herself and one. They wound their way through her: 2, 3, 5, 7, 11, 13, 17, 19, 23, 29, 31, 37, 41, 43, 47, 53, 59, 61, 71, 73, 79, 83, 89, 97, on and on.

I could still hear Esmeralda and Jay-Tee talking, but if I didn't focus on them, their words broke apart and became unrelated sounds. I stood up, the thickness giving way around me slowly, like jelly, only softer, more buoyant. As if gravity had halved. The door pulled at me, drew me with its magic lights that were the sixteenth Fibonacci. I slid through.

12
Everything Changes

"Whoa," Jay-Tee said, blinking rapidly. "Where did Ree go? She was just here."

"She went through the door," Esmeralda said, grabbing her winter coat from the back of the door.

"The door? Then how come I didn't see it? Was I daydreaming?"

"I'm going after her. You know how to dial my mobile when I'm in New York?"

Jay-Tee shook her head. Esmeralda wrote the numbers down and handed them to her. "I want you to call me if anything happens. Anything at all. Let me know when Tom turns up. If Kalder—"

"The social worker," Jay-Tee said. "Weren't you supposed to call the social worker? I think it was important. You know? Taking-Reason-away important."

"Shit," Esmeralda said. "I'll have to call her from New York."

"Have you got her number?"

"She left voice mail." Esmeralda pulled on her coat and opened the back door. "Call me, okay?"

Jay-Tee nodded, peering over Mere's shoulders, eager for her first glimpse of New York in days, but all she saw was the backyard. The back porch, the big old tree, light stained green by the dense leaves, a flock of those stupid red, blue, and green birds that never ever shut up.

"Wait," she said, but Esmeralda was already gone and the door closed.

Why hadn't she seen New York City?

Jay-Tee felt good, better than she had in ages. No dizziness, no fading away, no floating. She felt solid, grounded. Reason must have given her a *lot* of magic. More than Tom had.

They'd both saved her life now. That must mean they were all going to be best friends forever, even though Tom's forever wasn't very long, and hers was even shorter. They didn't have enough magic to keep saving her over and over again.

This time, she swore, *this time* she really would be careful. She wouldn't waste the little magic she had left. It was better to go crazy than to die.

Had she felt like this after Tom gave her his magic? She'd felt better, yes, but *this* much better?

How had Reason managed to find so much magic to give her? She couldn't have given her the sharp, cutting Cansino magic, because then Jay-Tee'd be on the floor writhing in agony, or probably dead. Had she given Jay-Tee regular magic? But how much of that did she have left? Not much. She'd been as stupid with it as Jay-Tee had been with her own.

So where did this new magic come from? Could Reason pull it out of the air? Was that another one of her brand-new superpowers?

Wherever the magic had come from, Jay-Tee was going to be very, very careful with it. She owed Tom and Reason that much for saving her life. It would suck if they'd given away their magic for nothing.

Especially Reason. What if this Cansino magic wasn't stable? What if it disappeared? Then she'd have nothing left. She would die. All because she'd saved Jay-Tee.

Why hadn't Jay-Tee seen New York City?

She got up, went to the fridge, and poured herself a glass of white wine, filling the glass near to the brim. Now that Mere wasn't here to say no, she could drink as much as she liked.

It had been really annoying watching Mere sipping wine while she questioned Jay-Tee over and over about stuff she mostly didn't have answers to. The whole time, Jay-Tee'd been wishing she could have some wine too. For all his evilness, at least *he* didn't care whether she drank or not. Jay-Tee took a big sip now in a stuff-you-Esmeralda-Cansino way.

It wasn't like Mere was *her* grandmother. Besides, Jay-Tee already had to stop doing magic, which meant no real running or dancing. What else was left for her? How else was she going to relax? Surely having some wine didn't matter.

Even if she did manage to stop using magic (and she really, really, *really* was going to do her damnedest), even so, how long did she have left? Weren't there little inadvertent uses of magic? When she ran just a little too fast? When she weaved her way through a crowd? Like at the airport. All of that added up. Sometimes when she was asleep and dreaming she would use magic. How could she control her dreams?

And even if Jay-Tee did manage to never use the tiniest trace of magic ever, ever again, then what kind of a life was she going to have off her rocker?

She had another sip of the wine, because, well, she needed it.

Jay-Tee wished she'd been able to go through the door with Reason and Mere, then lose them and move in with Danny. Her brother'd let her drink. At least, she thought he might. She missed him. But going through the door meant magic.

But the door had opened and she hadn't seen New York, she hadn't seen the East Village, Seventh Street; she'd seen a Sydney backyard. Was that a sign of how little magic she had left? Too little to even see through the door. Had *trying* to see through to New York cost her? When she'd peeked through the keyhole it had been blurry. That must have been because she had so little. Now she couldn't see it at all, not even blurred.

Jay-Tee took another gulp of wine, feeling it turn acid on the back of her throat. She coughed. Put the glass down, got herself water, gulped that down. Stupid Esmeralda with her crappy wine.

When her throat calmed, she drank some more, and then more, until the glass was empty. Jay-Tee found the idea of being drunk appealing. She didn't like the direction of her thoughts. Better to be silly and raucous, anything that would lead her away from thinking what she didn't want to think.

The door had opened and she'd seen that big-ass tree, stupid chirruping birds, the part of the garage door not obscured by the big-ass tree. Everything green and summery and light and Sydney. Not wintry New York. Not the dirty, comfortable, beloved East Village.

Did it mean she was going to die soon? Who'd rescue her this time? She'd lived her life so recklessly it was pathetic to discover that, after all, she didn't want to die young.

She wanted to live.

The wine was starting to uncurl inside her, to smooth things out, make them seem better than they were. She opened the fridge, looking for more. Found three bottles, unopened, lying on their sides at the bottom of the fridge. One of them was champagne. Easier to open than normal wine, but it seemed kind of pathetic to drink bubbles on your own.

She pulled out one of the other ones. It had a cheap-looking label: Moss Wood Estate Semillon. It was probably as crappy as the other one, but she didn't care. She found a corkscrew and opened it.

She poured herself another mighty glass, picking out bits of cork with a finger. The sour taste made her grimace. *Oh well,* she told herself. *It'll get me where I want to go.*

The house hadn't shaken when Reason and Esmeralda went to New York, she realized. Normally the door opening and shutting sent a shudder through the house. She hadn't felt it. She hadn't heard it. What did that mean?

It meant, she decided, that she should have more wine.

The door opened. Tom stepped through, head swathed in hat and scarf, so that all Jay-Tee could see was his red nose and eyes.

"Tom!"

He grinned, started to take off his gloves, turned to shut the door behind him.

"Don't shut it!" Jay-Tee yelled, jumping up.

"What?"

She grabbed the door, pushed it wide open. The backyard. Green leaves, brown bark, fallen brown leaves and twigs on the wooden porch. The last of the day's sunlight. Long shadows.

She stepped through. One step to the porch, wood under her feet. Not New York.

Jay-Tee heard Tom shout something from inside the house. He sounded scared.

She went down the rest of the steps to the backyard. Tom's house over that fence, past the red spiky bushes. Mere's magic cottage on the other side, its dark brick wall right up to the fence. It seemed to glower.

This was not New York City. She wasn't cold; she was hot.

She sat down on the steps.

"Jay-Tee?" Tom called. "Are you there?"

She turned to where his head was sticking out the kitchen window.

"Bugger, you just disappeared! Scared me to buggery." He climbed through the window, dropped onto the porch, where he wobbled. He'd taken off his coat, hat, and gloves, but he was still dressed too warmly. A scarf hung loose around his neck. "What's going on? Are you all right?"

Jay-Tee returned to staring at her hands. She was thinking

about Reason's. They hadn't been glowing. She'd said so, and Mere had looked at her weird.

No. It couldn't be true. It couldn't.

Tom sat down next to her, a little unsteady. "You don't look okay."

She turned to him before he could say anything else. She leaned forward and kissed him. Lips against lips.

He pulled away, startled. "Jay-Tee? Are you sure you're—"

"I'm fine. You're fine. I like you."

"I like you too. Kisses are lovely," he said, tripping over the word *kisses*. She understood. It was a tricky word. "But you seem so—"

"Fine," she said, and kissed him again.

"Fine?" he asked, and kissed her back. She opened her mouth: they kissed properly this time. She ran her tongue over his teeth. His tongue found hers. She reached her hands up to his cheeks, careful to avoid where Jason Blake had cut him. Smooth, soft, still chilled from the— She pushed that thought away. Felt his hands on her waist. Moved hers into his thick white-blond hair.

All the sensations, their bodies so close, so intertwined, all of it was making Jay-Tee tingle. A buzz spread through her; something in the pit of her stomach flipped, but it was a good flip. She let out a little sigh. Tom's hands moved on her waist and the sensation shivered through her body, all the way to her toes. It felt like magic.

It wasn't magic.

No. She wasn't going there.

She pulled her mouth from Tom's, touched his bottom lip with her fingers. Her face was so close she could see the little freckles on his lips. Pale brown on pale pink. She kissed each one. She could feel him breathing. "Pretty," she said.

"Jay-Tee," he said. "What's—"

She kissed him again, properly, with more passion, more oomph. He responded. He liked it, she could tell.

She pulled his hand from where it lay on top of her T-shirt and slid it underneath so she could feel his skin on her skin, just above her hip bone. His fingers were still cool but warming fast. His hands circled her waist. She shivered.

The phone rang. Sharp and loud, cracking open the heavy hot air.

Briiiiiing. Briiiiiiing.

"Phone," Tom said. She felt the word against her lips. Their mouths were still close.

It could be Reason or Esmeralda, Jay-Tee thought. *It could be important. I should get it.*

She untangled herself from Tom, stood up unsteadily, pushed back her hair, wiped her mouth. Put her hand on the door handle. It opened easily. Because it wasn't . . . She wasn't—

Briiiiiing. Briiiiiiing.

She stepped through. From Sydney back porch to Sydney kitchen. *Whoosh!* Magic. Not. She giggled. Wobbled to the phone and picked it up.

"Hello," she said, imitating Tom. "Esmeralda Cansino's residence."

"Hello, Jay-Tee," said a voice that chilled her. "I was hoping it would be you."

Jay-Tee's brain stalled. It was *him*. He scared her and she hated him. She didn't want to talk to him. She didn't even like to *think* about him. But it was his voice on the phone. He'd hurt her. He'd hurt Reason. Stolen from them. He would do it again if he could. He was a bad, bad man.

"I have a message for you to deliver to Esmeralda. . . ."

She wasn't listening. Thoughts were multiplying in her head. He'd hurt her by taking her magic. But she didn't—she forced herself to follow it through—she didn't have any magic. Not anymore.

Reason had taken it, or switched it off, or done something that had left her alive but as magic-free as big a dead spot, as her brother, Danny. She had no magic anymore, which meant that—

"Who is it?" Tom whispered. He must have clambered in through the window.

She shook her head.

"Jay-Tee? What's going on?"

What did it mean? It meant that *he* couldn't do anything to her. Nothing. She didn't have to be scared of him. She didn't have to think about him. He wasn't part of her world anymore. She was free.

"Did you get all of that, Jay-Tee?" he asked.

Jay-Tee giggled. "Nope. Not a word. I wasn't listening to you, Alexander, or Jason Blake, or Stephen Collins, or David Johnson, or whatever boring-ass white-bread name you're calling yourself this week. You can go shit in a bottle and eat it for all I care." Jay-Tee almost started laughing. She'd called him by name. All of his names!

"You can't do anything to me, not anymore. I'm not afraid of you. You can't touch me. You can't take my magic, 'cause I haven't got any! Go sit on that and rotate! Asshole!"

With a flourish she hung up the phone and fell into Tom's arms, which should have been all romantic and sexy and stuff, but she was wobbly and so was he, and they fell.

It hit her again: she had no magic, but she was alive. Everything had changed. Her whole life.

She *had* a life. She kissed Tom's confused and anxious face. His cheeks and then his mouth, which was when another thought hit her:

Jason Blake's—See? She could think his name, she could say it aloud if she wanted to—Jason Blake's message *had* been important. It had been for Esmeralda and Reason. It was about Reason's mother, Sarafina, who he was holding hostage, because he did still have power: he could hurt Jay-Tee's friends.

"Oops," she said.

She wasn't magic anymore. She burst into tears.

13
Hot and Bothered

"Oops?" Tom asked. He sat up, wishing his head was clearer. "What's going on, Jay-Tee? What did Jason Blake want? How can you not have any magic? You're alive!" Unless she'd gone mad already. Which was why she thought her magic was gone and spat the dummy at Jason Blake. And had kissed Tom? Well, no, he didn't want to think that was madness-induced.

She was still lying on the floor, still crying.

"Jay-Tee."

She groaned. "N'magic, Tom," she mumbled.

No magic? Was that really what she'd said? Tom's head was still fuzzy from the wine he'd drunk with Cath in New York City. They'd stayed up talking for hours. They hadn't talked like that, *really* talked, in such a long, long time. Not since before he met Esmeralda, found out what he was. He felt good. Fuzzy, but good.

Well, not all good. Not if Jay-Tee really was crazy. Lying on the floor and crying wasn't exactly a sane activity, was it?

But she'd kissed him. She'd kissed him, and *that* had felt very good indeed. He'd thought he was going to burst into flames, and not just because he had too many clothes on for a

Sydney summer. He was still vibrating. He took his jumper off.

"Are you okay, Jay-Tee?"

She moaned again. Was that a crazy moan?

"Jay-Tee," he said, stroking her hair. "Jay-Tee? You should sit up. Let me get you some water." And himself some water. He was suddenly parched. Water was a really good idea.

She moved her head in what might have been a nod. He stood up, grabbed her hands. "Come on, Jay-Tee. Help me, here." He pulled and she practically flew up into his arms. She was little. Littler than Reason. He hadn't noticed that before, because she was so big in other ways. Big personality, big mouth. Nice mouth, he thought, now that he'd explored it some. He blushed.

"You're cute, Tom," she said, tears wet on her cheeks. "I like your eyebrows."

She really was mad. He walked her across to a stool and slid her onto it. She leaned her forearms on the table as if that was the only way she could stay upright. "My head is all . . . What do you say? What's that Tom word? Buggery! My head is all buggery." She hiccupped.

Tom didn't bother to tell her that the word she meant was *buggered*, not *buggery*; instead, he handed her a glass of water. "Drink this." She did.

"See that?" she said, pointing to an almost empty bottle of wine on the table. "I drank all that."

Tom had had four glasses of wine. Well, three and a bit. He hadn't come close to finishing the last one. He'd've preferred

Coke. So Jay-Tee must be drunk, not crazy. That was a relief, though it still meant she'd probably only kissed him because of being drunk. But she'd kissed him this morning too! Right here in the kitchen. She hadn't been drunk then.

But it had been a little kiss. A very little kiss.

"You drank all of it?"

Jay-Tee nodded. "I think it might have been too much. I can't believe it's gone."

"Well, if you drink it, that's what happens."

"Not the wine, Tom! My magic."

"Don't be sill—"

"*I'm* gone. How can I be me without magic?"

"Jay-Tee—"

"Aaargh!"

Tom jumped; Jay-Tee was crying even louder now. Her head sank down onto her forearms. Tom stood beside her and patted her head, feeling useless. "Do you want some more water?" he asked.

Jay-Tee made a noise that he decided was a yes. He filled her glass from the tap and put it next to her forearm. She sat up—her eyes were red, her nose too. There were tears and snot on her face and on the table. Fortunately there were tissues left in the box he'd used to mop up her earlier bout of tears. He hadn't pegged Jay-Tee for a sob machine.

"I might have no magic, but I can still drink water."

"You're just drunk, Jay-Tee. You're still magic. Otherwise you'd be dead. Remember?"

"Oh, no," she said. "It's different now."

"How?"

"I *did* drink too much. But that's just because I was scared. It's really, really gone, Tom. I'm not kidding. I'm a hundred-per-cent honest."

"How's that possible?" Tom said, humouring her. He reached out and touched her cheek. "You're warm. You're definitely alive."

"I drank too much." She drank the rest of the water. He got her more.

"You drank too much and it made your magic disappear?" Tom asked. He sat down next to her, wondering if there was anything to eat. He was starving. Bloody vegetarians and their budgie food. Jay-Tee hiccupped again.

"No, I drank too much *because* my magic disappeared." Jay-Tee shook her head, as if she was trying to shake something clear, or maybe she was just trying to stop the hiccups. "But that's not the only important thing. Jason Blake has Sarafina. That's what he called about. I was supposed to give Esmeralda a message. But I—"

"I heard. Pretty excellent. 'You should shit in a bottle. . . . '" Though it was also definitely a sign of insanity. She never would have done that before. She'd been too scared of Jason Blake to even say his name out loud. "Hey! You said his name!"

Jay-Tee grinned, then hiccupped. She shook her grin away. "No, it was a *terrible* thing to do—not the saying-his-name bit—that's no big deal. But I didn't take the message. From him, I mean, from Jason Blake. I don't know what the message was."

"What message?"

"He wanted me to tell Reason and Mere something, but I didn't listen." Her next hiccup was even louder.

"Drink a glass of water backwards."

"Do what?"

"You take a glass of water, like this, then you lean over. Look, let me show you."

She spilled some of it, but when she stood back up, swayed, grabbed the back of the chair, and told him that it was stupid, the hiccups were gone.

Jay-Tee was muddled. Tom wondered if he was muddled too. "You kiss really good," he said, though he'd been planning to ask her where Reason and Esmeralda were.

She smiled. It wasn't a crazy smile. "You do too. 'Cept for using a bit too much tongue—"

He smacked her lightly on the shoulder. "Do not!"

"Do too!"

"Do not!"

"Do!"

"Not," he said, leaning forward, careful to hold onto the table and avoid touching the nasty bruise on her cheek, kissing her lips gently. She kissed him back. They exchanged more kisses, gentle as butterflies, one after another, lips on lips, mouths opening only slowly, tiny hints of tongue. Tom felt his ears get hot. He'd never kissed anyone like this before. "You're not hiccupping anymore."

"No."

They kissed again until she pulled away. Tom wondered if it was ethical for him to be kissing a drunk person. Or a crazy person, for that matter.

"Esmeralda," she said firmly. "Reason."

"Right," Tom said. "Jason Blake has Reason's mum? That's what you said?"

She nodded.

"Where are they?"

"New York," Jay-Tee said. "They're in New York." Her lips were bigger and redder than usual, almost like she was wearing lipstick. Looking at them made Tom feel even hotter. He hoped he wasn't blushing.

If she was mad, was any of this true?

"Tom! Why are you looking at me like that?"

"Looking at you like what?"

"Like you think I'm making everything up. My dad used to look at me exactly like that. I'm not making this up! Why would I? Why would Jason Blake be calling here? Where do you think Reason and Esmeralda are?"

"But . . ." he said. "Well, you think your magic is gone. And you're clearly alive, and you've been saying mad—"

"You think I've gone nuts?"

"No," Tom said. "Well, um, sort of, maybe . . . "

"How do you think I went through the door and ended up in the backyard? If I was magic, I'd go to New York, wouldn't I? Look at me, Tom, look really closely. Do you see any magic?"

Tom looked at her and then closed his eyes, focusing his own magic. There were no shapes, no emeralds, no triangles.

No magic.

He opened them again.

"See?"

He nodded slowly, trying to make sense of what he'd seen. Of what he *hadn't* seen. "No magic?"

"No."

"What happened?"

"I almost died. Again. And Reason fixed me, but she didn't give me magic, she took it away. I don't know how she did it.

"I'm a dead spot."

Tom's mouth opened, but no words came out. How could . . . He couldn't imagine not having magic. It would be like losing an arm—no, much worse than that. It would be like losing the special, talented, cool part of yourself. Being all three-dimensional and colourful and then waking up one morning 2-D and grey.

"I told you she would save me."

She didn't sound very happy about it. "You're sure?" he asked.

"Stop saying that, Tom! I'm sure! Okay? You're sure too. You just saw it. And stop looking at me like that!" Jay-Tee wiped her eyes. "I can't think about it right now, okay?"

Tom nodded, took a deep breath. "So, Reason and Esmeralda?"

"They're in New York City, waiting for Jason Blake to get there. He kidnapped Sarafina."

"He kidnapped Sarafina? From Kalder Park?"

"Yes."

"But my mum is there. Is she okay?"

"I think so," Jay-Tee said. "He only wanted his daughter. He didn't care about anyone else."

"So he just casually strolled into Kalder and took his daughter away? How come they allowed that?"

"We don't know. It has to have been Cansino magic. You should see what Reason's like now, Tom. She glows. And she moves like she's some kind of . . . I don't know, alien or something. I think she's becoming just like her ancestor dude. It's freaky."

"And Jason Blake is like that too?" Tom tried to imagine Jason Blake being even scarier than he already was.

"No. Well, we don't know, but Mere says Raul Cansino chose Reason, so she's the only one he made like him."

"Well, that's a relief."

"I guess. It's too weird, though. It's like she's not Reason anymore. But if she weren't like that, I guess I'd be dead."

Tom didn't want to think about Jay-Tee being dead. "What have the Kalder Park people said? Why would Reason's mum go with Jason Blake?"

"They haven't said anything so far, I don't think. They haven't called here, but maybe they've called Mere's cell phone." Jay-Tee shrugged.

"Great. Nice to know their security's so ace. Hey, wait a minute. How did Blake get here? Did he come through the door?"

"Nope. We think he took a plane."

"A *plane*?"

"Yeah, Tom, you know, big metal thing? Fly through the sky?"

Tom ignored her sarcasm. "But why? Why come all this way to steal Sarafina? Why would he do that?"

"Well, if I hadn't told him to go to hell, we might know."

"Point," Tom said. "We have to call them."

"Yes!" Jay-Tee said, then stopped. "Call who? Kalder Park?"

"No. Reason and Esmeralda."

"Right," Jay-Tee said.

"I'll get my phone." Tom picked up his backpack where he'd let it drop when he first came through the door and fished out his mobile. He turned it on and it beeped excitedly at him. "Huh. Lots of messages."

"You had your phone with you the whole time? You had it turned off!"

"Well, yeah. I forgot. Mere only just gave it to me so hardly anyone knows the number."

"But we called you like half a million times!"

"You called me?"

"We were worried, Tom," Jay-Tee said. "You were gone for ages and you said you'd come back right away. You know, after your sister called."

"Yeah," Tom said. "I meant to. But . . ." he waved a hand. "Stuff happened. Nothing bad."

"Here's the number." She slid a piece of paper at Tom.

"You want me to call?" Tom asked, marvelling at how sober he'd become. "You're the one who talked to Jason Blake. Not me."

"But I'm drunk." She hiccupped to prove it. It sounded forced to Tom.

"No, you're not." Jay-Tee's magic being gone was plenty sobering. "You're not even wobbling anymore," he said, though she was a little bit.

"Yes, I am. See!" She demonstrated the worst drunken wobble Tom had ever seen.

"Why do you want *me* to call?" he asked. "'Cause you're embarrassed that you stuffed it up?"

"Pretty much," Jay-Tee agreed. "I don't want Esmeralda mad at me. Not that she can do anything. Magical, I mean. Though, come to think of it, she can do plenty. Throw me out onto the street. I mean, it's not like she can teach me magic, is it? What use am I now?" Her eyes went wet again. She grabbed another tissue to blow her nose.

"She wouldn't do that." Maybe Esmeralda wasn't as wonderful as he used to think, but he still couldn't imagine she'd throw Jay-Tee out. Then another thought occurred to him. "So you want her cranky with *me*?"

"But she won't be mad at you, because you're just telling her what happened—you're not the one who did it. None of it's your fault. It'd just be nice if you could, you know, make it seem a little less like it was my fault. Oh, and tell her that the line he was on was all echoey and hard to hear. That could mean he was calling from a plane, right? I mean, we already knew that, but even so."

Tom sighed and flipped open the mobile. "You really don't

have any more magic? How does that feel?" The thought of losing his magic was so horrible he couldn't go there. He'd rather die.

※

Esmeralda didn't get angry. She accepted Tom's explanation that Jay-Tee had been too freaked out to talk to Blake. She asked lots of questions about Jay-Tee's non-magic status. That's what she called it, "non-magic status." As if Jay-Tee had been a spy for some government magic department and now had to be reclassified. Tom wondered if it was actuary talk. The kind of thing that filled up the memos and reports at Esmeralda's work. Magic actuary talk.

"Can you stay there? Answer the phone next time?"

Tom said that he would.

"How is Jay-Tee doing?"

"She's fine," Tom said, though she was sitting beside him looking decidedly less than fine. "How's Reason? Jay-Tee says she's been really weird."

"She's fine too," Esmeralda said. "We'll call if anything happens. You do the same." And that was that. Tom put the phone down. Outside, the sun was setting, orange-pink light making its way through the dense foliage of Filomena.

He thought about his own mother in Kalder Park, barking mad like she'd been his entire life. If Esmeralda hadn't found him he'd've gone that way too. His mum had never known about magic, never known how to stay sane.

"Whatcha thinking?"

"About my mum. I mean, at least now you're never going to go mad like she is."

"Oh," Jay-Tee said. "Oh! Your mom! Of course! Oh, Tom, that's a genius idea! If Reason can turn my magic off, then she could turn your mom's off too! Your mom would be sane again!"

Tom felt like he'd been punched. He heard what Jay-Tee said, heard each individual word, but he couldn't believe them. "My mum," he said.

"Yeah," Jay-Tee said. "Wouldn't that be amazing?"

"Yes," he said, but he was too afraid to believe it. He had no memories of his mum ever being normal. Not one.

14
Skin

The 610 Tiny smudges of light smeared across space, swirling into a spiral that opened out into infinity. I tumbled into it, falling round and round, then sliding into space even more crowded with lights than Sydney had been.

New York.

This was what a door was truly like: a swirling bridge between two points in magic space. So much more fun than simply opening a door and stepping through. The real world was so clunky, so constrained.

I surveyed the magical landscape, looking for other doors. I saw groups of lights threaded together as the door to Sydney was—seventeen of them. A prime number. All around me there were many prime configurations. I wondered if primes were one of magic's building blocks. Or maybe it was the other way around?

Some of the doors seemed near, others less so. But I wasn't sure what that meant here.

The door swirled again, and Esmeralda's bright lights appeared. And something began pressing in on me; noises leaked in from the other world.

"Rea-son. Rea-son. Rea-son."

I pushed up against it to where this world thickened into the other world. "Esmeralda," I said.

She told me something else. But the words muddled as they floated by.

"All right," I said. Maybe she had news of Sarafina.

I made myself leave pure magic and mathematics behind.

This time I stumbled on re-entry, slipping down the steps and landing heavily on the footpath. I felt like I was being crushed by normal gravity. I looked up at Esmeralda standing in front of the door to Sydney, rugged up against the cold. She came down and grabbed my arm to steady me.

"Are you okay?" she asked. Above the door I saw the face carved in stone with the crudely painted eyes and moustache. He seemed amused this time, not sad.

"I'm fine," I said, even though I felt horrible. I couldn't stop thinking about Sarafina. Was she still alive? I'd stopped wobbling, but my heart beat faster than it should. When I was in Cansino's world, I couldn't feel my heart.

"How can you be fine? You must be freezing! You have no hair and no hat. You're not even wearing a coat!"

"The air's heavier here."

"Here? What?" Esmeralda asked, putting her hands in her coat pockets. Her breath turned into puffs of condensation.

"In the real world." My breath didn't.

"What do you mean?"

"I've found some doors," I told her, because I didn't want to explain about the other world.

"How many?" she asked, shifting back and forth.

I shrugged. "Seventeen. But there might be more. There are other things there that could be doors. I'm not sure."

"Are they close by?"

"Maybe. I can lead us to them. I just don't know how long it will take."

"But you can see them from here?"

"Yes."

"Can you see when someone opens one?" Esmeralda said.

"Yes. I saw you."

My grandmother laughed. "The door's right there. How could you *not* see me?"

"I saw you in the other world, not here."

Esmeralda shivered. "If we go to my flat here, will you still be able to see the doors?"

"Is it near here?"

"Yes."

"Then I think so. But we could just walk to them. Find out what's on the other side. See if we can find Sarafina."

"But, Reason, you said there were seventeen of them. You don't know how close they are. Maybe some of them aren't even in Manhattan. It could take us all day just to look at two or three. And even though you suddenly seem to be immune to the cold, I'm not.

"If we go to my flat, we can wait, and as soon as Alexander or Sarafina shows up, we can go to them. Doesn't that make more sense?"

"I could examine the doors by myself. It probably wouldn't take me very long," I said.

"And if Alexander showed up? He's devious. He'll try to trick you, Reason. You'd be better off with my help. I'm not as strong as you, but I'm strong."

"Okay," I said. I wasn't convinced, but if there was a chance of real-world news of Sarafina, I didn't want to miss it.

Esmeralda stuck her hand out to make a taxi stop. "Too cold to walk," she said.

A taxi stopped almost immediately. That was easier here. In New York there were more taxis than normal cars.

I slid in. Esmeralda leaned forward to give the address. Thirteenth Street. Good. A prime number. Almost as good as those divisible by nine.

I thought about Jay-Tee again. Would she really stay alive without magic?

I hoped we'd find Sarafina quickly. And that I wouldn't see Danny again.

❀

Esmeralda's New York flat wasn't as big as Danny's, but it had more furniture, pictures on the walls. It seemed more lived-in. How often did she come here?

The flat had a long, narrow corridor with a kitchen, study, bathroom, and two bedrooms off it.

"You can sleep in there," she said, showing me the smaller bedroom. "If we end up having to stay a night."

A large Escher print hung on the wall, lizards entwined and crawling off the edges of the drawing. Sarafina had used Escher to teach me about tessellation and tiling. We'd spent hours designing our own mosaics, laying triangles and polygons edge-to-edge on paper, graduating to more complicated shapes, mixing them together. None of ours were as fine as Escher's, but it had been fun.

The next room was the bathroom. I peeked inside and caught a glimpse of myself in the mirror.

I had no hair.

Seeing it gone was completely different from *feeling* it gone. My eyelashes and eyebrows were missing too.

I wasn't looking at myself. I was looking at someone else: a hairless alien with golden skin that glowed like a statue's.

My eyes. They weren't . . .

The irises were bigger, pushing the whites away. They were without variation, one uniform colour: brown. The way pupils are black and nothing else. There were no feathering strands of colour radiating out from the pupil, no bits of yellow or green or black. Not like normal eyes. They were brown and only brown. The same golden brown as my skin.

They were like Raul Emilio Jesús Cansino's eyes.

That couldn't be me.

I stared harder, past my skin, I stared inside myself. It hurt to do it. Like something was tearing. I'd never been able to do that before. My cells were not what they had been. I found the pulsing life of my baby, those few scant cells that were not mine, but that were as changed as I was.

A monster. I was pregnant with a monster.

"You see," Esmeralda said. "You're hardly you anymore. And Jay-Tee couldn't see it."

She led me to the end of the narrow hallway, to the largest room in the flat. It had five windows, two couches, a coffee table, a piano and stool, and two bookcases filled with books. On one of the walls was a photo of an enormous tree. It looked like the Moreton Bay fig in her backyard in Sydney, Filomena.

I blinked and caught a glimpse of the tiny magics in the room, too numerous and too smudgy to count. Was that leakage from my grandmother's magic?

Esmeralda took off her coat and laid it on the edge of the nearest couch. Then she sat down, crossed her legs at the ankle, and waved at me to take a seat. She looked calm and relaxed. Not like a woman whose daughter had just been kidnapped.

"You're changing very quickly, Reason. When I look inside you," my grandmother said, "even your cells are different. If you become any more like him, you won't be human anymore."

"I know," I said. I had seen it.

"Do you still feel human?"

"I guess." I didn't know. I missed my mother. I was still angry with Danny. Those were human feelings, weren't they?

But when I was in Cansino's world, I hardly felt them at all. Was I beginning to feel them less strongly here too?

I looked up at Esmeralda. There were so many traces of Sarafina in her. The same colour hair and eyes. They were the same height, had the same olive skin, brown eyes. But it was her voice that was most like. If I didn't look at her, if I just listened, I could almost imagine it was Sarafina.

Esmeralda was staring at me like she wanted something. Sarafina would never stare at me like that.

"I wonder why he chose you?"

"Well," I said, "it's not like he had heaps of people to choose from, is it? How many Cansinos are there? Just you, Jason Blake, and me."

"And Sarafina."

"And Sarafina. So we each had a twenty-five-per-cent chance."

"But he chose you."

"And my baby."

Esmeralda nodded. "That's why, I think. Because of the baby. You'll become even more powerful as you change. I think you'll be able to do whatever you want."

I wanted to see my mother again. I wanted Tom and Jay-Tee to live long, happy lives. I wanted my baby to be born safe and sound and for Danny to love me. Or did I? I wasn't so sure about that last one.

"Have you thought about what's happening to your baby?"

Of course I had. When I didn't say anything, Esmeralda made

a little sound, half a cough, half a *tsk*. She raised an eyebrow, delicately, as if it might break. "Your baby is changing too."

"I know."

"You might want to be in that other place you won't tell me about, but is that what your baby will want?"

I didn't say anything.

"If you keep going there, you won't have any choice but to stay there forever. Your baby won't have any choice."

"Raul Cansino didn't stay there forever."

"But what was he, Reason? What was his life?"

Wonderful, I almost said. No pain. No hurt.

"I think you could stop the changes. The same way you turned Jay-Tee's magic off but kept her alive. You can do the same thing to yourself, to your baby. You don't have to turn into him.

"You can do whatever you want now."

"Like take away your magic?"

Esmeralda shivered, shifted back further on the couch. "Or make my magic stronger. More like yours."

"But I'm turning into a monster. You said so yourself."

"No, I didn't. I said you're becoming like him. Do you want to be all the way like Raul? Barely human?

"I'm just saying that you can do anything now. I saw what you did to Jay-Tee. She would have died. She's alive because of you."

I nodded. "But we don't know for how long."

Esmeralda shrugged. "How long do most people have? She's normal now."

Normal, I thought. Was that a good thing? Sarafina had never thought so.

"I bet you can use your magic to find Sarafina right now," Esmeralda said, as if she'd heard my thoughts.

"Maybe," I said. I wasn't sure how far I could see in Cansino's world. "But it wouldn't help finding her here."

"Aren't the two connected? You can see doors there. You said you could see me there."

"It's not like there are street signs. When I'm there I can't navigate the way I can here. There aren't any roads or trees or rock formations or any other way for me to find my bearings. I can figure north, south, east, and west. And whether something's far or near. But far could be twenty K or two thousand. I can't tell."

Esmeralda leaned towards me, an intense expression on her face.

"Why are you looking at me like that?"

"Like what?" She shifted back again, crossed her legs the other way.

Greedy, I decided, she looked greedy. She wanted what I had.

"You've changed."

"You said that already." I glanced down at my gleaming hands. The nails weren't broken and uneven. They were smooth and tapered.

There weren't any scars. No nick on the third right knuckle of my left hand from where I'd cut it peeling a yam. No long faded burn mark on my right palm from where I'd picked up a billy can from the fire. I'd only been little, I was trying to help. But it had hurt so much I'd cried and cried and cried. We had no ice, so Sarafina picked me up, carried me to the creek, plunged my hand into the icy water. At first the scar had stretched across my palm, but as I got older it got smaller and smaller and faded from bright red to white.

Now it was gone.

My hands weren't my hands.

"Not just physically," my grandmother continued. "You're not entirely you anymore. When was the last time you laughed?"

"There hasn't been much to laugh at, has there? My mother's been kidnapped." I paused. I wasn't going to tell Esmeralda about Danny.

"If you keep changing, will you even *want* to save your mother?"

I blinked and caught a glimpse of a familiar light. I closed my eyes, felt the weight lifting from me, the soft thickness of Cansino's world surrounding me.

The new magic was strong. It started to move—in its wake a glittering spiral.

Jason Blake.

"He's here," I said.

15
Dancing

They sat in front of the tellie in Jay-Tee's room. Something dramatic set in the American West with lots of cowboys, but so underlit, everyone was lost in shadow. Tom had no idea who was who. The costumes were pretty excellent, but. Even if they were all in dark, dirty colours, with the occasional shock of white or red.

Tom felt like he was floating. His little trip to New York to talk to Cathy had brought the door lag flooding back. It was night, and the sun had set, but it felt wrong. Maybe because he'd barely been outside since he got back. He'd just hung out with Jay-Tee while she tried to make sense of what had happened to her.

She'd rung her useless brother and left messages on his mobile, his landline, and with about a dozen of his friends. They all promised to tell him to call her when they saw him.

Esmeralda had rung to tell them that Jason Blake (or Alexander, as she called him) was in New York City and Reason was tracking him down, which gave Tom an incongruous image of Reason with her nose to the footpath, sniffing.

He was more than a little relieved that he and Jay-Tee

weren't in New York. That their job was, as Esmeralda put it, "to hold down the fort." Whatever that meant.

"Do you think she's going to be okay?"

"Who?" Jay-Tee asked. "The blonde one? Nope. I think that creepy guy's going to kill her. He'll probably kill all of them. He's clearly got issues."

"No. Reason's mum."

Jay-Tee turned to him and smiled. "I hope so. I mean, I'm pretty sure. You haven't seen Reason. She's changed. There's nothing she can't do now. She'll find her mom and save her, just like she saved me."

Tom wasn't sure Jay-Tee had been saved. Yes, Reason had stopped her from dying, but . . . well, he wasn't sure *saved* was the right word. She didn't have any magic. Tom couldn't imagine what that would be like.

He was also thinking about how his hands had felt on Jay-Tee's bare waist. About kissing.

Who'd've thought someone else's tongue in your mouth would be so tingle-making? He'd known that was how it was supposed to be, and he'd really wanted to try, but he'd had his doubts. It looked gross. He'd worried that he'd get a major dose of tongue-awareness right in the middle of kissing properly for the first time, and he'd be thinking about tongues being worms, or worse, slabs of meat, and, well, gross.

It hadn't been like that at all, and now here he was wondering—and not for the first time since they'd been interrupted by Jason Blake calling—if there'd be more.

He didn't know if Jay-Tee felt the same way. Right now, she didn't look like she was thinking about what he was thinking about. Yes, she'd kissed him first. But it could've been one of her strange moods: first worried about dying, then about going mad, now coping with her magic being gone.

It would do anyone's head in, wouldn't it?

What if she'd kissed him rather than think about it? Did Jay-Tee even like him? She said she did. Tom liked her, but he hadn't known how much until she kissed him. Not many hours ago he'd only wanted to kiss Reason. Would he be feeling this way about *anyone* who kissed him?

Tom wasn't sure. He hadn't felt much when Jessica Chan kissed him. It'd been okay, but he wasn't desperate to do it again the way he was with Jay-Tee. He hoped it hadn't been a spur-of-the-moment freak-out thing. After all, he'd given Jay-Tee some of his magic. Didn't that mean they were connected?

Or maybe not, now that she wasn't magic anymore.

Jay-Tee giggled, but nothing funny had happened on the tellie.

"What?" Tom asked. For a stricken moment, he thought she knew what he was thinking.

"I just tried to make light. And I really, really, really can't."

"And that's funny?"

She nodded. "Very. I'm concentrating on my mom's leather bracelet. I've got the tooth. See?" She showed it to him. It was the one Esmeralda had given her that had been in the Cansino family for generations. "And now—" She held out her hand, palm up. "Now I'm *not* making money out of nothing."

"You used to do that?" Tom asked. He hadn't known it was possible.

"Uh-huh. All the time." Jay-Tee grinned. "I was a very bad witch. Not a good idea, though. Uses lots of magic. I guess that's why I almost bought it twice. Okay, watch this." She stood up and held her arms out in front of her, Superman style. "Now I'm *not* flying."

"No way," Tom exclaimed. "You used to fly?!"

Jay-Tee sat down with a huge grin on her face. Then she cracked up.

"Bitch!"

"Gotcha!" She punched him lightly on the shoulder. Tom felt it through the thin cotton of his T-shirt. He thought about leaning forward and kissing her.

"I wonder if I can still run," she said, playing with her bottom lip. Tom found it hard to look anywhere else. "Not how I used to, obviously. But I wonder if I'm still fast."

"You'll be faster than me, that's for sure."

"Big deal. Hey, do you think I'll still be able to dance?"

"Well, that we can test. Esmeralda's stereo is grouse. Wanna go dance in the dining room?" Dancing could definitely lead to more kissing, couldn't it?

"Sure," Jay-Tee said. "I'd love to."

Esmeralda's music either sucked or Jay-Tee'd never heard of it. They went through every CD and found nothing she deemed even slightly danceable.

"Mere's forty-five," she said, as if she were saying, *Mere's an alien*. "Old people's music always sucks."

"How about this?" Tom asked. He'd turned the tuner on and pressed FM, then turned the dial to a best of the seventies, eighties, nineties channel, pretty sure that Jay-Tee would hate it.

"Vile!" she said instantly. "Top forty crap. It smells so bad it might as well be rotten meat."

"Let me guess," Tom said, trying not to laugh. "You don't like it?"

She grinned. "It's disgusting. Guitars, bass, crappy singing. Boring old-people music."

He switched the dial, got Triple J. "How 'bout this?"

She shook her head. "Guitars, Tom, guitars! They're *so* over. Dance music! It's gotta, gotta, gotta be dance music."

Tom turned to the three other stations that were actual possibilities. On the second one, Jay-Tee nodded. "*That's* more like it. Feel that bass? It's skittering and thrumming. There's reverb. Perfect."

They drew the curtains so no one could see in from the street. Then got good and sweaty pushing Esmeralda's dining table, chairs, and the other moveable furniture against the walls, which left plenty of space.

Tom turned the music up two more notches and walked into the middle of the room. "Ready?" he asked, though he was nervous. He really liked dancing, but most of his friends didn't. So he'd mostly just danced in his bedroom, which was deeply pathetic. He'd also danced some at the year nine formal last year, but then Scooter and Ron had started snickering. So he'd stopped and joined them in mocking everyone else, even though he'd rather have kept on dancing. He didn't want Jay-Tee to think he was unco at dancing, given that she was so good.

Or used to be, when she was magic.

Jay-Tee stayed next to the stereo, with her back to Tom. He could see her move the tiniest amount, as if she were measuring the beat without actually dancing.

He took a deep breath for courage and walked over to Jay-Tee, taking her right hand in his and moving her into the centre of the room.

"I don't do that kind of dancing," she said.

Tom laughed. "Me neither, dancing holding someone— that's the daggiest dancing ever," he lied. He really enjoyed watching ballroom dancing and had wanted to try it himself for ages. He could certainly make way better costumes than those dancers normally had. "But there's more room to move here. Are you going to dance or what?"

"Dunno. Not sure I feel like it."

Tom dared himself to just start dancing in front of her. Even though he knew she'd laugh at him. Instead he did something almost as brave. He kissed her. Quickly, on the cheek. "You had plenty of rhythm when we were kissing out on the porch. I'm sure you've got heaps left over for dancing."

"It's not the same thing," she said. The expression on her face was so sad, it made Tom want to cry.

But then Jay-Tee smiled, put her arms by her side, and started jumping pogo-stick style. Tom joined her. They bounced like crazy all around the room, staying in rhythm, laughing like they would explode.

And then, after two songs of silliness, Tom watched Jay-Tee slide into proper dancing. As if her arms, her hips, her legs were disconnected, moving in a separate space of their own, yet connected too. He'd never seen anyone move as fast, as smooth, as charged as her. He followed as best he could.

Jay-Tee hadn't lost any of her dance.

16
Sweating

It wasn't the same. Jay-Tee couldn't feel the dance sweep through her. She hoped she would find her rhythm, but when she didn't, and her eyes came close to leaking even more tears, she turned to Tom instead and kissed him.

He kissed her back, less tentatively than he had out on the back porch. They were both sweating from throwing themselves around the room. Their hands kept sliding off their damp clothes; they almost fell over.

Tom giggled. His cheeks were red and hot. So were hers. They fell back against the table. Jay-Tee grunted where the side of it dug into her lower back. Tom tried to kiss her again, but his lips landed on her cheekbone and then slid down to her chin.

"Sorry," he said. "Slippery."

It was a hot night. The whole room seemed to be sweating. Even without the dancing, they'd've been dripping. Even without hugging each other, they'd still have fused together.

She wondered what this would feel like if she still had her magic. How many threads would connect them? Without magic, Jay-Tee couldn't see the web that tied them together. Without magic, there probably *wasn't* any connection.

She pulled away from Tom, trying to see what wasn't there. He looked back at her, started to say something, but she put her hand up.

His skin was so white. He was so skinny.

"You glow," she told him. But not scary, like Reason. "A good glow."

He looked at his arms. His face went even redder. "I'm pretty white, eh?"

She put her fingers around his wrist. "Check that out." They both stared at Jay-Tee's brown hand against Tom's white, white arm.

"You're so much darker than I am," he said. "You're lucky. I get burnt really—"

"I like how white you are. I can see the blue veins so clear. It's pretty."

"Not as pretty as you. Not as gorgeous as—"

Jay-Tee put her mouth to his, hoping to get lost in kissing. With her eyes closed, she could remember what the web had looked like. All the magic catching between all the magic-wielders, pulling them together. What was pulling her and Tom together?

"Do you want to go upstairs?" she asked. The music was pounding, but without being able to catch its beat, it had become just noise. Something that verged on giving her a headache.

Tom blushed again. Though it was getting hard to tell. They were both so hot, so sweaty.

"I mean, upstairs'd be more comfy."

"You sure?" he asked, anxious.

"Yeah. The edge of the table's really digging in."

"I meant . . ."

She laughed. He was so anxious. "I know what you meant. It's just kissing, Tom. Relax."

Jay-Tee didn't want to have sex with Tom. She'd had sex three times. Twice it had hurt and the third time it was uncomfortable. Two different boys. One back in the Bronx, before she ran away. Diego, but everyone called him Dig. He was one of Danny's friends, another basketball nut, though not nearly as good as Danny.

They'd done it in his parents' basement, with her lying down on the unopened ironing board. Twice. Both times it had hurt so much she had to bite her lip not to cry.

There hadn't been any magic threads binding them together. Dig wasn't a complete dead spot, but he was close.

The other time was at Lantern, in one of the stalls in the girls' bathroom. She didn't know the guy's name, but he was a great dancer and she'd liked his smile, though now she couldn't remember what he'd looked like. Someone needed to go and banged on the door and screamed at them, even though there were other stalls.

But he had been magic. She hadn't realized till they were kissing and these strands unwound from him and unwound from her and tangled together, pulling them to each other. It was like fighting, each keeping their magic balanced—not giving any away, but not taking either. Like balancing a balloon on a pin, scared that it will pop.

Jay-Tee still hadn't liked the sex bit, but at least it hadn't hurt, and the kissing had been okay. And the magic had been strange and kind of cool.

She knew it was what you were supposed to do, so she'd done it. Already, kissing with Tom was better than kissing anyone else. The touching too. So maybe with Tom, a boy who'd never done it before, the sex wouldn't be too bad. Maybe it would bring the magic back.

"I like kissing you," she told him.

"I like kissing you too," Tom said.

She took Tom's hand and led him out of the dining room, up the stairs. He stopped her halfway and kissed her again. It was a warm, slow, gentle kiss. She felt it all the way to the soles of her feet, like getting caught in the right kind of beat, which she never would again.

She had to not think about that, to concentrate on Tom. He'd gotten a lot better at kissing really, really quickly. For a few seconds the kiss stayed slow; then their hearts heated up again, and they were kissing messily and fast.

Tom lost his footing, slipped down a step. Jay-Tee fell with him. She broke her fall on Tom; he broke his on the stairs.

"Are you okay?"

He nodded and was wrapping himself around her and she around him, with the stairs digging into her ribs and thighs. But kissing was too good.

Jay-Tee had no idea how long it took them to get to her room. But when they did, she was suddenly so tired she couldn't keep her eyes open. It felt like everything was hitting her all at once and the only way she could cope was to sleep.

For the first time in her life, Jay-Tee started to fall asleep in someone else's arms. And it was nice, even though he was bony, and she knew she was going to wake up bruised.

"You're lovely, Tom," she said, half asleep.

"You're lovely too," he said, and kissed her cheek.

17
907 Lights

I stayed close to the surface so that I could hear Esmeralda but still be in Cansino's world. "Alexander?" she asked. "Here?" Her words went past me like rippling water.

"Yes," I told her. Until she replied I couldn't tell whether I'd spoken or just thought those words. I wasn't a body in the same way I was in the other world. My limits were a long way past the edges of my skin. Space leaked into me; I leaked into it. Esmeralda's magic danced nearby. If I wanted to pull it towards me I could. But I didn't know what that would do to her. Could I do that with Jason Blake? Pull him here?

At that second his magic disappeared, swallowed by the spiral door. Could he hear my thoughts?

"You've found the door he came through?"

"Yes." I stood up, sliding through the thickness. I could see the door Jason Blake had emerged from and just as quickly disappeared back into. I wondered if there was a way to slide through Cansino space that was quicker than the way I had been moving. Raul Cansino had seemed to appear out of nowhere. Could I do that?

I looked at the door again, but it wasn't one door; it was two. How had that happened?

"And it's not far?" Esmeralda asked.

"I don't know." I still didn't understand the correspondence between the real world and Cansino's world of lights. The two sets of light tightly bound together—the two doors—seemed to be side-by-side. Just a smidgen of textured darkness between them. The stuff that Jay-Tee was now entirely made of.

I doubted that they would seem like that in the real world. "There's two doors," I said.

"Two?"

"I can see two."

"Which one did Alexander go through?"

"They're too close. It's hard to tell." Jason Blake had disappeared so fast, I didn't know which was the one he had gone through.

I pushed my way back to Esmeralda's flat. This time the weight of normal gravity was too much. I crashed. And even though my eyes were wide open, I could still see Cansino's magic world in the corners of my eyes. It had eaten my peripheral vision.

"Reason? You okay?" Esmeralda poked her head out of her bedroom, squashed-up woollen things in her hands.

I nodded. "Just the heavy air. Should pass in a second. It did last time."

"You sure?"

"Uh-huh." I stood up, feeling the movement of each muscle.

In the corner of my eyes, the three doors gleamed. My mother could be behind one of them. "Are you ready? We should go."

"Just let me grab a scarf. I left Sydney a bit empty-handed. Will you be okay dressed like that?"

"I don't feel the cold anymore."

"No," she said, staring at me. "I guess not."

❊

The first door was close by, only a block away. First I recognised the street; then I recognised the building. Jay-Tee had taken me here. We'd had a snowball fight on the roof. But the door wasn't on the outside of the building.

It was inside.

I recognised the huge foyer with its floor of swirling coloured marble tiles and ornate plaster ceiling of interwoven doves carrying roses in their mouths.

The lift, I thought. This was where Jay-Tee had taken me up in the temperamental old lift to the roof, where we'd thrown snow at each other. She'd said the lift liked me. The lift was a door.

I walked towards it.

"Can I help you?" asked a white man in a black suit and red tie, seated behind the big wood-and-leather desk. He looked at Esmeralda and then at me. Not the same man as when I'd come here with Jay-Tee. This man was much older. He didn't sound or look like someone who wanted to help anyone.

He had the smallest amount of magic I'd seen so far, but it

was there, a fraction of a micron-thin layer sprinkled between his cells.

"I'm here to see Rebecca," Esmeralda said. She was concentrating hard. I could see her calling his infinitesimal fragments of magic to her.

"In 8C?" he asked, frowning. "She knows you're coming?"

Esmeralda said, "Yes."

She nodded. I stared at the 250 brass tacks that held the green leather to the wooden desk, all the factors tumbling through my head. "We haven't seen each other in ages," Esmeralda added.

"Was she your teacher?"

Esmeralda nodded. "She was wonderful. And now I want Rebecca to teach my daughter."

I had a sudden vision of a white-haired old woman teaching students to play violin. I'd always wanted to learn an instrument, but it had never been possible. Sarafina didn't play anything so couldn't teach me: besides, we travelled too light to carry any but the tiniest musical instrument. But we'd never had the money to spend on such non-essentials. I'd never even touched a harmonica.

"I miss her," Esmeralda said.

The man smiled. "She's a lovely old lady. Go on through. Eighth floor."

The lift looked as forlorn as it had before, but this time I could see its magic: all 907 of its tiny smudges, bound together with threads of misty light. A delicious prime. I could taste it on my tongue.

I pressed the button, waited with my breath held for the doors to open. Surely this door would co-operate, let me through to my mother. Jay-Tee had said it liked me.

Nothing happened.

Then I remembered that Jay-Tee had spoken to it. "Please," I said softly. "Please." When I got to Fib (17), 1,597 (also a prime), the metal doors groaned open.

I stepped inside, Esmeralda behind me, onto the carpet worn so thin in places I could see the metal floor underneath. There was no panelling on the walls, nothing covering over the nuts and bolts holding the lift together.

"Please," I begged the lift in a whisper. "Please show me the other place you're connected to. If you want to. If you'd like. It would mean so much to me." I wondered if Jay-Tee had known it was a door. Or had she simply been attracted to its magic?

The lift did not lurch into motion—its doors didn't even close.

I reached Fib (43), 433,494,437, and the doors were still open.

"Maybe the door doesn't like you," I told Esmeralda. "It didn't take this long last time."

"Last time?"

"When I was here with Jay-Tee. I didn't know it was a door then."

"The lift is the door?" Esmeralda asked. She didn't sound like she believed me. "And it doesn't like me?"

I shrugged. All around us I could feel the lift's impatience. I was increasingly sure it didn't want Esmeralda to be there. "If you wait in the foyer . . ."

Esmeralda cut her eyes at me. "Wait?"

"The lift doesn't like you." I was at Fib (61). "It would have moved by now if it did."

"It's only been a few minutes. You can't be sure."

The lift groaned, a high-pitched sound of metal scraping against metal, but its doors stayed open.

"See? If you'd just wait outside. Jay-Tee says it's cranky."

The groan got even louder.

"All right," Esmeralda said at last, stepping out of the lift.

The doors shut so fast they caught the back of her coat. I heard her yelp from the other side, and then her coat disappeared, and the lift shuddered, creaking into motion. I couldn't tell if we were moving up or down. I couldn't see out of the doors the way I'd been able to when me and Jay-Tee had gone to the roof. None of the buttons for the floors were lit up.

Fibonaccis stuttered in my head, giving me only primes: Fib (3), 2; Fib (4), 3; Fib (5), 5 (yes, that's right, Fib (5) is 5); Fib (7), 13; Fib (11), 89; Fib (13), 233; Fib (17), 1597; Fib (23), 28,657; Fib (29), 514,229; Fib (43), 433,494,437; Fib (47), 2,971,215,073; Fib (83), 99,194,853,094,755,497.

The doors concertinaed open, groaning so loudly I had to cover my ears. I blinked in intense sunlight. Keeping one foot in the doorway, I put the other foot on the step in front of me and peered at this new world.

Opposite me was a long wall. Every ten metres or so it changed colour, from brilliant blue to yellow to faded red-brown. Each section had a door and a window. The doors were small, the windows large. I was looking at a blue painted door and a large stone window, pots overflowing with flowers resting on the wide sill behind rusting metal bars. From the top of the wall, vines dotted with tiny blue flowers cascaded towards the street.

Three white butterflies fluttered by. Then a huge yellow one with a black stripe at the bottom of its wings. I'd never seen such an enormous butterfly before. So big it could simply glide rather than constantly flutter its wings. Bells tolled in a tumble that made it impossible to count how many there were.

I wasn't wearing a watch. I peered up at the sky. The sun was high, in more or less the same position it had been in New York. If I'd been able to see the sun there, that was. So roughly the same time of day. Was this another city in the United States? It didn't look like New York.

The door snapped shut on my heel, pushing me out of the doorway and stumbling onto the street, where a car honked at me. I jumped out of the way, back onto the step, which I now saw wasn't a step but a narrow, raised footpath. On the other side of the street was a path just like it, made of the same large, uneven stones as the road.

I turned to the door. On this side, it wasn't the entrance to a lift: it was a wooden door with a brass knocker in the shape of a hand, set into a stone wall.

I grabbed the handle and pulled. It didn't budge.

I took a deep breath. The door had let me through without a key, which meant that Jay-Tee was right: it liked me. Of course it was going to let me go back to New York City when I needed to.

I sat down on the stone step and worked on breathing evenly, not panicking. I closed my eyes, and the calm of Cansino's world washed over me. I searched for Sarafina. There were fourteen strong lights close by: none of them was my mother. Jason Blake wasn't here either. There was not nearly so much magic here as in Sydney or New York City. The bindings between the 907 lights were pulled tight and did not respond to my probing them.

I opened my eyes, felt the weight of the real world fall on me. I gasped, wondering why I had bothered to return to the real world. The few strong lights—none of them Sarafina—floated in my peripheral vision. I tried the door handle again. Nothing.

I leaned back against the door, looked at the plants cascading down the wall towards me. These were studded with white, red, and yellow flowers. I peered up at them. More butterflies drifted by, more of the white ones, and a lone yellow, and then a tiny bird zipped past, stopping to stick its long, narrow beak into one of the flowers, and, more remarkably, hovering in place, its wings beating so fast they were a near-invisible blur. Its tail feathers bobbed back and forth. Then, just as my eyes adjusted to seeing it, the bird zipped away, faster than I'd ever seen any bird fly. What was it?

Where was I? The same time zone as New York, more or less. Was it the same hemisphere? I'd have to wait for dark to see if it was a southern sky or not.

An old man with skin darker than mine and as wrinkled as a walnut walked by, leading a donkey carrying two large baskets full of firewood down the hill.

He tipped his hat at me and said something too fast to catch. I wasn't sure, but I didn't think it was English. But the only language I knew other than English was Kriol, and I suspected they didn't speak that much outside the Northern Territory. I smiled at him, pretty sure now that this was not the U.S.A., wondering if I was ever going to see Sarafina alive again.

Two old women, skin dark like the old man's, trudged up the hill. They held bunches of dried flowers, offering them to me. I shook my head and they continued on their slow way. They were dressed in colours as bright as the walls.

The sky was almost as big as it was out in the deserts of home. Brilliant and blue, threaded with cumulus clouds fluffier than balls of cotton and a contrail left by a passing plane. When I looked down again I half expected to see spinifex, a wedge-tailed eagle snatching up a rabbit.

Instead a four-wheel drive made its slow way down the narrow, steep, unevenly paved street. Beyond the car, a whole town was laid out. Square houses of faded yellows, browns, blues, and reds; flat roofs; trees and bushes and gardens; the occasional church steeple, arrayed in tiers down the hill. And

past them a plain of greens and brown, and then, in the distance, a ridge of blue mountains.

I turned back to the door, reached for the handle that still
didn't turn. "Please," I whispered as I had before. "Please. I'm
ready to go back now."

The door would not open.

18
Morning After

Tom woke to the smell of something clean and damp roaring in the distance, and a hard, cold floor under his back. He shivered and sat up, blinking to unglue his eyes. He was on Jay-Tee's bedroom floor. He rubbed his neck and turned to look at her, asleep, sprawled across her bed.

He grinned.

The roaring was getting louder. Rain, he realised. Drops were hitting the glass doors that opened onto the balcony. The clean, damp smell was ozone. He tried to remember the last time it had rained. Must have been when he'd shown Reason the cemetery and old lady Havisham and the Cansino family monument, but that shower hadn't lasted long. He hoped it'd last longer this time.

The phone rang. Tom jumped up, groaning at the effects of a night spent on the floor. There wasn't a phone in Jay-Tee's room. Was there one in Reason's room? He opened the door, and just as he found it on a small table in the hall, the ringing stopped.

Tom thought about lying down on Reason's bed and getting more sleep. He was tired. Somewhere outside someone was playing loud dance music. He smiled, thinking of the two of them dancing last night, of all their kissing. He wondered how late it was.

A different phone started ringing. His mobile. He lunged back into Jay-Tee's bedroom, to his backpack, fishing it out and answering softly as he slipped out into the hallway.

"Tom?" It was Esmeralda.

"Yes, it's me." The music was a lot louder out in the hall-way. He wondered where it was coming from.

"How are you and Jay-Tee going?"

Tom glanced at the door to Jay-Tee's room. His cheeks went hot. "Good. We're good."

"Really? Jay-Tee hasn't been acting strange at all?"

"You mean about her magic being gone?"

"Yes."

"She's cool about it. She's fine."

"You're sure?"

"Uh-huh."

"Can I talk to her?"

"I, er," Tom stammered. "I just woke up."

"I thought she might be with you. She didn't answer when I rang my place."

"Huh," Tom said. "Have you found Reason's mum?"

"Not yet. Reason's looking. We haven't given up hope. Has the social worker phoned again?"

"Not yet, but we'll call the second she does. How's Reason?" Tom asked. "Jay-Tee said she was getting kind of weird. Glowing or something."

Esmeralda didn't say anything.

"Is she okay?" Tom asked again, wondering how powerful Reason had become. Turning Jay-Tee's magic off was intense. He wondered what else she could do.

Behind him he heard Jay-Tee yawn. She came out of her room still in her pyjamas and sat on the floor beside him, leaving enough space so that they wouldn't touch. He wondered why.

"She's changing," Esmeralda said at last. "It's hard to describe. Listen, I should go. If anything happens, let me know. And keep an eye out for Jay-Tee. I'm worried about her."

"Of course." He pointed at the phone and mouthed, "Esmeralda." Jay-Tee put her hand out for it.

"Thanks, Tom. I'll talk to you soon. Oh," Esmeralda said, as if suddenly remembering. "Where were you?"

"Oh, you know," he said, wondering why he didn't just tell her. "Around."

"That's what I told the girls. They seem to forget you have another life."

Tom laughed. "Them and me both. Listen, Jay-Tee just came round. Do you want to talk to her?"

Esmeralda said she did. As he passed the phone to Jay-Tee, she didn't meet his eyes and managed to avoid touching his fingers. He stood up and she sat down, turning her back.

Okay, he thought, checking his watch: just after nine AM. Plenty of time before breakfast with his da. At least his father wouldn't give him the cold shoulder. Or maybe Jay-Tee just wasn't a morning person.

✹

The dance music was still playing loud outside. Then Tom thought he heard a crash from downstairs. It was a second before he recognised the sound: the front door opening.

Bugger, thought Tom, *who the hell could that be?* He dashed down the stairs, realising halfway down that the dance music wasn't coming from outside. It was coming from the dining room. They'd left the radio on. Bugger.

Rita, Esmeralda's cleaner, stood in the hallway, hanging her bag and raincoat up on the hallstand. She smiled at him. "Hi, Tom. What's up?"

"Oh, nothing," Tom said.

"That music's pretty loud, isn't it?"

"Yup," Tom said. "I was just about to turn it off. Lot of rain out?"

"Cats and dogs."

"Brilliant. So, um, Mere's not here."

"Well, no," Rita said. "She's at work, isn't she?"

"Nope, she's in the city. The other one." He gestured back at the door.

Rita nodded but didn't look in that direction. Like Tom's father, she wasn't comfortable about magic, didn't like to talk about it. "What happened to your face?"

Tom touched the bandage covering Jason Blake's handiwork. "I was climbing. It's nothing. I thought you only came on Mondays?" he asked.

"Mondays and Thursdays. But it's been mixed up a bit

lately. Appointments," she said, shrugging. "Is that something on your neck? Did you do that climbing too?"

"My neck?" he asked, thinking, *Oh crap! What's on my neck?* He put his hand to his throat, as if he could feel whatever it was. Unsurprisingly, he couldn't.

"Looks like a bruise."

"Huh," he said. *Jay-Tee had marked his neck?* He moved so that he stood between Rita and the dining room door. No way did he want her walking in on the mess they'd made. Not when she'd already noted the bruise—or rather, hickey—on his neck. She'd tell Esmeralda. He blushed thinking about Esmeralda knowing about him and Jay-Tee. If there was a him and Jay-Tee. Why was she avoiding touching him? Why hadn't she said anything to him about last night? *Why did she give him a hickey?!*

"And how have you been, Tom?"

Tom's cheeks got hotter. Stupid blushing genes. "Good," he said, "you know." He shrugged, and leaned back against the door as if it were the most natural thing in the world to do. At least, he hoped it looked that way. Then his bum slipped across the wood and he almost went arse over tit.

Rita smiled. "Been on holidays too long, have you? When my ones were still at school, I used to think the summer holidays lasted forever." She sighed. "How's that sister of yours? Still overseas studying?"

"That's right. She's going good. Cath really likes it there. Sometimes I don't think she's ever coming home." He wished

Rita would keep heading to the kitchen. Wasn't that where she normally started? He had to get in and clean up the dining room and turn the music off. How did you get a hickey off your neck?

"It's always the way. So many young people go away and then never come back or don't for years and years and years. My brother Simon lives in England, so my nieces and their children all have proper English accents. Very strange."

"Must be."

"Well, I better get on with it. Nice chatting to you."

He nodded. "Yeah. Grouse."

"Don't forget to turn that music down."

"No fear." He waited until she was in the kitchen and then eased himself into the dining room, where he turned the stereo off. His ears buzzed in the sudden silence.

The dining room was a catastrophe, the carpet crooked. Two of the chairs lay on their sides, one up against the folding wooden doors that when closed (which they never were) divided the big room in two. The chair had left a scratch. Tom could only hope Rita and Esmeralda wouldn't notice. He didn't remember knocking either chair over.

"Tom," Rita called, opening the dining room door closest to the kitchen. "I'm just putting the kettle on. Do you want a cup . . . ?" She took in the room. "Oh, my. Had a party, did we?"

Tom's face got hot all the way to the top of his neck. "No, no. Jay-Tee was just teaching me how to dance. And we needed space."

"I see. *Lots* of space, eh?" Rita looked at Tom with an expression that made the blush extend down to his chest. "Jay-Tee's that American lassie who's staying here?"

Tom nodded.

"Yeah, that's me," Jay-Tee said, coming through the other door. She stopped to stare at the room. "Oh." Tom could've sworn that she was blushing. He hadn't known she could. She was still in her pyjamas. Bugger. That would just make Rita think . . . Tom looked at Rita, who was staring at Jay-Tee. Too late. She was already thinking it.

"You're the dance teacher, then?"

Jay-Tee shot Tom a look. "Um, yeah, that's right."

"I'm Rita," she said, and held out her hand. "Pleased to meet you."

"Likewise," Jay-Tee said in a tiny voice as they shook hands.

"I was just offering Tom a cuppa. Would you like one?"

"No, thanks. I'm fine," she mumbled, staring at her feet.

Embarrassed, Tom realised. She was embarrassed about them. *Oh great*, Tom thought, even though he was embarrassed too. But he wasn't embarrassed because they'd gotten together. He wasn't embarrassed about Jay-Tee. He was just, you know, embarrassed.

"Tom? A cuppa?" Rita asked, looking from him to Jay-Tee and back again. Tom could've sworn she was smirking. He was so mortified he didn't know where to look. Though his feet seemed like a good idea.

"Nope, I'm good, Rita. Ta, but."

"Well, I'll leave you two to straighten up. Careful with that table. It's heavy." Rita closed the door behind her. Tom tried to think of something to say to Jay-Tee but couldn't. She must've thought he was a total dag.

"What's a cuppa?" she asked.

19
A Different Sky

i ran through the first two hundred Fibonaccis before I tried the door again. It didn't budge. "Please," I whispered, wishing there was a way to beg that didn't sound pathetic. Jay-Tee'd given me the impression that the door wouldn't open if it didn't respect you.

I put both hands flat on the wood, feeling the ripples become more and more agitated. I whispered to the door to hush, that I meant no harm. I had to get back. "You don't understand," I told it. "My mother is dying. I have to save her. Please."

The ripples stopped. But the door didn't open.

I wished Esmeralda had come through with me. Maybe she'd have remembered something out of one of her books, something that would lead me to Sarafina.

I closed my eyes, probed between the 907 lights and the cords that bound them. This time I found tiny fissures that closed tight as soon as I approached. I opened my eyes, laid my cheek against the door, whispering, begging it to please, please, please open for me. I offered the biggest prime I knew as a precious gift: $2^{2976221}-1$.

The door stayed deaf to my offerings. I apologised for whatever it was that I might have done wrong. I promised not to do it again. I said I would do whatever it wanted, though I had no idea what a door would want.

I slid down onto the raised footpath, then crossed my legs under me and leaned back against the wall.

Sarafina was dying somewhere.

Another car drove by, this time struggling up the steep hill. The road was so narrow the driver had to stop to let two men walk by carrying slabs of beer. They called out to each other, but I couldn't understand what they were saying. They laughed.

There were other doors in this town. But not so many as in New York City. I could see them. But even if one opened for me, what then? The odds were long of them leading back to Sydney, or New York, or to wherever it was that Jason Blake had hidden Sarafina. Most likely they'd lead to another strange place like this, where I couldn't understand what anyone said.

If my mother hadn't been dying, if she'd been here with me, it would've been fun. Find another door, see where it led. Travel the world. Discover how many doors there were. Hundreds? Thousands?

If I waited long enough, would the door change its mind? I knew I could wait. I hadn't needed to go to the toilet since Raul had changed me. I'd stopped being thirsty or hungry. This new body didn't even want food. If I ate, I vomited.

For me, waiting was easy, but Sarafina couldn't wait.

The people walking past me were dressed warmly. Jumpers,

shawls. Winter, but not a New York, cold-all-the-time winter—
a desert winter, warm during the day, cold at night. The northern hemisphere, then, but a lot further south than New York
City. What was south of the United States? South America:
Argentina, Brazil, Nicaragua. But they would be in summer
now, like Australia.

A few of the people smiled at me; others spoke, but I
couldn't understand them. Mostly, though, they avoided my
eyes, made gestures across their chests, like Jay-Tee sometimes
did when she was nervous or scared. They could see that I was
gold. It frightened them.

One woman spoke to me directly. I could separate the
words, but I didn't know what they meant. She had dyed-
blonde hair and was brown-skinned, but in an over-tanned way,
like her skin wasn't meant to be that colour. She didn't look
like the other people I'd seen. When I didn't understand her,
she spoke to me in English, with an accent like Jason Blake's.

"Are you all right, honey?" She had so little magic that I
doubted she could see my glow. "You've been sitting outside
there for a while."

"I'm fine," I said, though I wasn't. Sarafina was so far away.
"I'm just waiting for my friends to get back. They shouldn't be
much longer."

"You're sure?"

I nodded. "I'm good at waiting."

"You're really okay? You must be so cold. Can I at least loan
you a coat?"

"I'm fine. Really. I don't feel the cold. Honest."

"Well," the woman said, obviously not believing me, "if you need anything, I live in that house over there." She pointed up the street to a wall painted yellow with another blue door. "Number forty-nine."

I nodded. "Thank you."

She paused as if she was going to say something else and then nodded. "You take care of yourself, okay?"

I said that I would and watched her walk slowly up the hill to her blue door in the wall that bounded that side of the street. It was hard to imagine an entire house lying behind it.

I whispered reassuringly to the door, asked it again to let me through, reminded it about Sarafina. "Please," I said. The door ignored me.

Two small children hanging from their father's hands and slapping at one another came walking up the hill towards me. Their skin was as brown as mine. Or as mine had been before it had turned to gold. The little girl pointed at me and said something. The man smacked her hand and spoke to her sharply. Then he made the Jay-Tee gesture. He nodded to me but did not meet my eyes. He said something I couldn't quite hear that might have been an apology. His pace picked up, until he was almost dragging his children up the hill.

The little girl turned her head, stumbling as she walked half backwards, still clutching his hand. She stared at me, curious and avid. Her plaits bounced and twisted with her uneven gait.

She was magic. As magic as I had been, as magic as Tom or Jay-Tee, but her magic was strong and crackling because she was still so young. I wondered if she knew what she was, if she knew how to keep from going mad, how to keep from hurting anyone. Did she know about this door? Her brother and father had very little magic.

As the little girl disappeared around the corner, I stood up and followed.

A few narrow, winding streets later, the man and his little girl and boy disappeared into a door as small as the one I had come through, set into a long wall dotted with other windows and doors. I had begun to realize that different-coloured stretches of wall indicated where one house ended and the next began. The street was just as steep as the one I'd started from, almost at a forty-five-degree angle. This whole side of the town climbed a huge hill, the houses stacked like uneven books on a shelf.

In my Cansino vision, I could see right into the house: two strong magics stood close together. The little girl was one. The other one felt related to her.

I raised my hand to knock on the door, then lowered it. I didn't know what to say and doubted they would understand me.

A group of boys further down the street kicked a soccer ball up and down the angled street. I turned to look at them. One of them saw me and started, eyes wide—the ball shot past him down the long, steep hill. The other boys cried out in dismay; one punched his shoulder. With a last suspicious look at me, he took off at a flat-out sprint to retrieve the ball, one of the smaller boys trailing behind. As the rest waited, they glanced at me warily and moved further away down the hill.

All of them had tiny bits of magic. Not nearly enough to be wielders, but enough to know there was something strange about me. This town seemed full of magic. Every time I blinked my eyes, more glimmers stole into view.

Through the wall, I saw the little girl and her magic relative moving about the house together.

The sun was sinking, stars starting to dot the sky. It wasn't a southern sky: no Southern Cross or pointers, no Sagittarius. I was still in the northern hemisphere.

The two boys returned, dripping with sweat, the ball wrapped in the shorter one's arms. They laughed and—I imagined—launched into an account of where it had gone and what chaos it had caused. Soon they were back at it, kicking the ball back and forth, careful not to let it escape again, or to come anywhere near me.

I raised my hand and knocked on the door.

The little girl opened it, looked at me, started giggling, and then shut the door in my face.

"Wait!" I yelled. I knocked again, louder this time. I could hear her still giggling on the other side. It wasn't funny. "I need your help!" I called through the keyhole.

I could feel people looking at me and turned. The soccer-playing boys were staring at me openly now. Most of them backed away, making the Jay-Tee gestures across their chests.

The biggest one spat a long stream of phlegm that landed just half a metre short of my feet. He lifted his chin up, as if to say he wasn't afraid of me.

The door opened. A tall man—a boy, really, he didn't look much older than me—stood there. He was magic too, the other light I'd seen in Cansino vision. The little girl held his hand, smiling up at me. The boy wasn't smiling.

He asked me a question.

"I don't understand," I said.

"You speak English?" the boy said in a strong accent. He made the *sh* of *English* sound like an *s*. His skin was a shade or two lighter than the little girl's, the colour of Jay-Tee's.

He waved at the boys on the street, calling out something to them before turning back to me. "What do you want?"

"Help," I said. "I have to get back to New York." Behind him I could see a courtyard with a fountain and lots of greenery.

"Why should I help you?" the boy said slowly.

"I know you're magic," I said.

"Not as magic as you are. You are glowing."

The little girl said something in the language I didn't understand. The boy answered, shook his head, and shrugged. She spoke again, staring at me.

"What did she say?" I asked.

"She wants to know where your hair went."

"Oh, um, tell her I don't know."

She grabbed my hand and pulled me into the house. The boy shut the door behind us.

Her hand was small and soft. It made me think of the baby growing inside me. Would I be the mother of a child like this in five or six years' time? Or would old man Cansino's magic make my child something else entirely?

She led me to a bench in the courtyard. I sat and saw that the house was spread out around a huge courtyard split in half by four palm trees. On the other side of the trees was a glass wall, behind it a kitchen.

The little girl jumped up and pressed a switch on the wall. Lights came on in the fountain, making the bubbling water glitter.

"Do you know about the door to New York City?" I asked as the boy sat beside me.

"Yes," he said. "You came here through the door? But you don't have a key."

I nodded. "I didn't need a key. But now I have to get back."

"She won't let you?"

He meant the door, I realised. "No, she won't."

He spoke to the little girl rapidly and they both laughed. I didn't think they were laughing at me.

"She does that a lot?"

"A lot? No, but she does it. She is very . . ." He frowned, searching for the word.

"Stubborn?"

"Yes, she is a stubborn door."

The little girl said something else and then touched my skin, peered into my eyes. She asked me a question, giggled again. I looked at the boy.

"She wants to know why you are so soft. You skin. Why you eyes are so different. She wants to know if you are a genie."

"A genie?" I asked. "I don't think so. I don't know what I am. Another magic person changed me. I don't know what he did."

He explained to the little girl, then said, "I don't think you are a genie. I think you are stopping being a magic person and becoming magic all the time."

"What do you mean? Aren't *you* magic all the time?"

He shook his head. "Not like you. The magic is becoming all of you. In me it is just a part. I am a person too. You are changing very fast?"

"Yes," I said.

"When you are all magic, you won't have any more troubles."

"What do you mean?"

"My mother's mother told her that sometimes the magic takes one of us completely. Takes us and makes us part of it. No troubles then. Just magic."

"Just magic," I murmured. In Cansino world there were no troubles. No dull ache when I thought of Danny not wanting me. No fear and anxiety over Sarafina. He was describing what it would be like to stay there. My future.

"Are you sad?" the boy asked.

That wasn't the question I was expecting. "Yes. My mother is dying. On the other side of that stubborn door. I have to get to her."

"You don't seem so sad. I think if you change more the sadness will go away."

"The magic will make everything okay?"

He shrugged.

"Do you know long it takes?"

"*Rápido*. My mother said it happened very quick."

"Then I have to go," I said. "Will you help me get back through the door?"

He nodded. "You will come with me."

20
Becoming Magic

They led me out of their home, past the soccer-playing boys, who studiously avoided looking at me. We went further up the hill, and then across, and downhill a bit to yet another house hidden behind a wall like all the others. The outside of this place was green except for where the paint was worn away to reveal sand-coloured stone.

He knocked on the door and then opened it with a key. "My mother's grandmother's house. She is very old."

"And magic?"

"Magic? No. She guards our magic *cosas* and our silver."

This house was dark and much smaller than the first one. The courtyard was tiny and had no palm trees, no plants at all. Lines were strung across the open space, heavy with clothes. In the corner was a cage with two yellow birds inside.

"Wait here," he told me, going up grey concrete steps with the little girl. I sat down on an upturned bucket. I thought they would come straight back. I could see the lights on in this house. But all I could hear were laughter and voices coming from the street. Somewhere further away a dog barked and a car backfired.

At last the boy came down the stairs carrying a bowl with steam rising from it. He held it out to me, then handed me a spoon he took out of his pocket.

I put the food on the ground. "Have you got the key?"

"No. My great-grandmother has it hidden. She will not give it to me. She says you are not family. I ask her to speak to you so you may convince her. She says it does not matter. You are not family."

"But she's not magic. Why does she even have the key?"

The boy looked at me like I was mad. "That is why: because she is not magic. Magic people are not always trusted."

I grinned. "I've heard that. How about if I just appear out of the floor in front of her?" Though I wasn't entirely sure I knew how to do that. "You know, kind of scare her into giving it to me?"

This time he looked at me as if I was stupid. "She is not magic *at all*. You cannot make magic against her. She does not see it."

The little girl appeared at the top of the stairs and waved at me. I waved back. She giggled and disappeared into the house.

"I'm sorry I could not help you. After you eat your food, my great-grandmother wants you to go."

I didn't know what to say. I *had* to have that key.

"Chago!" someone called from above.

"My great-grandmother."

"Is that your name, Chago?"

He nodded. "My short name. I am Santiago David Cuervo."

"I'm Reason," I told him.

"Reason," he repeated. "My mother said it was good. The magic. You can live inside it forever. She said the closer you get to the magic, the more beauty there is. You are lucky that you will see it. Soon you won't need any keys. You won't need any doors."

"Chago!"

"I must go."

I watched him hurry up the stairs. Maybe in the future I wouldn't need doors. But right now I had to get back to New York. I needed that key. I had all this magic. Now I would use it.

Raul Cansino had made himself disappear, melted into the ground and out of it. I concentrated on my hands, but instead of turning them into wires, I willed them to dissolve. I stared at the space between the cells, thought about them collapsing in on each other.

My hand wilted, hung from my arm as if it were rubber. Slowly I melted the rest of my body. By the time I was fluid enough to sink into the ground, it was damp with my sweat. I pushed my way through the concrete and the soil just underneath it as though they were cotton wool. Then I snaked up the stairs and into the grouting between the tiles, weaving past the hairy clumps of mould. I could hear their slow growth.

Further above I could hear voices. I slithered away and into the walls. When I couldn't hear them anymore I unvanished, fleshing myself out and pulling away from the wall with a pop. But my legs were still too much like rubber; they gave way beneath me.

I closed my eyes, searching for magic nearby. I could see the boy's magic and his sister's, but they were too big. I was looking for smaller lights. I found them, glittering like tiny stars.

I eased my way back into the real world slowly, minimising the punch of gravity. The tiny lights twinkled at the corners of my eyes, above me.

I melted back into the wall and then into the ceiling. It was easier this time, less painful. I popped through onto the roof, pulling myself back into flesh. I was greeted by a sky full of real stars, more stars than I'd seen since being sent to Sydney. I was standing in between seventy-eight terra-cotta pots overflowing with flowers.

The magic items glittered so close I could smell them. Magic mixed with dirt. I knew where the old woman hid the family's magic and silver. Now all I had to do was dig around in the soil of all seventy-eight pots.

Behind me I heard a giggle. I turned. The little girl was just climbing onto the roof. She grinned at me, walked over, slipped her hand into mine, and pulled me over to one of the smaller pots. She pushed her hand in and then pulled out a large key. She said something to me, then placed it in my hand.

The key was big and solid, a dark metal that was beginning to rust. It wasn't ornamental like the one that opened Esmeralda's door, but it radiated the same kind of magic. I knew as soon as it touched my skin that it would take me back to New York.

21
Fragile

"Rita seems nice," Jay-Tee said. She was still fasci-
nated by her own feet. Her hair was slightly damp and had
curled up even tighter around her face. *She's really pretty,* Tom
thought, wondering why it had taken him so long to notice.
Just as pretty as Reason. Her profile was lovely. Her nose was
almost dead straight.

He could see the dress that would suit her perfectly: A-line,
with no sleeves. Sky blue with navy blue trim.

"I guess we should straighten up, then."

"Yeah," Tom agreed.

Jay-Tee picked up the chair that had crashed against the
folding doors, saw the scratch, and said, "Oops." She looked up
and half smiled. He liked the way she smiled. But her eyes still
weren't meeting his.

"Yeah," Tom said. "What are the odds of them not noticing?"

"Not good. I don't remember doing that. Do you?"

"Nope. I think we were maybe preoccupied."

"I guess," Jay-Tee said, but she didn't giggle or smile or anything. Did that mean it really *hadn't* meant anything to her?
"Should we start with the carpet?" she asked.

Tom nodded and took the corner closest to him, pulling it into place, while she took the other side. "So what did you talk to Esmeralda about?" he asked. He didn't really care. He wanted to talk about what happened last night. Or not talk about it, exactly, but he wanted . . . Tom wasn't sure what he wanted. Well, yes, he was. He wanted to kiss her again. And dance. And all of that. Like last night. And he wanted Jay-Tee to want that too.

"Stuff." Jay-Tee still wasn't looking at him. Was it because she was religious? Did she think she was going to go to hell for kissing him?

"Like what?" He smoothed out a bump in the carpet with his foot.

"Table next?" she asked.

Tom grabbed the end nearest him. It was huge and made of solid wood. They moved it only a few centimetres before resting.

"So, Esmeralda?" Tom prompted.

"Oh," she said. "Well, I wanted to ask her about something. Something I've been wondering about."

"What?" Tom said.

"Well . . . " She trailed off, still not looking at him.

"What?!"

"Okay," Jay-Tee said. "You know how Reason's been acting weird? I don't mean her old-man-magic weirdness. She's been weird about Danny too. Whenever he's mentioned, she's all . . . I don't know, weird. And, well, it just got me thinking."

"Thinking what?" Tom asked. Why were they talking about this? Why weren't they talking about them?

"Also, yesterday morning, you know, when you were off drinking with your sister—"

"I only had a few glasses. And I didn't even like it. Not to mention that I didn't drink a whole bottle like some people."

"Whatever," Jay-Tee said. "Anyway, the three of us—me, Mere, and Reason—were talking about Reason's morning sickness. But Mere said that it couldn't be morning sickness, 'cause that doesn't start until you've been pregnant for months. She was trying to figure out how long Reason had been pregnant. Don't you think that's odd?"

"Huh?" What was odd was that Jay-Tee still hadn't looked him in the eye.

"Why would Mere have to think about how long it'd been when we all know it was the old man who got her pregnant, doing magic on her? Anyway, all of that got me thinking. And I was wondering, you know? So I asked Esmeralda . . . " She trailed off again. "Should we finish the table?"

"Asked her what?"

"Table first." They lifted it again, grunting, stepping, grunting, stepping, and finally got it back into position.

"Damn, that's heavy!"

"Yup," Tom said, leaning forward and panting more. "Chairs are easier, but. And you can tell me what you asked Esmeralda while we put them back."

"I don't want you getting weird or mad or anything, okay?"

"Why would I?"

"Well, you like Reason, don't you?"

"Sure. Don't you?" Tom said, putting the last chair in place.

"Not like that, I don't."

"Oh," Tom said. "Well, yeah, I did, a bit, but, not like, you know, not like, um." He stopped. He couldn't go there, not without knowing what Jay-Tee thought. "I don't like her that way anymore. I'm not sure I did before, you know? Not really. It was just kind of, ah, um, and anyway, because, er . . ." Tom didn't want to be the first to mention last night. He was embarrassed. He was nervous. He didn't know if she still felt what she'd felt last night. He was starting to be pretty sure that she didn't.

"You sure?"

"Uh-huh."

"Okay, then, Danny and Reason did the nasty. Danny's the father of Reason's baby. I asked Mere. She said it's true."

"*Danny*? And Reason? Whoa." He felt sick, but also not. The thought of it split him in half. Part of him was grossed out, but the other part was just puzzled and maybe concerned. Other things worried him more. A lot more. Like, did Jay-Tee like him? Was Reason going to find her mother? Were they going to be okay? Another thought struck him. "Hey," he said, "that means it's a normal baby. Not a freaky scary child of a monster. That's great news!"

"Great news! Are you kidding? Danny's going to ignite! A baby? Do you know how many girlfriends my brother has? And he doesn't give a damn about any of them. All he cares about is basketball. A baby? Are you nuts? It's a disaster. Oh my God, he's going to break her heart! It's going to be *horrible*!"

"I guess."

"You guess!"

Tom flopped down onto the couch. It was strange, how calm he was. When he'd first thought about the possibility of Reason and Danny together, he'd thought his brain was going to explode. Now, not really. All he felt was relief. Because Reason being pregnant to Danny was a *million* times better than her being pregnant to her creepy ancestor.

And, besides, he didn't want to be with Reason anymore. Did it only take getting with another girl to take your mind off the first? How shallow was that? Especially when he wasn't at all sure how the new girl felt about him.

Jay-Tee sat at the other end of the couch, pulling her legs up underneath her. Tom wondered if she was making sure they wouldn't accidentally touch.

"Sorry," Tom said. "I don't know why we didn't figure it out earlier. It definitely stands to reason. Occam's razor."

"Occam's what?"

"Razor. It's something Da says. The most obvious explanation is usually the right one."

"Yeah, well, Danny and Reason doing it might be Occam's razor, but that doesn't mean it's a good idea. Do you know Danny's never, ever been dumped? Not once. And if he was, he wouldn't care. And he's never dumped anyone either. He just stops calling them, stops returning their calls. And if he runs into a girl who thinks they're still going out, he's all, 'Baby, how you doing? Haven't seen you in ages.' He's the worst. He hates confrontations. You know, unless it's on a basketball court. Basketball, that's it for Danny. The beginning and the end. Poor Reason."

"Well, yeah, but it's still better than her being up the duff to someone who's *hundreds* of years old."

Jay-Tee sighed. "I guess."

"You guess? C'mon, Jay-Tee. It's a normal baby, not some kind of freaky—"

"It'll still be magic."

"How do you know?"

"You should've seen her skin yesterday, Tom. Freaky. And Raul Cansino did something to her belly. In the cemetery. I saw him do it. Not only is Danny the father, he's the father of a freaky supermagic baby."

"It's still better than—"

"Okay, yes, it's better than that, but not a *whole* lot better. You don't know my brother, Tom."

Tom shrugged. That was true. He didn't really *want* to know him. Tom might not be jealous about Reason anymore, but Danny still didn't sound like the nicest guy on the planet. Thousands of girlfriends? Bastard. Plus it was all his fault they were talking about this instead of them. Double bastard. "Why do you reckon she didn't tell us?"

"C'mon, Tom! Are you going to tell everyone about you and me?"

"Well . . . " Tom paused. Did that mean she thought there *was* a him and her, or that she didn't want anyone to know about it?

"I didn't think so."

"But," Tom stuttered, "but not because I don't want them to know. I mean. I do. Sort of. It's just that, well . . ." He stopped, feeling his cheeks get hot.

"What?"

"I like you."

Jay-Tee smiled, though it was a wary smile. "I think you're okay too."

What did that mean? Was she breaking up with him? Thinking someone was okay was a lot weaker than *liking* them. "Well," Tom said, taking the plunge, wondering if he'd regret it, "I think you're more than okay."

She didn't say anything.

"Um, it's not that I don't want anyone to know 'cause I'm embarrassed or anything. It's because it's all new and kind of . . . " He must sound like a total dropkick.

"Fragile?"

"Yes!" Tom grabbed at the word. "Fragile! That's exactly what it is. I want it to be just for you and me. I want it to stay our secret. Something special. Private. We don't have to tell anyone until we want to." He suddenly realised he was talking about him and her being a real thing, when Jay-Tee hadn't actually agreed there was any him and her. She was looking at him, but she wasn't saying anything. Tom felt sick, and not the halfway kind of sick he'd felt when he realised that Danny and Reason were into each other.

"I don't mind," Jay-Tee said at last, and Tom almost laughed out loud, he was so relieved. "Us having a secret will be fun." She reached out her hand and slid it into Tom's. He enjoyed the warmth of her fingers tangled with his.

"Are you hungry?" she asked. "Wanna get breakfast?"

"Breakfast. Oh, bugger." Tom checked his watch: twenty past ten. "Bugger! Sorry, Jay-Tee. I promised Da I'd eat with him, but I'll come straight back after."

"You promise? You're not going to disappear to New York like last time?"

"I'll be right back. I promise," he said, kissing her lips, filled with relief that there were going to be heaps more kisses.

22
Another Door

The doors closed in front of me and the lift spun, round and round and round, until I was unable to tell what was up and what was down. I closed my eyes. Immediately the disorientation was gone. I was surrounded by little lights strung together with filaments. But each of the lights was made up of even more lights, and as I got closer, I saw that each one too was made up of still more. Infinity.

It was so beautiful. I could have stayed forever. Santiago was right. I wasn't sad. In Cansino's space, there wasn't any sadness.

But then the spinning stopped and I could see other lights beyond those of the lift-that-was-a-door. I could feel the real world pressing up around me.

I could see the lights that were Esmeralda. They were in motion. She was using magic, I was sure of it: filaments stretched out from her, groping through Cansino's space towards me. She was looking for me, I realised.

I opened my eyes. The lift doors were open again. My body felt clumsy and heavy. I was dizzy too. I stumbled out, past the doorman—a different doorman—onto the street. It was so unlike where I had just been. No scent of flowers in the air. No bright colours. Everything was closed up, shut off. I could see the dull grey-brown buildings on the other side of the street and a little further down the block, but not much else. The people who passed me disappeared into their winter coats. They moved fast, their heads down.

The ugliness of a New York winter had made me forget how beautiful the real world could be: flowers, stars, butterflies. All with their own mathematical patterns. Where Santiago and his sister lived was almost as beautiful as Cansino's world of magic and lights and mathematics.

In my peripheral Cansino vision I could see Esmeralda coming towards me. I turned and saw her in both worlds: a glittering assemblage of magic and a tired, slow-moving figure buried in coat, hat, and gloves.

"Reason," she called.

I couldn't see Sarafina or Jason Blake.

I raised my hand. My golden hand.

Esmeralda nodded. Under her wool hat, her eyes were glassy and shadowed. "I'm glad you came back. I was beginning to think you wouldn't. You've been gone a long time."

"It's good to see you," I said, surprising myself. It *was* good to see her, and not just because she looked so much like Sarafina. "Getting back turned out to be a lot harder than getting there."

She smiled but didn't meet my eyes. The goldness was still too much for her. "Are you . . . " She trailed off. "How do you feel?"

"Strange. Strang*er*. I didn't find Sarafina. Have you heard anything?" I asked.

She finally looked me in the eye but shook her head. "Nothing. Tom and Jay-Tee are fine, though. Better off than me. You mightn't feel the cold, but I do."

"Sorry. I'm glad Jay-Tee and Tom are okay." I just wished my mother was too. "Sarafina has to be behind the other door."

We walked. I'd expected it to take minutes, but what seemed close in Cansino vision was thirty-eight blocks away. We waded through a sea of names: Horatio, Jane, Perry, and Charles. Then the numbers returned.

Esmeralda kept looking at me, as though that would help her see what I was seeing. "Where did that lift door take you?"

"I don't know. It seemed like the same time of day as here. Maybe an hour or two different. I think it was winter too. But not as cold as here. The people weren't wearing heavy coats. Lots of them had brown skin."

"Sounds like Mexico. Any further south and it would have been summer again. Did they speak Spanish?"

"I don't know. It wasn't English."

"What a shame Sarafina didn't teach you any. You know the Cansinos are from Spain, don't you? It's your ancestral language."

I shrugged. Something else to add to the long list of things Sarafina never told me.

"You were an awfully long time there. What were you doing?"

Should I ask Esmeralda if she knew anything of what Santiago had said about the magic I was merging with? The humanity I was losing and the intense beauty I was gaining? But there was still so much greed in the way she looked at me. She wanted what I had. "The door was kind of stubborn," I told her. "Didn't seem to want to let me back to New York City. I'm starting to think that doors are kind of like that." We'd already been walking for twenty minutes and the door seemed no closer than it had been when I started. It was as if the door moved at the same pace as us, always staying just ahead.

"Unless you have the key."

"Uh-huh."

We turned the corner and there it was, at the end of a narrow, dead-end lane, lined with piles of garbage, two rats skittering out of our way as we walked towards it. The biggest rats I had ever seen.

The surface under my feet was sticky with layers of filth and rot, as if it had never been cleaned. Esmeralda's nose wrinkled.

"That's it?" she asked. "It doesn't look very old."

The door didn't look like anything special, except that Jason Blake might be on the other side, which meant that Sarafina could be too. Plain metal, painted blue-grey, with many dents and rust where the paint had peeled away. In the middle was a white sign with red letters warning about high voltage.

The door glittered with 756 pinpoints of light (divisible by nine, and many of the lovely nine family, as well as two, three, six, and twelve), tenuously strung together with wires of light so fine I could barely see them. Like those stars you can only glimpse when you catch them out of the corner of your eye.

Esmeralda put her hand to it. There wasn't a handle or a doorknob. "It's locked."

"Don't look at me." I shrugged.

"Can't you just *make* it open?"

"That didn't work for Raul Cansino, did it? If he'd been able to blast through, he would've gotten to Sydney without grabbing me."

"We had protections, remember? This door might not," Esmeralda said. "He sent part of himself through before we put them down. You could do that."

True, Raul Cansino had squeezed a small part of himself through the door to Sydney. We'd thought he was a golem.

But I didn't know how to do that. Although I did know how to melt. . . . Was it the same thing?

I reached my hand out towards the door, but just before I touched, it seemed to shrink away from me. Ripples ran across its surface. I pressed my palm against it, spread out my fingers, felt the ripples of magic. They were moving faster now, skittering away from my hand. Like many tiny lizards, too wary to come near.

I slid my hand to the lock, made my fingers slender as wire, pushed them inside the mechanism, tinkered with it, trying to find a way to make it click.

The door's ripples trebled in speed. Then quadrupled. The door started to shake, trying to throw me off. A sound like metal on metal started up, a loud, harsh grinding. The vibrations ran up my arm, shaking me, then suddenly throwing me backwards. . . .

I landed on my arse.

"I believe someone else knows how to lay protections," Esmeralda said.

"Yup."

The door still trembled. I put my hand on it and closed my eyes, and the shaking, the vibrations, fled. Calm, silence. I narrowed my vision until all I saw were those 756 lights. I searched for a gap between them, some weakness, a way to push them apart. But they were roped tight. I saw no gaps, no fissures. No way to make them unbind.

I pushed as hard as I could, throwing my magic at the door. The lights shone brighter, hung together tighter. If they could speak, they would have told me, *No*.

I opened my eyes. The door was rippling even faster, convulsing. My bones shook, my teeth rattled, but the door did not open.

I removed my hand. I'd failed.

Sarafina *had* to be behind that door, but I couldn't get it open. How much magic did she have left now?

And me with so much magic I could've floated up into the sky if I wanted, yet I still couldn't find my mother. What was the point of so much magic if I was powerless?

I kicked the door hard as I could, but instead of the jarring impact I was expecting, the door swung open and I stumbled through.

"Wha—"

I was on a city street. Wider than most I'd seen in New York City but with a narrower footpath. The streetlights were on, though it was beginning to creep into morning.

"Hello, Reason," Jason Blake said.

Esmeralda and I turned. He was leaning against the building we'd emerged from, well dressed and smiling. "I've been waiting for you. Are you ready to see your mother?"

23
Blue Silk

It was after two in the afternoon. The house was spotless. Rita was long gone, the rain continued bucketing down, and Tom still hadn't come back. He'd promised. How long did it take to eat breakfast with your dad anyway? Or Da, as he called him. Pretty stupid thing to call your father, like something a baby would say: *da da da!* Jay-Tee was half tempted to go next door and yell at him, but she didn't want to show him how pissed she was. They'd only just started going out. . . .

She grinned. That was what they'd agreed, wasn't it? A secret going-out. Something special just for him and her. Well, she didn't want to start out by being the demanding, cranky one. Tom should have to wait for *her*, not vice versa. She was the cool New Yorker, not him. It really sucked that he was standing her up like this. How long had they been going out? Four hours? And he was already dissing her.

On top of that, the waiting was driving Jay-Tee crazy. Mere had called again and been all, "Are you okay? Are you sure you're okay? Are you really, really sure?" until Jay-Tee wanted to scream, though instead her eyes had filled with tears. (Again! Stupid leaky eyes.)

Of course she wasn't okay. But talking about it wasn't going to change anything. You could say every word in the universe and at the end of them she'd still be the same way, wouldn't she? Less than she had been. Much, much, much less.

While she waited, it was really hard not to think about all the things she didn't want to think about. Like her not-okay-ness. Much better to think about having a boyfriend, about positive, I-have-a-future-now things.

Was it selfish to be thinking like that when she didn't know if Reason and Esmeralda were okay? Probably. But there were too many things to worry about. She needed some rays of light. A boyfriend was a good start. Even though the brand-new boyfriend(!) was already not turning up when he'd promised.

She'd have gone out and done something herself, except that it was still pouring, and anyway, she wanted to be here so she could yell at Tom. Stupid, unreliable boyfriend Tom. If he didn't show up soon, she was going to dump his ass. That'd be a record, wouldn't it? World's shortest relationship.

Plus, if Esmeralda called again, she'd kill herself if she missed the call. She'd promised Mere she'd stay put.

Jay-Tee went outside and sat on the step between the back door and the porch and watched the rain thundering down. It came down so hard it bounced back several inches. Jay-Tee wondered if that was normal for Australia. She'd seen rain fall this heavily before, but not for this many hours.

The rain had brought the temperature down too, which was a relief. It was still warm, but it wasn't sweat-when-you-take-a-step warm. The ground and the trees and bushes and other plants seemed to be enjoying the rain too, sucking up the moisture greedily. Everything was green and glistening and sighing with contentment.

If her whole world hadn't crumbled—*No, not thinking about that*—if Tom wasn't being such a jerk, she'd've really enjoyed watching the buckets of rain changing everything.

When Tom showed up, she was going to be supercool. She'd act like she hadn't even noticed that he'd been away for hours and hours after he'd promised. She wouldn't even mention it. That would serve him right.

Maybe she would go back to New York. Not much point staying here now that she wasn't—

There she went again, thinking stuff that was too, too, too hard and horrible to think. Tom. When Tom got back, she was going to cuss him out like he'd never been cussed before. She was going to make his ears bleed with the force of her cussing. That would show him!

Her cheeks were wet. She rubbed them with her palms, mad at herself for getting all leaky again. She stood up and walked the length of the back porch and then turned to walk it again. What had happened to her wasn't so bad, was it? Not compared to Reason. She was all glow-in-the-dark with m—. Jay-Tee pulled up short from thinking the word.

She wished Esmeralda would call again. Let her know they were all right. Distract her from thinking about her own problems. Her complete absence of . . .

It hurt, she realized. Just thinking that word—the word she didn't have anymore—made her sides throb. Like she had appendicitis or something. Reason might be changing, but at least there was a gradualness to it. Jay-Tee'd been changed all at once. *Whooosh!* No choice, no questions asked.

One minute she was herself: Jay-Tee full of dance, and running, and connected to the world. Next she was not. Not any of it. She wasn't even sure she was herself anymore.

What would she do now? Go back to New York? And do what? She'd missed a *lot* of school. She'd probably have to start high school over. But at least she'd be living with Danny, so it'd be a whole different school, different people. She could start out fresh. This time, she was going to take running seriously. She paused. That was, if she *could* still run. Would she even be able to make the track team anymore?

She had a future . . . but what was it?

Jay-Tee sat back down on the porch, stared at the rain running down the trunk of the big ol' tree, Filomena.

Everything was different now. She and Tom might be boyfriend and girlfriend—or *not*, if he didn't show up soon—but he was . . . He was and she wasn't. That changed everything.

Was it like having a rich boyfriend when you were poor? Or was it more like having a boyfriend with cancer? Tom was where she'd been. Well, not quite—he had more magic left than she'd had—but he was still going to die young.

For a few minutes there she'd been happy. She'd been

revved up at the thought of living and having a normal life and not dying at fifteen. She couldn't wait to tell Danny—he was going to be thrilled. Realizing that Jason Blake couldn't do anything to her anymore—that was all good too.

So why did she feel so sad?

"Hey, Jay-Tee," Tom called from the top of the fence, rain running down his face. "It's pissing down."

Well, duh. Did he think she was blind? Tom dropped to the ground with a squelch, backpack over one shoulder, grinning hugely, like he'd just won the lottery.

"You are so dead," she said, scooting away from him. "You said you'd come straight back. Liar!"

"But I did, Jay-Tee. Honest. Look. I'm here!" He jumped up onto the porch and shook himself. Water went flying everywhere.

"You're getting me wet!"

"Sorry," he said. He didn't look even slightly sorry.

Tom wiped his hands on his jeans and then pulled something blue out of his backpack. "Look, I made it for you. I got the idea when I saw this blue silk fabric poking out from under the bed. I don't know when I bought it, but just one look at it and I realized . . ."

Jay-Tee looked. He was holding out a gorgeous top. All blue and shiny, but not in a tacky way; it looked soft, not plasticky. She could imagine wearing it to a fancy restaurant and everyone staring at her 'cause she looked so cool.

"Wow," she said.

"It's yours. I made it for you."

"What?" She stared at him and then at the top he had made. Along all the edges—at the neck, at the bottom, and at the ends of the tiny little sleeves—there was a line of black. He must have sewn that on. "In the last few hours?"

"Yup. Went as fast as I could without, you know, buggering it up. You like?"

"You were *sewing*?" She'd been going crazy waiting and he'd been *sewing*.

"Uh-huh," he said, grinning, looking unbelievably proud of himself.

Jay-Tee felt her pissed-offedness start to crumble.

"So what do you think?"

What *did* she think? That it was lovely and that he was completely crazy. "It's gorgeous, Tom. Really, really beautiful."

"Well, you going to try it on, then?"

Jay-Tee nodded, taking it from him. It felt even softer than it looked. "Wow, Tom. It's like holding a spiderweb or something. Though, you know, not sticky or gross."

"Like gossamer, you mean."

"Gossamer," she repeated, turning it around. "How do I put it on?"

"Put your arms through the sleeves so the opening's in back. Got that?"

Jay-Tee nodded and pulled off her T-shirt, feeling a bit self-conscious about Tom seeing her in her bra, and slipped her arms through the sleeves. She reached with her hands to do up the fastenings in back, but she didn't know how they worked and there were so many of them—she couldn't see if they lined up. "Um, help? How am I going to do this up on my own?"

Tom laughed. "You can't. You'll have to have me around every time you wanna wear it."

"Jerk!" She grinned and swiveled so her back was toward Tom, giggling as he took forever with the buttons, and kept slipping and touching her back. "Stop it! You're tickling me!"

When it was all done up, the fabric relaxed around her and then shifted, tightening in places, loosening in others, until it fit perfectly. She'd never worn anything like it before. It must be some kind of special fabric. She stood up, turned around. "What do you think, Tom? It feels great."

"It's perfect." His smile was huge. "A perfect fit. I am a genius! You look amazing, Jay-Tee. Even better than I thought. Or, you know, you would if you weren't wearing those crappy shorts."

"Hey," she said, smacking his shoulder lightly. She looked down and giggled. They *were* pretty spazzy. "Mere said she'd take me shopping for clothes, but it keeps not happening." She grinned. "Weird that she hasn't made it her top priority. It's not like there's anything else going on."

Tom snorted. "Nope, nothing else. Teenage pregnancies. Social workers. Missing mothers—"

"Lots and lots and lots of strange happenings."

"But you don't need Esmeralda. You've got me. I'll make you clothes. You'll need a skirt or pants to go with the top. But, you know, a decent pair of jeans would look great too."

"You can make jeans?"

Tom snorted. "Of course. I can make anything." He pushed her toward the bathroom. "Go take a look. Tell me what you think."

❋

In the bathroom mirror, Jay-Tee saw herself dressed in a top so beautiful it could have been spun out of—what had Tom called it?—gossamer, or out of an elf's breath. *Elf's breath? How lame is that?* But then Jay-Tee thought of the golden Cansino man. His breath made solid, that was what this fabric was.

Tom was right. It fit perfectly. Jay-Tee'd never worn anything so gorgeous. She hadn't *seen* anything as gorgeous before, not even in a movie with the hugest special effects budget ever.

She twirled, stopped with her back to the mirror, and craned her neck, trying to see what it looked like. She caught a neat row of black buttons on rich blue. "Pretty."

Jay-Tee couldn't believe Tom'd made this for her. She wanted to hug him so tight he burst. It was the most spectacularly beautiful top in the history of tops. Hell, it was the best piece of clothing ever. Way better than any crappy wedding dress. Or whatever it was people thought was the most beautiful clothing ever. They were all wrong. This was it.

She spun again, admiring her reflection, the way it shimmered. Just like . . .

Oh, she thought. *Magic*. Her eyes began to sting.

She stopped twirling, stared.

How else could it fit her like this? Tom hadn't even measured her. The fabric moved, had shifted around her until it was just right. No fabric on earth did that. No normal fabric.

Tom'd made it the same way he'd made Reason's pants. He'd pushed his magic into the cloth so it would do whatever he wanted. Tom'd used his precious magic to make her a pretty top.

All her joy slid from her. How could he throw it away on something so unimportant?

Tom came into the bathroom, still grinning, still pleased with himself. He stood behind Jay-Tee. She watched his reflection in the mirror, saw all the freckles across his face, each hair of his sandy eyebrows and lashes. He seemed farther away than he was. "You like?" he asked.

"How could I not like?" Jay-Tee said, looking at the way the fabric fit her. Her eyes were wet, but she was determined not to cry. "But you shouldn't have done it."

He smiled broader, proud of himself. "I had to. Soon as I saw the fabric, I finally knew who it was for: you. I'm so glad you like it, Jay-Tee." He slipped his arms around her waist and kissed the top of her head. Which felt nice, but how could he be so careless? Didn't he even want to live to see sixteen?

"Tom!" she yelled, spinning to face him.

He jumped. "What?"

"Are you insane? Do you not pay any attention? Didn't you notice that I almost died? Twice!"

"Well, of course, I saved your—"

"Yes! You saved my life. With magic! Have you not been

listening? Are you blind? It runs out. It ran out on me. I was so close, Tom. I saw the light. I saw the gates to heaven opening." She hoped it had been heaven. "I really, really did. And you? You're throwing yours away making me pretty clothes! Jesus, Mary, and Joseph!" She crossed herself. "And you, Mr. Atheist, you don't even have the hope of an afterlife!"

"It wasn't that mu—"

"It doesn't matter how much! What does Esmeralda say? Once a week. Use it *once* a week and only a little bit. When was the last time you used yours? Ten minutes ago! And then the day before that and—" She broke off to keep from crying.

"Wow, Jay-Tee. I'm sorry, okay? I won't do it again. Really, and it's not like I can help it. When I make clothes it just—"

"Then don't! I don't want you to die, Tom. Not because you made me pretty clothes. Not because you already saved my life."

"I'm not going to die, Jay-Tee."

"Yes, you are, Tom. Ask Reason. I bet she can see how much magic you have left. How much *life* you have left. You're going to die, Tom, and you're going to die while you're still young."

He was like the boyfriend with cancer—with lung cancer, and he keeps smoking. It'd been one thing when she'd been careless with her own life, another thing entirely now that it was Tom, and he was being careless to *impress* her.

Jay-Tee wasn't sure she could stand it. The pain in her side had gotten bigger, but she wasn't sure if she was mad at him for using his magic or for still having it when she didn't.

A sob escaped her lips. She dodged past Tom before he could grab her and sprinted up the stairs, slammed the door behind her, locked it, and threw herself on the bed.

Jay-Tee sobbed so hard her throat and chest almost burst; she sobbed so that she almost drowned the tiny thought in the back of her mind: *Hey, I can still run fast.*

24
Jason Blake

We were standing on the footpath outside a tall building in front of a nondescript wooden door. My grandfather headed across the street to a small park without looking back at us.

I searched the scattered lights in the corners of my eyes and sighed. None of the magic in this new place was my mother's. "She's not here," I told Esmeralda.

"He's lying, then," Esmeralda said. "No surprise there. But at least we're still in the States. See?" She pointed to a car that drove past. "Wrong side of the road. Those billboards over there are English. And it's the same time of day as in New York."

I nodded. The light was very close to what it had been in New York City, very early morning, with the sun low.

"Do you think you can get the key from him?" Esmeralda asked in a low voice. My grandfather stood on the other side of the street, hands in pockets, watching us.

"Yes," I said, though I wasn't sure.

"Well, let's find out what he wants, then. Maybe he *will* tell us where Sarafina is."

I doubted it but crossed the street. If I was strong enough

to take the key, then maybe I was strong enough that I could *make* him take me to my mother.

"She won't thank us for bringing Esmeralda," he said, walking towards a low bench beside a path. "She isn't fond of her."

"You're the one who let us through the door. Besides, Sarafina's not here." I searched further but still couldn't find her.

"No," my grandfather agreed, staring at my eyes, his gaze greedier than Esmeralda's. "She's on the other side of a different door. I doubt I can keep your grandmother from going through. It won't make your mother happy."

"Let's go, then," Esmeralda said.

"Did you not hear me? Your daughter doesn't want to see you."

"And I'm not leaving Reason alone with you."

"Just take me to the door," I said.

My grandfather put up his hand: for a moment, I thought he was going to touch me. "First we need to talk, you and me."

"No, we don't. You kidnapped Sarafina. You've been draining her of magic. I have to go to her." Before it was too late.

"She came with me willingly." He stared at me as if he couldn't not look. The opposite of Esmeralda, who could hardly look at me at all. "I've taken nothing from her."

"I don't believe you," Esmeralda said.

"It's true," he said, staring at me. "Unlike your mother or your grandmother, I've yet to lie to you, Reason."

Esmeralda snorted.

He sat down on a bench, his eyes never leaving me. Esmeralda and I remained standing. A huge, long truck rattled past. I could feel his gaze. It made my skin contract. I looked closely at the pattern of numbers that held him together and then laughed.

Perfect numbers: 6; 28; 496; 8,128; 33,550,336; 8,589,869,056; 137,438,691,328. Numbers that equal the sum of all of their factors. Six is the first one, because $6 = 1 + 2 + 3$. Six is also a triangular number and hexagonal too. A very perfect number. Jason Blake would be pleased. Didn't he think he was perfect? I wondered what would happen if I shifted them, turned them into Mersenne numbers, or primes, or Fibonaccis. Would that make him a better person?

"How do you think doors are made, Reason? Who do you think made them?"

It wasn't what I expected him to say. "Where's Sarafina?"

"I will tell you, Reason. I promise. You'll see her very soon. But there are things we must discuss first. You need to trust me."

"I trust you even less than I trust Esmeralda."

Esmeralda looked away.

"I'm sorry," I told her, because I was. I *did* want to trust her. I wanted to feel like there was at least one adult on my side. But she'd lied to me and she'd kept things from me. Who was to say there wasn't more she hadn't told me?

"Don't trust me, then," my grandfather said, "but listen. Then I'll show you the way to Sarafina."

Up above, a plane flew over. I had been in a plane. It flew

me from Dubbo to Sydney, to Esmeralda and her house with its
door to New York. Getting on that plane had completely
changed my life. Danny was probably on a plane right now. Or
had he already arrived in Sydney?

Just two weeks ago the world had been so much smaller.
Much less overwhelming. I had to make myself stay in the real
world; the temptation of retreating into Cansino's world was
growing every minute.

"Doors, Reason. How are they made?"

"Why are you asking?"

"Just answer me, Reason."

I remembered what Esmeralda told me and Tom and Jay-
Tee in our one and only formal magic lesson. "Accretion of
magic over time. One magic family in the one house—"

"Really? That's the garbage you've been telling them,
Esmeralda?"

"It is *not* gar—"

He waved his hand as if he were sweeping away everything
Esmeralda had ever said. "Forget it. How much magic do you
think it takes to make a door? Don't you think it would need a
giant kick to collapse space, to contain it between the frames
of two doors? Do small amounts over years sound enough to do
that? You've seen real space now. You've flown in it."

Real space? Was that what he called Cansino's world? He
thought *it* was the real world?

Was he right?

"Just show me how to get to Sarafina."

"There's more than one way, Alexander," Esmeralda said. "You know that."

"Think about how much magic it would take, Reason."

I thought about the magic that made up all the doors I'd seen. Magic I couldn't break.

"See this place? I grew up here. This is where my family is from. My hometown."

"We're in Texas?" Esmeralda asked. He ignored her.

I looked around. The park was mostly grass, not trees. Other than that there was no greenery at all. I could only see two stars above. What a bleak place to grow up.

"I made that door." For a moment, he took his eyes off me to look back at it. A plain wooden door in a six-storey brick building.

"You made it?" Esmeralda asked, staring at him.

"I did," he said, pleased with himself. His eyes were back on me. "You glow much brighter than Raul Cansino did."

"How did you make a door, Alexander?" Esmeralda asked.

"With magic. *Lots* of magic."

Esmeralda snorted. "Very informative. How many others have you made?" she asked. He had made a door. I wondered if I could do that. Was that how I was supposed to get to Sarafina?

"None."

"None? You only made one door?"

"These are the only two places I know well enough. New York and here, where I grew up."

"Why?" Esmeralda asked.

"You of all people should know. To learn more about what magic is, what we can do. If you knew how to make a door, surely you would."

Esmeralda looked down, but I could see he was right.

"Okay," I said. "You made a door. Now take me to my mother." He wasn't bargaining with me. He wasn't attacking me. He wasn't doing any of the things the Jason Blake I knew would have done. Even the staring was out of character. The old Jason Blake wouldn't have been so obvious. But now he looked at me as if he was a magpie unable to keep from something shiny.

"You'll see her, Reason. You'll rescue her like you want to."

"How did you make the door, Alexander?"

"You can do anything now, Reason," Jason Blake told me. Then he turned to Esmeralda. "I drew points of light together. From here to New York City."

Esmeralda clucked her tongue.

Lights flickered in the corners of my eyes. I thought about how much magic it would take to draw them together. "It was easy?"

He laughed. "Easy? No. But it was the best thing I've ever done in my life."

"Now *that* I believe!" my grandmother exclaimed. "Other than fathering Sarafina, your life has been a selfish waste."

Jason Blake fished something out of his pocket and held it out: an ordinary key. "I fashioned it out of air." I could imagine doing that. He watched my reaction, waiting for me to say something. When I didn't, he continued. "All I've ever wanted, Reason, was to live. To live and use my magic."

"And steal other people's," Esmeralda said.

"Like you haven't?" he said to her without taking his eyes off me. "You're no better than I am. You just pretend harder."

"That's a lie!"

"And you've never lied, have you? When I take magic, I always ask."

"Because it's no good to you if you don't," she said. "Not because you give a damn about anyone but yourself."

"You didn't ask me," I said, interrupting them. "That first bit of magic Raul Cansino gave me—you stole it."

"That's true. I was desperate. I knew he would choose you. I wanted . . . That was an exception. The only time I stole."

"Liar," I said. When he first asked me a question it had been to get magic from me, but his question hadn't been clear. He had tried to trick me out of my magic. "You might've asked, but you didn't make clear what you were asking for, did you?"

My grandmother looked down again and I knew she had done the same thing, but Jason Blake just shrugged. "It's not stealing. Technically, anyway. Stealing requires too much magic, not much of a net gain. I was a good little magic-wielder: eking out a life, a tiny bit of magic here, a tiny bit there." He spat. It landed two metres away.

"When you took Raul Cansino's magic from me it almost killed me."

"I knew Cansino would give you more."

I doubted that. "What about Jay-Tee? There was no Raul Cansino to save her."

"It's true. I cared more about living longer, having more magic." He was still staring at me. "We can't afford to care too much about other magic-wielders. It's dangerous. My own mother tried to trick me out of my magic, as she had my father. In the end I tricked her out of hers. That's how it is. How it always has been. We eat one another."

Esmeralda opened her mouth to speak, then closed it.

"Is that why you don't use your real name?" I asked.

"My real name?"

"The name you were born with."

"I was born Alexander Tannen."

"You told Esmeralda your real name?"

"I was young."

"And in love?"

He laughed. So did Esmeralda.

"I didn't woo Esmeralda out of desire for anything but her magic. And if there was a child—and I saw there would be—that magic too. Like my mother tried to do to me. Like every magic person I have ever known. Esmeralda too, of course."

"But you didn't get mine," Esmeralda said.

"Nor did you get mine. Stalemated each other, didn't we?"

"I was just glad to be free of you."

It was one of the first things Esmeralda had said that I believed a hundred per cent.

"None of that matters, Reason. Raul Cansino's magic sets us free." He laughed. "We don't have to turn on one another anymore. What he gave you—it changes everything."

"What about what he gave you and Esmeralda?" I asked. "You made a door. If you can do that, why do you need me?"

"I don't. I don't *need* you. But I want to be like you. I want to have all of Cansino's magic. He showed me what I would become if he chose me. He showed me real space. How I could change what I was. Change anything I wanted—"

"You want me to give you *more* magic?" I asked. Was he mad? "I'd much rather turn your magic off."

Jason Blake blanched. It lasted only a moment, but I saw it. He *was* frightened of me. Esmeralda saw it too.

"What did you mean when you said this new magic doesn't last?" she asked him. "How long do we have?"

"I don't know. A month. A year. The rest of a human life span. But not the centuries she has."

"But I feel so strong," she said. "And I've done things I never dreamt of."

"He left us powerful," Jason Blake agreed. "Not as powerful as you, Reason, but powerful. He left me human. Do you know what you look like now? You vibrate with power."

"But I'm changing. I'm losing—"

"Your humanity? Why care? I don't. I don't care about people. I never have. I don't want to feel greed. Or guilt. Or love." Esmeralda laughed, but my grandfather ignored her. "Or lust.

I want the life he had. Your life. I want to be stripped down to curiosity. I don't want anything else. I want to explore, to have the universe unfurl for me. It's all I've ever wanted. Not love, not money, not fame. I've never wanted human things."

"But Raul wanted them," I protested. "He wanted to make sure there were more Cansinos. He wanted to die and be with the rest of his family."

Jason Blake laughed. "Every living thing wants to pass on its genes. And, eventually, every living thing dies. Not many get to explore for centuries before it happens."

I could see it. The shimmering lights, shifting in the margins of my sight. No discord there. All I had to do was close my eyes completely to be there . . . to stay there forever.

"He's wrong, Reason," Esmeralda said. "Raul Cansino didn't want to live forever. It wasn't enough for him. In the end he chose to die."

"Rubbish," my grandfather said. "No one has ever been as content as he was. Or as you'll be once you accept your gift. You can do anything you want. Go anywhere. Raul Emilio Jesús Cansino showed me what he was."

I looked at Esmeralda, but she was looking at Jason Blake.

"She can't go through doors that don't want her," Esmeralda said.

He laughed. "Neither of you understand, do you? Reason, you don't need doors. Those lights you see? The magic? Concentrate on any one you recognise and you'll fly through space until you're there."

Esmeralda turned to look at me. "Really? She can do that?" The greed had returned to her eyes.

"You can go to Sarafina anytime you want. If you can see her magic, you can go there. Your magic is inextricably linked to hers."

"Then why didn't Raul fly to me? Why did he need the door?"

"He didn't know you. He had to know you first. Then, wherever you were, he could go there. He was in the room when you and your Danny boy went at it, making sure you conceived. He pushed you at him." His smile turned feral. "That's why he chose you, after all. For the baby."

As soon as he said it I knew it was true. I *had* wanted Danny—he was so beautiful—but I never would have kissed him, not without Raul Cansino pushing me. He'd even made Danny smell of limes, of lightly toasted bread, of cinnamon. I'd seen Danny since then, and all I'd smelt was soap. Those other smells—they'd been from Raul Cansino.

He really had been in the same room with us. I shuddered. Jason Blake smiled.

"You are repulsive," Esmeralda said, glaring at him.

"But," I began, pushing thoughts of that night away, "why did you steal my mother?"

Jason Blake laughed. "Why don't you ask her yourself? Go on. Concentrate. Find her."

"Reason, be careful!" Esmeralda said. "You can't trust him."

I looked from him to her and back again, not sure what to do. I had to get to Sarafina. I had to save her. I closed my eyes.

"No," my grandfather said. "Don't shut your eyes."

I opened them. He was still staring at me.

"Can you see her?" he asked.

I couldn't. "She's not here."

"Careful, Reason," Esmeralda said.

"Search further. Push yourself. Concentrate on her. You've seen her magic; now find it!"

I was already searching, pushing further than I ever had before. I heard them yelling at each other, but not what their words were. My peripheral vision was growing, eating into everything I saw.

I found her.

So far away. She was even fainter than when I'd last seen her, almost as faint as Jay-Tee before I'd saved her. "What have you done to her? She has almost no magic left."

"Go to her, then," my grandfather told me. "Ask her yourself."

"How?"

"I don't know. He didn't show me how. I just saw him do it."

"Don't," Esmeralda said. "It might not be safe."

I retreated into the lights floating in my eyes. Sarafina's was so faint. I concentrated on it, until it spread out and was almost all I could see. My vision stretched out. My skin prickled. I moved forward. I panicked, stutter-stepped, tripped.

A huge semi trailer zoomed past; wind pushed my hair and

clothes wildly around my face and body. I was on the edge of the highway. I took a step back.

Behind me Esmeralda called out, "I'll find you!"

I didn't turn. I'd moved. My grandfather was right: I could be my own door. But I had to concentrate or—another semi trailer rushed past—or I would be squished flat as a bug.

I turned my attention to Sarafina, let her fill my vision, until the highway in front of me drifted into my peripheral vision. My skin contracted, then expanded, shifting across my flesh. And my vision stretched again. Streets unfurled beneath my feet, countryside, ocean, ocean, ocean, but her light always there.

I could feel the panic rising. The rushing ocean began to take up more of my vision. For a brief moment I thought I could feel spray, smell salt. I pushed my thoughts back to Sarafina. Sarafina, not ocean—Sarafina. Ocean changed to land; green, blue, brown flashed by.

Then my mother's light grew sharper and sharper, until I was standing in front of her.

25
Without Tears

Tom was banging on the door and calling out to her to let him in, that he was sorry, and that she should stop being such a bloody pain. Jay-Tee lay in bed and listened, which was easier than it had been, because the rain had finally started to ease off.

She wasn't crying anymore. That hadn't lasted very long. She wondered if she was about to get her period or something. This wasn't her. Having tantrums, slamming doors, crying over nothing. Well, not nothing—her whole life gone splat was not nothing—but she hadn't cried when her dad started beating her. She hadn't cried when she ran away from home and thought she'd never see her brother again. She hadn't cried over Jason Blake stealing her magic. Or over her dad dying. Or when she thought *she* was going to die. Except for the last few days, Jay-Tee honestly couldn't remember the last time she'd cried. Now all she seemed to do was blub.

She got up and opened the door. Tom stood there, mouth open, still red in the face from yelling. He closed his mouth, then opened it again, then closed it. She could see all the different thoughts flickering across his face: being mad at her, worried about her, wanting to make it up, wanting to kiss her, back to mad again. "You okay?" he said at last.

"Yeah." No. Jay-Tee wasn't magic anymore. And Tom was. She was jealous of him. She was sorry for him. She didn't know what she was.

"I'm really sorry."

"You should be." She leaned forward and kissed him. A demure little mouth-closed kiss.

"That's better," he said, reaching forward and taking one of her curls in his fingers. He stretched it out and then let go so that it bounced, which normally would've made her totally lose it. But she didn't mind Tom doing it.

"I'll be careful," he said. "I really, really will. Until you and Reason showed up I always had been. Careful, I mean."

"I'm the bad influence, then?"

"Reckon. Before you came I hadn't hardly done anything. Catholic girls!"

She smacked him lightly. "Least I'm going to heaven."

"You'll be lonely there without me."

She crossed herself and smacked him again.

"Reckon there'll be any kissing in heaven?" Tom asked.

"Nope. Angels are beyond earthly things like kissing."

"So we should get as much in now as we can, eh? Before it's too late?"

Jay-Tee laughed and opened the door wide for Tom to come in.

"Sorry 'bout the tantrum."

"'S'okay. I was being a dropkick." He kissed both her cheeks and then her chin, her nose, her mouth. She opened her lips a little, kissing him back. "But I'm not sorry I made it. You look gorgeous."

She ran a finger down his cheek. "Plus how am I going to get the damn thing off without you around? It's lovely, but I want to change back into normal clothes."

She turned her back to him and Tom started to unbutton her.

"Mere called a few times."

"What'd she say?"

Tom undid the last button and she shrugged the gorgeous top off and put on another one of Mere's T-shirts. "She was just checking on me. Wanted to know if I was okay. Blah, blah, blah."

"Did you speak to Reason too?"

Jay-Tee shook her head. "No, she didn't mention Reason. I wonder if she's still . . ."

"Still what?"

"Human."

"What do you mean?" Tom asked. "Of course Reason's still human."

Jay-Tee didn't know what to say. Reason had looked so strange. All glowing and gold. At least she had until she'd turned Jay-Tee's magic off.

"What did Esmeralda say about Reason's mum?"

"She didn't mention her either. Or Jason Blake. And she would have, right? If they'd found him, I mean."

"I guess." Tom looked down. "Hope they're okay."

"Sure they are," Jay-Tee said. "I mean, Reason's like a superhero now, right?"

"You keep saying so."

"'Cause it's true. Anyway, I'm glad you're here to wait with me."

"Um," Tom told his feet.

"What?"

"Well, that's the thing. I kind of rushed through brekkie with Da. You know? So I could make your top. And he wants me to come home and then stay for dinner and stay tonight as well. He said he missed me. And it's true I haven't seen him properly since Reason got here."

"But." Jay-Tee really hated the idea of spending the night alone.

"I'll call you. I'll go to bed early and I'll call you straight away, okay?"

Jay-Tee didn't say anything, but she was really hating Tom's dad.

"We can talk until we fall asleep and then I'll race around first thing in the morning. Just call me if Esmeralda and Reason show up or if they call or anything, okay?"

"Sure," Jay-Tee said. "But what's your number?"

Tom went out into the hall and returned with the notebook from beside the phone. "This first one's my house and the second one is the mobile."

He tore the paper off and handed it to her. There were two

love hearts under the numbers. Jay-Tee grinned and mock-punched him.

"It's going to be okay," Tom said.

"I hope so," Jay-Tee said.

She walked downstairs with him hand in hand. He climbed out the window to the back porch and she went through the door. They kissed for a while, neither of them wanting to stop, until finally Tom pulled away. "I've really got to go."

"I know," she said. "See you tomorrow."

"Talk to you tonight." He jumped off the porch steps and landed with a soft squelch. The rain had slowed some, but he was still pretty wet before he was over the fence.

"See ya!" she called.

"Later!"

She realized that she wasn't worried about Reason. Reason was so powerful now, she could take Jason Blake. She could take anyone. She could turn magic off. She could probably do anything she wanted to do.

Jay-Tee had been right all along: Reason *was* going to save them. It was just that being saved was not so wonderful as she had imagined.

She missed her magic.

26
Sarafina Cansino

I staggered, tripping over a tiny rock wall into greenery. Ferns, I thought, as I closed my eyes and slipped into Cansino's space, so comfortingly free of sound and sensation. I took in the patterns of light around me: A door close by: 539 lights, divisible by 7, by 11, lots of pretty patterns there. And Sarafina. Her magic frail and tiny, her Fibonacci pattern starting to fray.

Sarafina was calling to me. Her words floated by. I pushed out of Cansino's world to where she was. I felt cool soil between my fingers, leaves against my face, rocks digging into my legs, but somehow muted, as if the real world were coated with the other world. Behind me she laughed.

"Hey, Reason," Sarafina said. "Get up!"

I rolled over, shifted onto a path made up of lots of tiny pebbles. Sarafina held out her hands to help me up.

"I'm here," I said.

"Yes, you are," she answered. "But it's not very comfy there. Come over here; it's much better," she said, pointing to a long wooden seat with shiny red cushions on it.

"I'm here to save you!"

She grinned and pulled me up, folding me into her arms. "Of course you are! Hey, darlingest daughter. Glorious child. So grand to see you! Though you're *so* slow—I thought you'd never get here." She squeezed me and then held me out at arm's length. "You have no hair! You weren't even that bald when you were a baby! But it looks wonderful. I love the bronze look. Very you. Have you grown? No, you can't have. It's only been a couple of weeks, hasn't it? But still, it looks like you have. It could be the baby inside you. Like mother, like daughter. What shall we call her? Glory? Brilliance? Beauty? Fibonacci?"

She looked and sounded just like the old Sarafina. She was rocking from heel to toe, her feet moving as fast as her mouth, giving me no time to respond to any of her questions. Full of energy, the way she always had been. Her eyes were bright. They looked into mine. "Extraordinary. Alexander said your eyes would change. But I had no idea. They're beautiful."

"They're—"

"And your skin." She touched my arm. "It's like you have no pores."

"Not *like*. They're gone. I'm poreless."

"The hair on your arms is gone too. Not just your head." She ran her finger over my scalp and then my forearm. "Not a single one. How odd. But it suits you. Come, sit down," she said, dragging me to the seat and chattering at me all the while. She folded her legs up underneath herself, wrapping the fabric of her skirt around her feet.

"Let me give you more mag—"

"No rush, darling. Isn't this lovely?"

"Well, yes, but—"

"Just look at it, Reason. See those fountains?"

We were sitting in a walled garden, with two fountains and a stream circling from one to the other. Plants everywhere. Many ferns, and vines I didn't recognise climbing the stone wall. The air shimmered, so it had to be warm. Little brown lizards skittered across the tiny pebbles that made up the garden paths and darted into the greenery.

There were butterflies, but they looked nothing like the butterflies I'd seen on the other side of the lift. I could hear traffic noise, honking, wheels on bitumen, but I couldn't see any of it.

"Are you listening, darling?"

I hadn't been. "I'm sorry. You don't have much time left. I need to—"

Someone gasped. I looked up at an Asian woman wearing a long, tight skirt in bright colours, and a white blouse, and carrying a tray. She was staring at me.

Sarafina laughed. "She loves your goldness!"

The woman lowered her head and placed the tray in front of us, then turned, revealing black hair spiralled on the nape of her neck. She retreated up the path to the house she must have emerged from. It had a low, sloping roof and a wall of glass cast in shadows.

"More tea," Sarafina announced, reaching down to pick up one of the tiny teacups. "Shall I pour you a cuppa? It's awfully sweet."

I shook my head. The magic within her was breaking up, her Fibonaccis unravelling. Just as Jay-Tee's had. My mother was dying. "You have to let me fix—"

Sarafina waved my words away. "There's plenty of time."

"No, Sarafi—"

"Even if you don't want it, they'll bring it to you. There'll be food along in a second," Sarafina said, screwing up her nose. Sarafina had never been much interested in food.

"Do you want to die?"

"Don't be silly, Reason. I'm not going to die."

She was wrong about that; I could see her pattern unraveling before my eyes.

"Do you know where we are? Bangkok. Outside these walls is chaos. Utter chaos. More people than I've ever seen in my entire life. Far too many. It's too much—I'm still not used to so many people. But I like it in here. The walls go all the way around, and you can't see the tiniest bit of the crazy city. It's just fountains and butterflies and giggling servants. Alexander's house is calm and full of number patterns. Especially the tiles. Wait till I show you the Fibonacci bathroom.

"His servants are all very kind. They smile a lot. They're always bringing me little things to eat. Pretty food on pretty platters. They get sad when I don't eat it all. But I can't explain that I only need enough fuel to keep going and that I don't really care what it looks like, because none of them speak English. Though actually that's kind of a relief, and I've learned to put my palms together, bow my head, and say, '*Kop kun kah*,' which I'm fairly sure means 'thank you.' They'll be thrilled that you're here. You'll love all the pretty food."

I didn't bother telling her I didn't eat anymore. I wondered if I ever would again. The stones that made up the narrow path that wound through the garden had felt so rounded and smooth. Or was that just the residue of Cansino's space around them, forever between me and the rest of the world?

More of Sarafina's pattern had unravelled as she spoke. Why wouldn't she let me save her? I was here to rescue her and she just wanted to chatter. She was just as she had been. The old Sarafina. No longer mad. Or at least she wasn't staring off into space, not recognising me.

She'd probably always been a bit mad, I realised. I'd simply never spent enough time with other people before to understand just how odd she was. But even as a small kid I knew she was different. I remembered one time when I was really little— I think it was up in Arnhemland—we'd just travelled three hours on foot to get to a billabong. She spent the whole journey telling me about it, jabbering like she was now about the carpet of lily pads, the brolgas, and the jacana birds that walked across the pads so that it looked like they were walking on water.

But when we finally got there, we couldn't find any of the birds she'd told me about. Sarafina made us walk on to the next billabong, and when there were only spoonbills, she pushed on to the next one and then the next, until it was dark and I was so tired and hungry I cried.

I remembered those emotions; I should be feeling them

now. She was killing herself by rejecting the magic I offered. But the Cansino magic blunted my pain. There were no tears left in me. No laughter either.

"This is Thailand?" I asked.

"Yes, darling. Bangkok, Thailand: 9,290 K from Sydney."

"Huh."

We'd always meant to come here—not crowded Bangkok, but Thailand. Once I was old enough for Esmeralda to have no claim on me, we were going to leave Australia and travel the world. She'd always told me about Angkor Wat in Cambodia, which wasn't so very far from here. Not compared to how far it was from Australia.

And here we were, overseas together. I watched Sarafina's lips moving, her hands too. She crossed and uncrossed her legs, rearranging her skirt around her. She had never been a still person, except when the doctors in Kalder Park had drugged her.

"You must listen. I'm telling you something very important, Reason. I was confessing. When I said insanity was preferable to magic, I was wrong. I didn't know there were other kinds of magic." She waved her hand and made a butterfly appear. It was bigger than any butterfly I'd ever seen before, with bands of red, green, and gold. Sarafina's light became so dim she was barely there.

"Sarafina!"

"Isn't it gorgeous? Almost as big as the largest butterfly in the world. See the wingspan? That's about thirty centimetres.

Isn't that incredible? What's better—I made it. I'm pretty sure it's a whole new species. Or if it's not new, then it's so rare no one knows about it, surely almost extinct. Perhaps I should make a few more?"

"No! That's mad! You don't have enough—"

"I know." She jumped up and spun, her skirt swirling out around her. She snapped her fingers. "But it doesn't matter. Esmeralda's version of magic was so grim. No fun. It was all dour survival and trying so hard never to steal it from anyone— though she did from me, and didn't that eat her up? What I want is my childhood back. I want the fun of magic. I want the play."

"We played all the time. *Without* magic."

"We did, didn't we? *Mostly* without magic. And I loved it, Reason, I did. You are the most wonderful thing I have ever done in my life. I don't have words for how glad I am that I made you. That I taught you. That we had so many years together. And we'll have many more too. I love you, Reason. More than I've ever loved anyone else."

I wondered if she'd ever loved anyone but me. I didn't think so. Back when we'd lived together, Sarafina had seemed capable of anything. But now all I could see were her limits. How she'd never connected to anyone but me. I knew I loved her, but the feeling was remote. It was like the memory of a feeling. I knew I should feel sad about her dying. But the most I could summon up was a vague sense of guilt.

"I love you too, Sarafina," I said.

"I'm not going to worry about my mother anymore," she

told me. "Not now that I've got my baby back. It's so wonderful to see you, precious Reason. So wonderful to *really* see you. Unclouded. Clear." She drew me into her arms again. I had always felt safe there, but not anymore. "I can't wait till we can go flying together. Alexander told me all about it. How wondrous!"

"Flying together?"

"Yes, after you've changed me to be like you."

Sarafina stretched out her hand, palm up, and her butterfly landed in its centre. She blew on it and the pretty insect disappeared. "There, that's about all my magic, I think. Oh, yes . . ." She sank to her knees, her eyes rolling up so I could see only the whites.

"Time to change me," she whispered.

27
Reunion

Jay-Tee woke to the sound of pounding coming from downstairs. She unglued her eyes, jumped up, and threw on clothes. She and Tom had stayed up talking for hours and hours. It was light outside but very quiet. It had to be early. She was so tired she almost fell down the stairs. The pounding on the door didn't stop. She turned the handle and threw it open.

"Hell, what are you—"

It was Danny, holding a winter coat. Beside him was a large suitcase.

"Oh my God! Danny!"

Jay-Tee's brother picked her up in a huge hug and twirled her around. "You're still alive! Thank you, God." He gave her a kiss on both cheeks and then set her down to look at her. "What happened to your face? Did someone give you that bruise?"

"What? That? No. It's nothing—a magic thing. I'm totally alive," Jay-Tee said, unable to stop smiling. "Reason cured me."

"She did! How? I mean what? Cured? Why didn't she tell me?! I came all this way—she made me think you were dying."

Jay-Tee pulled him into the house. He hefted his suitcase through, and Jay-Tee shut the door.

"Wow, you look terrible!" she said. His hair was matted to his head, and big black rings shadowed both eyes.

"Thanks. You try sleeping in a chair designed for pygmies. Two flights to get here, Julieta! And one of them was a thousand hours long." He rolled his shoulders and cracked his neck. "And it's so hot and sticky here. I forgot about the whole summer thing. Didn't pack anything but winter clothes."

Jay-Tee laughed, though she hadn't known about the whole winter-summer thing herself until a week ago. "Moron! Come and sit down in the kitchen. Just leave your suitcase and coat here. We'll sort it later. It's this way. What the hell are you doing here? Why didn't you call?"

Danny pulled up a stool. "To surprise you. Thought it would be fun!"

"You almost scared me half to death."

"You sorry I came?"

"No! It's wonderful to see you." And Danny wasn't magic. It would be great to hang out with someone who wasn't magic for a change. Maybe she wouldn't feel like such a freak.

"Damn, I'm thirsty."

"Water do?" Jay-Tee asked, opening up the fridge.

"There any beer in there?"

"Danny! It's like eight in the morning!"

"Oh, yeah. Well, it sure don't feel like it. There any soda?"

"Just water or OJ."

Danny grimaced. "OJ, then."

She poured them both a glass and handed Danny his.

"Cured like how?" he asked.

Jay-Tee sat down opposite him. "I was dying. And now I'm not. I don't have any magic left."

Danny's mouth dropped open. "Say what? I thought that shit was with you till you died?"

Jay-Tee nodded. "Me too. But Reason broke the rules. That's how she cured me. She took all the magic away. Now I'm just like you."

"Took your magic away? So you're like me now?"

"That's right. Except I still suck at basketball."

"That's wonderful!" He reached across the table and squeezed her hand. Jay-Tee tried to believe that it was too. "I'm so happy for you. For me too."

Jay-Tee smiled. "Yeah. I'm alive. It totally beats being dead," she said. "Wow, Danny, I can't believe you're here. This is great!"

"It is, isn't it? I mean, despite the flight. I was trapped next to this guy who follows high school basketball. Would you believe it? He recognized me. So I had to listen to him ranting about pro ball and how it ain't what it used to be and how the women's game is more old-school. I had to pretend to be asleep to shut him up. I don't think I can go back to the city. Don't think I can ever face that flight again." Danny yawned, rubbed his eyes. "I could go to sleep right now. You're really not dying?"

"Cross my heart."

"Well," he said, "I'm so glad." He started stretching his arms. "Man, I'm sore. Those planes ain't designed for people as tall as me."

Jay-Tee tried to imagine her brother cooped up in a normal-person chair, unable to fling his legs every which way. It was kind of impossible. But then, she wouldn't ever have imagined Danny crying either, and there he was sitting opposite her with his eyes full of tears. He squeezed her hand again, like he wasn't convinced she was real. This was not the Danny she'd grown up with.

"It's so great."

"Isn't it?"

"I can't believe Reason lied to me. She told me you were dying. Almost gone."

"She did? Is that why you came running?"

"Running? *Flying*, you mean." He made a face. "Nah, I'd already booked the flight. Why'd she lie?"

"I don't know. It doesn't make any sense." It really didn't. Reason didn't tell lies. She was completely allergic to them. "When did you see her?"

"Yesterday, I guess."

Jay-Tee thought about it. It was Saturday morning now. "Friday, you mean?"

"Friday? Nope. Being on that plane ate up Friday. That is one long-ass flight, let me tell you. Reason showed up Thursday afternoon as I was waiting for the car." He stretched his neck again. "I half wished I was magic and could come through that door of yours."

Jay-Tee winced. That door she was never going through again. She shook her head. Thursday afternoon in the city was when here? Reason would know. Jay-Tee was pretty sure it was

Friday already, yesterday. So Reason should've known that Jay-Tee was okay. Yesterday was when she'd saved her, and she hadn't gone to NYC until after that. "It doesn't make sense. She knew I wasn't dying anymore."

"She *was* being weird." Danny ducked his head. "It was awkward, you know? I had no idea what to say."

"About what?" Jay-Tee asked, and then she realized. Reason must've told him about the baby. And he hadn't taken it well, and *that* was why Reason hadn't told him about curing Jay-Tee. She'd been too mad. "Oh," she said. "*That.*"

"So you know?" Danny asked.

Jay-Tee nodded. "Yeah, we all do."

Danny swore. "I can't believe she blabbed to all of you."

"Well, she didn't blab. It was Mere, her grandmother."

"She told her grandmother! I thought she hated her grandmother!"

"Look, Danny," Jay-Tee said as soothingly as she could. "It's not going to wreck anything for you. Truly. Reason has Mere and her mother. . . . Well, sort of. Anyway, she won't need anything from you. Her grandmother has scads of money. You won't have to have anything to do with the baby if you don't want. You'll still get to play—"

"*Baby?!*"

"Um . . ." That wasn't what he'd been talking about. *Oops.*

"Baby? What baby?"

"She didn't tell you." *Always great to state the obvious,* she thought, *get it out there in the open.*

"She's pregnant? What's that got to do with me?"

Jay-Tee looked at her brother's open mouth. She couldn't believe he could be *that* low. "It's *your* baby. That's what it's got to do with you."

"She said that?! But there's no way it could be mine. We only just slept together. It was only a few days ago! She wouldn't even know she was pregnant yet!"

"Magic."

"What?"

"She knows because of magic. Mere saw the baby inside her."

"Jesus wept!" Danny ran a hand through his hair. "Ack. I need a shower so bad. It still don't necessarily mean it's mine!"

"It's yours."

"Her grandmother could see *that*?"

"Yes," Jay-Tee said.

"Because of *magic*?!" He rolled his eyes. "Of course, why did I ask? I s'pose the baby'll be all magic and shit too?"

"Seems like." Jay-Tee felt herself getting teary, thinking about her own lost magic. She blinked it away.

"Great. So I'm gonna have a kid who dies before I do? Wonderful. Though, wait, can't Reason fix it? She fixed you, didn't she?"

"She did," Jay-Tee said slowly, but she wasn't thinking about her unborn niece or nephew; she was thinking about Tom again. About Reason turning Tom's magic off. About Tom not dying young. About how Reason could give him a normal life like Jay-Tee, where all you had to worry about were little things like your brother getting your best friend pregnant.

"I really have a kid?" Danny looked like he was going to cry too. And not from happiness this time. "I *can't* have a kid." He stood up and started pacing the kitchen.

"Well, you're gonna." Once more on the obvious.

"Fu—"

"You did that already, Danny. Remember? Don't freak out. The baby's not going to stop you becoming the king of the NBA, okay?"

"Jesus wept! Jay-Tee, you can't tell me I'm going to be a dad and expect me not to freak. How do you know she won't come after me? This could be the end of everything. No college ball. No shot at the NBA."

"Danny, relax. You're just the dad. You won't have to do nothing. Dads never do."

"Hey! Our dad did." He paused. "I mean, before he went crazy and turned on you and . . . Look, there are good dads out there."

"You just don't have to be one of them. Seriously, Danny, you can go back to New York and never even see the baby."

Danny stopped pacing to stare at Jay-Tee. "What kind of a lame-ass loser do you think I am? My own sister! If it's my kid—*my* kid—of course I'll help out with that. Of course I wanna see it. Know it. Be its dad. Oh my God! *Be* its dad! I'm gonna be a dad. Man. Man! I am *way* too young to be a father."

"Dad was only nineteen," Jay-Tee pointed out. "That's only

232 of 308 Justine Larbalestier

a year older than you. And they didn't have any money at all hardly. You're loaded."

"*We're* loaded. It's your money too, Jay-Tee, remember? Dad did some of his magic hoodoo stuff and now money grows on trees. Anyway, that was the olden days. Back then, *everyone* was having babies while they were still babies."

Jay-Tee laughed. "What? And no one you were at school with had babies? You *did* go to the same high school as me, didn'tcha?"

"You are *so* not helping."

"I will, though. We'll both help with the baby." If it didn't turn out so scary-magic that Danny couldn't even see it, like Raul Cansino. Which would mean *she* couldn't see it either. "You'll go to Georgetown and be the best point guard in their entire history. I bet there are other basketball stars who've had babies. In college even."

There was a tap at the window; they both looked up to see Tom.

Jay-Tee waved at him to come in. He climbed through the window and dropped to the kitchen floor, his eyes wide.

"Wow, Danny, right? What are you doing here?"

Jay-Tee looked at the two of them looking at each other and wondered how she was going to tell Danny that Tom was her boyfriend.

28
Magic or Madness?

Tom sat down next to Jay-Tee, his eyes still on Danny.

"So, um," he said. "This is a surprise."

"Isn't it?" Jay-Tee said, beaming. Tom felt a tiny pang. How come he didn't make her as happy as her brother did? She hadn't grinned like that when he'd showed her the blue silk shell.

"When did you get here?" Tom asked.

"Just now."

"Huh. Long flight, eh?"

"Yup," Danny said.

The doorbell rang, and Tom almost jumped up to get it. Anything to get away from Danny-who'd-gotten-Reason-pregnant. But he paused. If he answered the door, would it look like he lived here, like he'd *spent the night* with Jay-Tee just yesterday? Even though they'd just kissed (a lot), how would Danny feel about that?

Jay-Tee stood up. "I guess I'll get that." She darted off. He wasn't thrilled at being left alone with Mr Thousands-of-girlfriends, Mr Breaker-of-hearts, whose sister was Tom's secret girlfriend. For one thing, Danny was a lot bigger than Tom remembered.

"You going to stay long?" he asked.

"I'm not sure."

"Right," Tom said, because he didn't think it would be a great idea to tell Danny that he looked *really* tired and that maybe now was a good time for a nap. Tom had come over to hang with Jay-Tee and get back to where they'd left off. Not likely with her insanely huge big brother hanging around.

Danny didn't say anything. He wasn't much of a talker. Tom wondered what Reason saw in him, other than him being tall, kind of okay looking, and wearing decent clothes. His shirt was made up of parts of three different shirts that had been sectioned and then sewn together with the seams showing. A Frankenstein shirt. Pretty cool, for a guy obsessed with sport.

"So are you cured too?" Danny asked.

"Am I *what*?" Tom wondered what on earth he was talking about.

"Did Reason cure you of magic?" Danny asked, as if he were asking if Tom had had a wart removed or something.

Tom's jaw dropped open. "No way! Why would she do that? I'm not dying!"

"But you will, though, won't you? Reason said you people don't live very long."

You people! What did he mean, "you people"? "Esmeralda's forty-five. That's heaps long."

"Isn't she about to die? Forty-five's not that old."

"Esmeralda is *not* about to die."

"Whatever." Danny shrugged in the exact same way that Jay-Tee did. "But Reason seemed to think you'd be lucky if you made it into your thirties."

"Reason said that?" Tom swallowed. "That's still heaps of time, but. And, you know, maybe then she can cure me. Right before I'm about to die."

"I guess."

"That's if Reason's still around to cure you," Jay-Tee said, coming in and sitting back down beside Tom. He reached under the table to briefly squeeze her knee. He was pretty sure Danny didn't notice.

"Who was it?" Tom asked.

"Mormons."

"You got those here too?" Danny said. "Huh."

"Reason might not be around that long," Jay-Tee continued.

"Of course she will be," Tom said. "She's got the super-duper, live-forever magic."

"Sure, but Esmeralda said she's changing so fast she might not be with us much longer."

"Huh? But you just said—"

"Not dying, Tom, *changing*. Becoming less human. Like the weird old guy. Remember him? That's where her magic came from."

Actually, Tom *didn't* remember Raul Cansino. He'd been on the floor unconscious when the old guy had made his little visit to Sydney.

"He was freaky as hell, and now Reason's turning freaky too. Who knows what she'll be by the time we see her again—forget about fifteen years from now when your magic's almost gone."

"Twenty-five years from now!"

"Does that matter?" Danny asked. "I think my sister's saying that Reason won't be around to cure you when you're thirty and dying."

Jay-Tee nodded. "If she comes back, this may be it."

"Wait?" Tom said. "*If* Reason comes back?!"

"She probably will," Jay-Tee said. "I mean, she'll want to say goodbye, won't she? And then she'll fix you. You won't have to worry about how much magic you use. You won't have to die. Not having magic, Tom, it's not so bad."

"You're not serious!" Tom didn't believe she really wanted this. "Turn my magic off?" No magic? Why would anyone *want* to live without it?

"I like my magic, Jay-Tee. It makes me happy. Plus I'm *not* dying."

"Not *now* you're not. But you will be."

He didn't know what to say. It meant a lot to Jay-Tee for him to be "saved," but he *didn't* want that. Not the religious kind of saved, and *definitely* not the losing-all-his-magic kind. No making clothes? No dreaming up new designs and making them real? No going through the door?

"She's right, man, what about your future? You might think making it to thirty or forty is a big deal. But it isn't. What if you have kids? You'll be dead before they're hardly grown up. That's what happened to us, you know. We're orphans now. I don't even remember our mom."

Tom stared at Danny. It was the most he'd ever heard him say. He couldn't help thinking the advice about having a family was a bit much, what with Danny just having gotten a fifteen-year-old girl pregnant. But he could hardly say that after Danny had mentioned the orphan thing. Danny looked completely knackered. Why didn't he bugger off to bed?

"Tom?" Jay-Tee said. "I know it doesn't seem that way now. There's all the good magic stuff, like dancing and running and—" She broke off, her eyes red. "But it's not that bad. You get to live. . . ."

Tom shook his head. He could see perfectly well that Jay-Tee was heartbroken that her magic was gone. Why would she want him to suffer too? It didn't make any sense. "I'll get to live *with* magic."

"There's your mom too. You want her saved, don't you?"

"Of course." They'd tried so hard, Tom and his da, to explain that if she just used a little bit of magic, she'd stop being crazy. But she hadn't understood. She kept screaming at them that they were mad. When he'd tried to convince her by demonstrating his own magic, she'd gone completely off. The staff at Kalder Park had to restrain her, strengthen her meds. And would taking her magic away really make her sane? She'd been mad for so long. . . .

"You're lucky you've got parents who are still alive," Danny said.

"You already said that," Tom said. "I get it."

Danny gave him a look that would have frozen him on the spot if it'd come from Jay-Tee. "I don't think you do," he said. "You should be thinking about them, not yourself. How do you think they'll feel knowing you're going to die before they do? That's harsh."

"I dunno," Tom said. "It's about as harsh as finding out that your fifteen-year-old daughter's up the duff to some random bloke she only just met. I wonder how Reason's mum will feel about that? I mean, aren't you like ten years older than her?"

"Tom!" Jay-Tee said. "He's only eighteen!"

Danny flushed and looked down. "You got me."

"But we're talking about you, Tom, and your mom. Danny's right. If Reason saves her, how's she going to feel knowing you're not saved?"

Tom decided not to argue about whether or not turning someone's magic off meant that they were *saved*. "I want my mum back. But that doesn't mean I have to stop being myself. I've been pretty sparing. I reckon I'll make it to forty."

"I wouldn't be so sure. You've used way more magic than Mere had when she was your age. I bet she never broke anyone's fingers with magic."

"You did that?" Danny said, turning to stare at him. "That's brutal."

"You had to be there," Tom mumbled. "Look, Jay-Tee, until I met Esmeralda I'd barely used any magic at all. So little by little, I was starting to go mad. Like my mum. Think of all the amazing clothes I can make by the time I'm forty. Think what a career I'll have by then. There'll be movie stars wearing my clothes—"

"Doubt it," Jay-Tee said. "Most of them have pukey taste."

Danny laughed and Tom had an urge to smack him. But

Danny was a *lot* bigger than him. He wondered again how Danny was going to react when he found out about him and Jay-Tee. Maybe he shouldn't have mentioned Reason being preggers.

"You know what I mean. All I've ever wanted is to design beautiful clothes. You're telling me to give that up. Danny, you're a really good basketballer, right? Would you give it up if it meant you'd live longer?"

"Basketball player," Danny said. "Not basketballer."

"That's not a fair question," Jay-Tee said. "Playing basketball doesn't mean he's going to live a shorter life."

"Actually," Danny said, "my high school coach told us once that a pro ball career takes years off your life."

"See? And have you stopped wanting to be a basketballer?"

"Basketball *player*," Danny said. "And no, but it's not the same. Lots of players live into their seventies and eighties. It's not a sure thing. *You're* guaranteed to die before you see forty."

"But you wouldn't give it up. See, Jay-Tee? You wouldn't ask him to either, would you? But you're asking me to give up something just as important to me. Without my magic, without the clothes I make—"

"You'll still be able to do that. Magic isn't why you do that. *You* are why you can do that. I can still run fast."

"And you can still dance, but it's not the same, is it?" Tom said. She winced.

"Magic is how I see the shapes, how I pull the threads together, how the ideas form, become real. My magic gets into every strand of fabric. Without it I might still be able to design clothes, but there'll be nothing special about them. They'll be completely av. *I'll* be completely av."

"Av?"

"Average. Ordinary. Not much chop. Nothing special. Lame."

"No, you won't, Tom. Magic's not the only thing that's cool about y—"

"How do you know? You don't know me any way but *with* magic. Magic's who I am. Without it I won't be anything. I might as well be dead."

"I don't have magic anymore! Is that what you think I am?" she shouted, her face turning red. "Nothing? Do you think I should be dead?"

"Hey, Julieta," Danny said. "That could well be just what he means."

Tom blanched. So did Jay-Tee.

Of course, it wasn't what he meant. He hadn't known Jay-Tee very long, but already he couldn't imagine life without her. How could she even *think* he wanted her dead?

"No!" he spluttered. "Of course not, Jay-Tee. You don't need magic, because you're already special. You're just as amazing without it as you were with. I'm not. I *need* my magic."

"You just think you do, Tom. You don't need magic. No one does. You can live without. I am." Her voice wobbled and she blinked rapidly.

Tom didn't say anything. He didn't know what to say.

Danny was looking at him; then he turned to Jay-Tee. "You two have hooked up, haven't you?"

29
Butterflies

Sarafina lay mostly on the path, her left arm stretched across into the ferns, the tips of her fingers in the small stream. A fern frond fallen into the water bumped against each of her knuckles, agitated by the tiny bumps and eddies, before floating past.

I closed my eyes, and calmness returned. My mother's lights were flickering out. It would be so easy to remain there, leave the world behind, leave Sarafina to die. I didn't belong with her or anyone else. I belonged in Cansino space.

I opened them again to brilliant light, the sun high, the shadows cutting. The ferns glowed green; the colour was reflected in my mother's skin as she grew paler. Next to her head a butterfly rested on a rock, its white wings vivid against the grey of the rock. But its body was as still as Sarafina's.

One of the women who had offered me tea ran down the path towards us. She cried out, leaning over my mother, trying to make her breathe. The woman's black hair was short and cut close to her scalp. She blew air into my mother's lips, thumped at her chest.

I could let the woman continue, even though it was futile. I could let Sarafina go. More of her winked out in the corners of my eyes.

Then a shudder went through me, a sudden horror at myself, at what I was becoming. Sarafina was my mother, no matter how many lies she'd told me.

I pushed the woman away. She cried out, trying to get her hands back in position over my mother's rib cage. I reached to the magic inside her, froze her with it, then closed my eyes, stretching out my fingers, thinning and sharpening them, cutting my way inside my mother.

I began to patch Sarafina's crumbling sequence, but it had frayed too much, had already lost so many numbers. And besides, that was how I'd turned Jay-Tee's magic off. Sarafina didn't want that; she wanted to be like me.

I pulled away from her, returned to shadow, light, and the movement of air. The woman knelt there, glaring at me, unable to move.

"You were in the way," I told her, though she probably didn't speak English. "I'm saving her."

For as long as I could remember, Sarafina had hated magic so much she'd denied it existed. But somehow Jason Blake had made her love it. How could I give her what she wanted?

Then I remembered Raul Cansino's golems. Before changing me completely, he'd given me pieces of himself.

But Sarafina was so faded now that I could barely see her.

I stared at my hands, sharpened my vision to see beyond the skin and meat and bone; I concentrated on pulling magic out of myself. Acid moved inside me, burning, moving up towards my skin. Stuff bubbled out beneath my fingernails, scorching.

It was the same colour as my new skin. I rubbed it onto Sarafina's feet, watched it disappear inside her. Blood dripped slowly from my fingers until it stopped, dried up, vanished, as if the skin had never been broken.

For a long moment, Sarafina didn't move.

And then she gasped, coughed, drew in air, expelled it.

I set the woman free. She glared at me, said something I didn't understand.

Sarafina shivered. Her eyes opened. "Reason," she said. "Am I still me?"

"Yes," I said.

She shivered again, the movement travelling from her shoulders down to her toes.

"You're okay," I told her, though I didn't know if that was true.

The woman looked at us. She said something to Sarafina, a question, I thought.

I shrugged. "I'm sorry. I don't understand." I held Sarafina's hand; the skin was covered with tiny dots of blood. "How do you feel?"

"It stopped hurting," Sarafina said. "I've stopped being so thin."

The woman bowed her head, stood up, and backed away. Three other women watched from the edge of the garden.

They all wore the same clothes: short-sleeved blouses, long skirts. One held a jug of water, the others towels.

Had they never seen anything this strange before? This was Jason Blake's house, after all.

The short-haired woman took the jug of water and a wooden cup from the others and placed them beside my mother, then helped her sit up. She poured water for her, held it to her mouth. Sarafina sipped, then gulped.

"Thirsty," she said, as the woman poured her more and she drank it all. She smiled at me, took the cup from the woman's hands, and poured her own water. "It tastes almost sweet."

Colour was coming back into her skin. She looked so healthy that I shivered again, remembering that I'd almost let her die.

She drained the cup and set it on the floor, crossing her legs and wiping her hands on her skirt. She nodded at the woman, who smiled and backed away, disappearing with the others into the house.

"They're very kind," Sarafina said softly, turning her hand palm up. Another one of her enormous butterflies appeared, red and green and gold. Its wings trembled. She turned to look at me. "Am I like you now?"

I didn't think so. I didn't need water; I didn't feel thirst. She was like Esmeralda and Jason Blake, with only a small piece of Cansino magic.

But she was alive, and sane again.

I had my mother back.

30
Greed

Sarafina stood up and took several steps away from me. The sun on her face was so bright it almost whited out her features.

I stared at my hand. It still tingled where I'd pushed the magic out. I'd done it: I'd made my mother whole.

The whole world was ours now, like we'd always planned. And there was no need for money or passports: We had everything we needed woven into every cell of our bodies.

This was the real gift Raul Cansino had given me.

"I don't think it's enough," Sarafina said.

I looked up at her. Her eyebrows pushed together and the corners of her mouth tightened, giving her eyes a fierce look as she stared at me. I'd never seen her look that way before, even when she'd been crazy.

"What do you mean?"

She took another step away from me and held her arms out, palms facing up, fingers splayed, pointing towards me. The air between us shimmered. My skin prickled.

"What are you doing?"

Sarafina said nothing, but her stare remained intent on me.

Then I felt something moving through me, a thin stream of

acid, burning out of my skin, across the air, and into Sarafina. I could see it too: motes lit golden in the sunlight, as if they were particles of sun.

"What are you doing?" I asked again.

"I'm making it better."

"Better?" I took a step closer to her; she took a step away. Her hands glowed, but not as brightly as mine. "Making what better?"

"See?" she said, shifting her gaze to the particles streaming out of me. "They're dancing! My father said they would." Sarafina smiled, but the tight, intense expression on her face didn't change.

"Jason Blake?" I asked. "He told you to do this?" I felt dizzy. I took another step towards her and swayed, grabbing at one of the ferns to keep from falling.

Sarafina laughed. "This is more like it. The world's getting bigger."

"It will get bigger and bigger," Jason Blake said, stepping from the shadows of the house into the radiant garden. He slipped a pair of black sunglasses on, hiding his eyes, but the expression on his face was identical to Sarafina's. As the two of them stared at me, it looked as if someone else were operating the muscles behind their skin.

He strode towards Sarafina.

"Let me help you," he said, putting his hand on her shoulder. "You can pull harder now."

She nodded.

The particles tore from me faster. I could feel cell walls begin to thin, then break. I turned my gaze inward and at last saw the sequence of numbers that made me—just like my mother's had a moment ago, they were breaking up: Fib (55), 139,583,862,445; Fib (37), 24,157,817; and Fib (13), 233. My Fibs were dissolving. I was getting lighter.

Sarafina loved me. Why was she doing this to me?

I opened my eyes, turned to her. "You're hurting me."

"It won't be for long. Alexander promised."

"I did." My grandfather did not look at me: his gaze was fixed on the magic flowing into my mother. Then I saw a single mote dance across the space between them, from her into him.

"It hurts, Sarafina. You have to stop." All the changes that Raul's magic had wrought in me were unravelling. My scalp was itching. My stomach contracted into a hard ball. Tears leaked out of my eyes. When was the last time I had cried?

"Soon, darling," she said, but she wasn't looking at me.

"No," I said. "You can't do this!" The motes floated as Raul Cansino's had in the cemetery, when he was dying, but now they floated out of me and into my mother and Jason Blake. "Stop!"

Neither of them said anything. They continued to tear the magic away, to rip me apart. They stood even closer together now. Shoulder to shoulder, father and daughter. Faces set like dolls.

I gasped, then pulled back with all my strength. But as the magic flowed away, my humanity came rushing back. Pain. Emotion. My love for Sarafina. How could she do this to me?

"You're killing me!"

I fell, landed heavily on my knees. Only the magic in Tom's trousers kept them from tearing.

"Sarafina!"

Her head tilted to one side as if she heard music. Jason Blake must have heard it too. The expressions on their faces were still identical.

But they weren't listening to me.

"You're killing me and my baby. Little Glory or Brilliance or Beauty or Fibonacci. If you don't stop, she won't ever be born. You won't get to name her. Sarafina!" As the magic slipped away from me, I could see more clearly, feel more clearly. I loved my child. I loved my mother. How could she do this?

Sarafina staggered. Jason Blake steadied her. Had she heard me at last?

"Fight back," someone said beside me, slipping their arm around my waist, keeping me from falling. "Pull it back towards you!"

"Look!" Jason Blake said to Sarafina. "Your mother's here to help your daughter. I told you Esmeralda owned her now."

"Esmeralda?" I asked. "Where did you come from?" The world—both Cansino's and the real one—was losing focus around me.

"Pull, Reason, pull," Esmeralda commanded. "I'm going to lend you all the strength I have. Don't waste it."

"He wants to be like me." He'd said he wanted to be like me, called me magnificent, an extraordinary golden creature.

"Of course he does. We all do. But you can't allow it. Fight him, Reason!"

Fight, I thought, watching the floating pieces of magic flow into my mother and from her to Jason Blake.

"He's using you, Sarafina," Esmeralda told her. "He's killing you as surely as he is Reason. You don't have to help him."

Sarafina didn't hear; she was too entranced by the dancing pieces of my magic—watching it become her magic, then Jason Blake's. She was too busy killing me to hear her mother.

31
Belly of the Beast

i could feel Esmeralda's magic inside me now, strengthening me just a little, easing the dizziness just enough to focus again. "Fight," Esmeralda hissed in my ear.

I held out my hands, pulled as hard as I could, but only managed to slow the flow, not reverse it.

I looked at my mother's face, at Jason Blake's. Both were set. Hungry. Identical. They didn't see me, just the magic they were taking. I faltered. At once the magic began to rip loose from me again.

"Don't stop. You can't stop." Esmeralda's voice was starting to sound strained.

I pulled, harder than I had before. Why was Sarafina doing this to me? She'd hated magic, had warned me never to use it. What had my grandfather done to her?

"Sarafina!" Esmeralda called. "Why are you killing your daughter?"

My magic was still being pulled from me. Slower than before, but still leaving me. It hurt. If I had my magic back, the pain would go away.

Sarafina and Jason Blake weren't feeling any pain.

That's when I realised.

Santiago David Cuervo had told me about becoming magic all the time. He told me how peaceful it was. No pain. His grandmother had seen it happen. Now my mother and grandfather were becoming the magic as they dragged it from me. I wasn't fighting them; I was fighting magic.

That was why they looked the same. Their faces were distorted with the same hunger.

That was what magic was: greed. They both wore magic's face.

It had consumed all my ancestors, turned them against one another. Just as Sarafina was now trying to consume me.

"Fight, Reason!" Esmeralda yelled at me, pushing even more of her magic into me. "Stop it, Sarafina. You have to stop it. You're killing her!"

But my mother wasn't just killing me, she was making me see. With the magic pulsing through me I'd been blind. But now I saw that Cansino's world—real space, Blake called it— was the belly of the beast. It was the centre of everything, where magic came from. Magic that was so seductive, so overpoweringly wonderful, you'd lay down your life for it, your daughter's life. Magic crooned to me, to all of us: *Leave everything else behind, become a part of magic, a child of magic.*

Magic-wielders didn't wield magic; it wielded them. Every one of them except that one chosen magic child. Everyone but Raul Cansino. And then me, and soon Jason Blake. Unless I could keep it.

Not just for me, but for my child. If I died, then it died too.

I pulled harder then, trying to haul the magic back. I wanted it, even knowing what it did. Knowing that it stopped me seeing, blunted feelings of love and hate and anger. I still *wanted* it.

Sarafina had been right. She'd always been right: magic was wrong. She'd told me over and over again that my grandmother's belief in magic made her evil. Sarafina had hated any signs of magic, wouldn't even let me read *The Magic Pudding*. I'd thought she was mad, but she'd been trying to keep the beast out of our lives. *Don't let her charm you*, she'd said. But really she'd meant, *Don't let magic charm you*.

Sarafina trained me my whole life to resist the temptation. That was why she called me Reason, so I could fight magic. This was what I'd been raised to do. If she'd raised me in Esmeralda's house, how could I have resisted?

Sarafina was right—there were worse things than madness. *This*, for instance, fighting my mother and grandfather to the death. But my mother was not my enemy, nor was Esmeralda, not even Jason Blake. Magic was, working through them, turning them into monsters.

"You were right, Sarafina. About everything. I'm sorry I didn't understand," I said louder, trying to break through its grip on her. "Remember Le Roi. Remember what magic made you do to him? What Esmeralda made you do? Remember your cat, Sarafina!"

"Good," Esmeralda said. "Keep talking."

Sarafina staggered, blinked. "Le Roi?" But her hands were still outstretched.

"Your cat, Sarafina," I said. "Magic made you bring it back from the dead. Remember? Esmeralda made you cut its throat."

"Didn't happen *quite* like that," Esmeralda murmured.

Sarafina brought her hand to her own throat.

"Magic, Sarafina, you hate it. Remember? You're right to hate it. It's the enemy, Sarafina. It eats us. Let it go!"

"Then why do you want it so much, Reason?" asked Blake. "Why does Esmeralda want it so much? You know she'll just take it from you. She's got her claws in. If you get your magic back, you won't keep it." He'd begun to sweat, his clothes growing damp, water dripping from his chin.

I stared at Sarafina, willing her to stop, willing her to look at me, still using Esmeralda's magic to stop the disappearance of my own. "I'll fix it, Sarafina. I'll turn your magic off, just what you always wanted!"

She looked at me, still pulling the magic, but the greedy expression was gone from her face.

"Le Roi," she said again. "In the southeast corner of the cellar." Her eyes, fixed on a point beyond me, were somehow blank. This was how she'd looked back at Kalder Park.

"Magic's evil. You always knew that."

Sarafina moved her head; I couldn't tell if she was shaking it or nodding. "Le Roi wasn't evil," she said, her hands slowing. "Not until he died. And that was my fault. I shouldn't . . . I should have accepted—" Her grip on my magic loosened.

"That's right, Sarafina. But it's okay now," Esmeralda said. "Everything's okay. You just have to stop." She lowered her voice. "Pull even harder now. She's weakening."

"Don't listen to them, Sarafina," Jason Blake said. "That's Esmeralda talking. Your mother is lying to you again, stealing from you again."

"No, she's not," I said. "Not this time. It was never your mother tricking you. It was magic. *Magic* is what eats us alive. You were right! You told me not to trust it. You told me to stay away. You were right and I was wrong. I thought you'd lied to me, but you never did."

"I never lied to you," she said, meeting my eyes, lowering her hands.

Jason Blake grabbed her hands and jerked them up. "You can't stop! They'll steal *everything*!"

She pulled away from him, took a few unsteady steps towards the stream. I pulled hard and fast, dragging back as much as I could. Esmeralda pulled with me. I couldn't let my grandfather have it. I could feel it clouding my thoughts again, filling me with the need for it. I wondered if my expression was changing. Was I wearing magic's face?

Jason Blake screamed. Sarafina looked bewildered. "Reason," she said, but I couldn't tell if it was a question or a statement. Her face melted of expression; she looked like a baby. Her hands fell to her sides.

Jason Blake leapt at me, as if he could claw the Cansino

magic out of me with his hands. I rolled out of his way, pulling back even more magic from Sarafina, from him, from the air around us. I wanted what was mine.

I wanted everything.

Esmeralda jumped in front of me. Blake punched her in the face. The blow made her stagger, but she remained steady on her feet, raising her hands, keeping her body between me and my grandfather.

I was getting stronger.

Sarafina sank to the ground, trembling.

Blake tried to lunge past Esmeralda. I stepped back, stumbling over the ferns. My left foot landed in the stream. A large black, gold, and white carp darted around it. I stepped back onto the path, ran to Sarafina's side.

"Are you okay?"

She nodded, staring at her hands. "What was I *doing*?"

"You still have the magic I gave you," I told her. "Will you help me?"

Sarafina sat up. She nodded. "But you'll turn it off, like you promised?"

Jason Blake knocked Esmeralda aside. I turned to him. My magic was wrapped up tight and strong. I could feel it calling to everything he'd stolen.

Back to me. *Mine.*

I would fight him until he was destroyed. Ever since I'd first met him I'd known he was a bad man, and now I was going to drain him of all Cansino's magic.

"No," Sarafina said, barely above a whisper. "Run away."

"What?" Every cell of my body was poised, ready to rip open his cells.

I shook my head, as if that would clear my thoughts. Jason Blake stood in front of me, teeth bared. Calling his own magic forth.

"Run," Sarafina said. "Like I taught you: *run away*."

Run away? Why should I? I was stronger than him now. I was sure of it. But all Sarafina's lessons came back to me: Always look for the escape route. Keep a bag packed, always ready for when the moment is right to slip away.

I knew a lot about running away.

Was it simpler to fight him or to run? What did the magic want me to do?

To stay. To drain every inch of him.

I reached out my arms, making them thin as wires.

"No!" Esmeralda shouted. She ran to Sarafina and offered her a hand. My mother hesitated but then took it. "Don't fight him!"

"What are you waiting for?" Jason Blake asked. He couldn't win, but the greed was too great in him not to try.

Esmeralda pulled Sarafina towards me. She put her hand on my shoulder. Sarafina grasped the other. "You can't fight all three of us, Alexander."

"I'm not going to fight him," I said, "I'm going to destroy him." I didn't feel angry at all. It was just what the magic wanted.

I began to drain him.

Jason Blake paled, took a step away.

I drew more of his magic, everything he'd taken, and still more.

"Can you take us back to Sydney?" Esmeralda asked.

I frowned. In the corner of my vision was the back door to Esmeralda's house, all 610 lights. I could go there. I could take them with me.

But that meant travelling through the beast, and it was already so strong inside me. All my pain was gone. My love for Sarafina too—I only remembered it. If I jumped into the belly, into the land of magic, lights, and numbers, why would I ever leave it again?

Of course, if I stayed here and drained Jason Blake dry, would I wind up any different?

"Can you do it?"

I nodded. "Hold on to me. Tight."

I focussed on the door. It was 9,290 K away, Sarafina had said, but it felt close and familiar. I took a step up into the air, clutching Sarafina and Esmeralda tight. Then something hard and sharp cut into me—Jason Blake grasping for me one last time with all his strength. I ignored him, took another step through space towards my grandmother's house.

Magic flowed through me, taking me over again. More than I'd ever felt before.

I fought to keep my mind clear. Magic was not good, I remembered that, but I felt exquisite, rushing across city, forest, ocean. The blues, greens, browns, purples of the world smeared into rushing black under my feet. Sarafina and Esmeralda were small and fragile as butterflies, as if I were their mother.

I could let them go. If I closed my eyes and plunged deeper into Cansino's world, then they'd fall. It would be quick. I would never have to worry about them or anyone else again. I would be free to stay in Raul Cansino's world forever.

The lights of the door drew closer.

Magic is the enemy, I reminded myself. It had killed my family, generation after generation.

It felt wonderful, better than the breaking of a drought, the first clear cold rain turning the dust to mud, streaming down my face; better than mango dripping over my face and hands. Better than madness.

Magic is the enemy, I chanted.

Sarafina raised me to reject magic. She was right. It fed on us, all of us.

She was wrong. It was beautiful. In the corners of my eyes it unfurled, purer than I'd ever seen it. I wanted it. I needed it.

Evil. Enemy. Didn't I want to be human?

Up ahead flickered the door between Sydney and New York. A door made from Cansino magic. I reached for it, felt the recognition of like to like.

As we landed in Esmeralda's kitchen, Sarafina slid from my arms and onto the floor.

Tom, Jay-Tee, and Danny stood staring at us. *Danny?*

"Jason Blake!" Jay-Tee screamed.

I turned. My grandfather stood behind me.

32
Full Kitchen

"What on earth?" Tom said. Standing in the kitchen were Esmeralda, Jason Blake, a completely bald, gold-skinned Reason, and a woman Tom figured had to be Reason's mum. The air crackled; the hair on Tom's arms stood on end.

Jason Blake raised his hand and Tom's legs buckled as if he'd been kicked from behind. He fell, letting out a yelp. He saw Jay-Tee falling too, and even Mere staggered against the icy diamonds spilling from Blake's fingers.

"Leave them alone!" Danny rushed forward and punched Jason Blake so hard he spun, slamming into the kitchen cupboards. Dishes rattled from inside them. "No magic in me, mister."

"Yes, I recall," Jason Blake said, wiping his mouth.

"Don't try anything else," Esmeralda said. "Either this young man will thump you again or Reason will drain you completely."

Blake raised his hands. "No need for either."

"Where did you all come from?" Jay-Tee asked. "The door never even opened!"

Reason didn't say anything. Tom wondered if she could still speak; everything Jay-Tee had said about her was dead-on.

Reason looked like an alien. She had no hair on her head, no eyelashes or eyebrows either. And she was completely golden: her skin, her fingernails, her teeth. Even the green pants he'd made her flickered with a metallic sheen.

Tom reached out for Jay-Tee's hand and squeezed it hard, but he was still looking at Reason. She was *so* golden.

"We didn't come through the door," the woman said. "We came from Bangkok."

"Bangkok?" Jay-Tee asked. "Are you Reason's mom?"

"Yes. I'm Sarafina. She rescued me."

Reason took a step towards Tom, and he saw that her eyes weren't human. It was as if they'd been removed and replaced with burnished gold. The irises were completely regular, like a doll's: no lines, no variation in colour.

Tom found himself edging away from her. He was too scared to get up.

She wasn't Reason anymore. She was bigger and golder, and looking at her made Tom feel weird. "Reason . . ." he said, trailing off, not sure what to say. It was as if he were attempting conversation with a wild tiger from the remote reaches of Kalimantan.

Sarafina pulled out a stool and sat down heavily, looking at everything going around her with wide eyes, as if it were action taking place in a movie she was watching.

"Are you okay, Reason?" Jay-Tee asked.

Reason didn't say anything. She took a step towards Tom.

"Better watch out," Jason Blake said. "She's hungry."

Tom wished Danny would punch him again.

"There's not much time," Reason said at last. It startled Tom that she sounded just like herself. He wasn't sure what he'd expected.

"Time for what?" he asked.

She bent down and looked at him, so close that he could see her skin was too smooth, like a retouched photograph in a fashion magazine: no hair, no pores.

"Reason?" he said. The muscles of his throat and mouth were tight.

She moved even closer. "I have to turn your magic off."

"No," Tom said. "No way."

"Magic is evil, Tom. Our enemy. It will kill you."

"I know that. Well, not the evil part." He wondered if the gold had eaten part of her brain. The only thing that looked evil right now was her. Her golden expression did seem hungry, like she was getting ready to snack on him. He realised that he couldn't even hear her breathing. "I like how I am, Ree. I want to stay that way."

"This is your only chance, Tom. Either I change you now or you stay that way."

"Fine," Tom said, taking a step back from her. "I'll stay this way."

"What do you mean, this is his only chance?" Jay-Tee asked.

But Reason was looking closely at Tom, like she was figuring out how best to cut him up.

"But what about my mum?" Tom asked, his voice shaking. "Can you change her?"

"Yes. I can make her sane again."

"Do that, then, Reason. Please?" Tom swallowed. His mum sane, living with him and Da. It was hard to believe it was possible. He wondered if he could love her if she was sane. He knew you were meant to love your mother no matter what, but he'd never felt it.

"Can you trust her, Tom?" Jason Blake asked. "She'll take your mother's magic as well as your own."

"No, she won't," Jay-Tee said. "She didn't take mine. Just turned it off."

Tom frowned. "I don't want my magic turned off. Just my mum's."

Reason nodded. "Okay. Just your mother's."

She grabbed hold of Tom and the kitchen floor dropped away. His body moved faster than his stomach. Wind rushed past his eyes, making them water. The ground beneath them, the trees and houses and roads, blurred into one another, becoming a dark grey stream. Tom wanted to scream at first, then thought he might chunder, but before he had time to do either, he found himself in a huge bathroom in front of a long row of sinks.

His mother's face was looking at him, reflected in the mirrors.

33
Asylum

Tom stumbled out of Reason's arms feeling like he weighed three tonnes. He grabbed one of the eight white basins to steady himself, then faced his mum's reflection. The mirror was so old that in places he could see the rusted metal backing.

His mum was washing her hands at the sink and staring back at him. She didn't scream or act startled. She wiped her hands on her jeans and nodded at them both, as if this was just what she'd expected.

"Mum." Tom turned to face her but didn't know what to say. His mum's eyes weren't right. Not freaky gold like Reason's, but unfocused, like they were when she was at her most—what did his da call it?—disconnected. She looked completely disconnected. She probably didn't even recognise him. "Mum," he said again, breathing deep. "Reason's here to fix you."

"Whose reasons? What are they? They'd want to be pretty good." She kept her eyes on the mirror. High above her head was a window covered with wire mesh. On the other side he could see metal bars.

"Mum, this is my friend Reason. That's her name."

"It'd have to be a bloody good reason. I don't need fixing. Why's your friend that strange colour?"

"She's not well," Tom said, pleased that his mum was making some kind of sense.

His mum nodded again. "She got the flu?"

"Sort of. She wants to help you."

"But she's sick. How's she going to help me? I don't like her looks." She put her hand over her eyes.

"She's, ah, she's a kind of doctor."

"Doesn't look like a doctor. She looks like a kid."

"Do you want to be fixed, Mum?"

"Not broken, am I?" she said, sneaking him a look from between her fingers. "What kind of fixed?"

"She'll make you—"

"Less confused," Reason said. She held out her hands. In her palms was a golden shape, quivering like those golems the old man had sent into the house. "I can give you this if you want."

"What—?" Tom began. That was Cansino magic! It would hurt his mum just as bad as it had hurt him.

His mother's eyes changed. Sharpened. She looked at the magic on Reason's hand and trembled. Slowly she reached out a hand towards it.

"You want it, don't you?" Reason asked.

She nodded. "Yes, please. It's pretty." Reason leaned forward and whispered in her ear. His mum nodded again, even more emphatic. "I want it."

"You see, Tom? That's the magic in your mother calling out to more magic. Even though it's the wrong kind. Magic is greedy, Tom. That's what you're clinging to: greed."

His mum lunged for the golden thing, but it disappeared back into Reason.

"Why not?" his mother cried. "Why can't I have it?"

"Because it will hurt you. You need to sit down. You need me to fix you another way. You're clearer now, aren't you? You want to stay like that, don't you?"

Her eyes did seem more focused, as if just a glimpse of magic had taken some of the insanity away.

"I can give you something better," Reason told her.

"All right, then." Tom's mum sat down on the tan tiles. The grouting between them had gone black. Tom suspected the tiles had once been white. Reason sat down beside her.

"Close your eyes."

His mother did, but immediately opened them again. "Will it hurt?"

"No."

"Will I regret it?"

"I don't think so."

"But you don't know so?"

"No."

She closed her eyes again. Reason's arms and hands began to change, becoming longer, skinnier, metallic. Tom's mum opened her eyes again, looking at Reason's hands suspiciously. "You're sure it won't hurt?"

"Yes."

Her gaze darted down to Reason's metal hands. "Really?"

"Yes."

"All right, then." She closed her eyes.

Someone started to open the door, but Tom dashed to push it shut. The man on the other side yelled and pushed hard, and Tom had to lean all his weight against it. There was no lock, and the old door rattled on its hinges. He shoved his foot against the bottom and turned around to put his back against it. Reason's arms were buried in his mother up past her wrists. His mum's eyes were wide open and staring.

"Don't hurt her, Ree."

"Open the door!" the man on the other side yelled. The door started to open. Tom's feet slid on the tiles.

"Use your magic, Tom," Reason said.

He opened his mouth to protest. He had to be sparing. He'd promised Jay-Tee. He wanted to make it to thirty.

"Tom!"

He felt for the jade button in his pocket, put his hand to the chain around his neck. He pushed the tiniest amount of magic into the door. It slammed shut. He eased off his pushing, but the door didn't budge. He wondered how many hours of his life he'd just used up.

Reason pulled her hands out of Tom's mother and laid them in her lap. Tom watched them turn back into normal hands. Well, not exactly normal; they were still gold. He was too afraid to look at his mother.

Reason stood up and then helped Tom's mum to her feet. She was wobbly, but her eyes were much clearer. She looked at Tom and her eyes went wet, but the tears stayed on the surface, not teetering out to spill down her face. She opened her mouth to speak and then closed it.

He stepped into her arms and she held him.

Tom couldn't remember her ever holding him. Her face was wet against his. The tears had escaped. He had to bite his lip to keep from crying too. She put her hands to his cheeks, pushed him a little away so that she could look at him. "You're so big," she said. "So big . . ." She ran her hand down his cheek and onto his shoulder. "I don't believe this. I'm so . . ."

Tears still poured down her face.

"What happened . . . ?" she began. "I don't understand."

The banging on the door got louder.

"We have to go, Tom," Reason said, grabbing hold of him.

His mother looked confused, but not disconnected, not lost. "What's going on?"

"Why can't we take Mum?" Tom asked.

"She's not magic anymore."

"We'll be back," Tom said. "Through the front door next time. I'll explain everything. Dad too . . . I love you." He kissed her cheek, but then Reason grabbed his hand and pulled, zooming him across the red terra-cotta-tiled roofs of Leichhardt and back to Esmeralda's kitchen. He hoped them using magic to leave wouldn't drive his mum mad again. She didn't know about magic. She didn't know why she'd gone mad.

It occurred to Tom for the first time that his mother's madness might have spared him. Jay-Tee and Reason had both had such a rough time because of their magic relatives. But not Tom. It was almost like his mum had sacrificed herself. Just for him.

"Is she okay?" Jay-Tee asked, rushing up and hugging him hugely.

Tom nodded, hugging her back. "I think so. It was a bit weird. I mean, she's not mad anymore." He could still feel his mother's tears on his face.

"It worked?" Esmeralda asked.

"Yes," Reason said. "There's no magic left in her." She turned to Tom. "Are you certain you want to keep yours? This is your last chance."

"You keep saying that. What do you *mean,* my last chance? Where are you going?"

"I'm changing fast. When I've changed completely, I won't want the same things. I'm not sure I'll care enough to do anything for you. I'm going to turn my own magic off before that happens."

"You what?" Tom, Esmeralda, and Jason Blake all said at the same time.

"Magic is wrong," she said once again. "I don't want it."

"And you can't change me once your magic's gone." It was obvious, but Tom had to say it out loud. He felt dizzy. His mother. Her face. She'd looked . . . He didn't remember a time when he hadn't been afraid of his mum. He didn't remember ever wanting her to hold him. And now he did. Because her magic was gone.

"But what about Esmeralda?" Jay-Tee asked. "She's still magic. And your mother."

"You don't want to do this, Reason," Jason Blake said.

"Why?" Esmeralda asked. "Is it really necessary?"

"Magic is wrong. It's always been wrong. I don't want to become the magic."

"No," Jason Blake said. "It's not wrong. It's beautiful. Why turn it off, Reason? You'd be throwing centuries away! Why would you do that? Give it to me instead."

"Will you turn mine off too?" Sarafina asked. "Will you turn it off for the baby in your belly?"

"She doesn't have to," Jason Blake snapped.

"What?" Esmeralda asked.

"Haven't you guessed? Hers is *the* Cansino magic. Like ours, only stronger—"

"If she turns it off, she turns off ours as well?" Esmeralda blanched. "Reason, no. You can't do that to me. I need it. I need this magic." She grabbed Reason's wrist, a horrible expression unlike any Tom had ever seen on her face. Reason just shook her off.

Jason Blake reached out towards her, and Danny punched him in the stomach, sending him to the floor. Maybe Danny wasn't *so* bad.

"Tom, I'm asking you," Reason said. "I don't have very long. Do you want me to save you from becoming like them?" She pointed a golden arm at their hungry faces, their grasping hands.

Tom didn't want to turn into a Jason Blake. Or Esmeralda, the way she looked now. But he couldn't imagine his world without clothes and patterns and magic pulsing through the jade button in his pocket. The shapes cascading through his head and the surge of it through him, the electrical jolt of it.

But how would it feel to be magic and Jay-Tee and Reason not. And to go mad, to die. He looked at Jay-Tee. . . .

"Tom," she pleaded.

"I can't wait," Ree said. "I have to change myself now. Or I . . . "

Tom squeezed his eyes shut against all their faces. Inside his eyelids, the world was made of beautiful shapes, all *his*.

"No, don't take it. I need my magic."

34
Cansino Magic

Cansino's world of quiet and beauty and light was calling to me so strongly, it was hard to focus on Esmeralda's kitchen, on all their questions that crashed around me in waves. Their arguments, yelling across one another. When they grabbed me, I pushed them away. They weren't anything to me anymore.

I could feel glimmers of how it had been. Of friendship. Of how Tom and Jay-Tee and me had been learning to look out for each other. Looking at Sarafina, I could almost remember the love between us, what it felt like to be held tight in her arms. Sarafina had made this possible. By trying to steal my magic, she'd made me see again, made me remember being human, made me understand what magic really was.

But those glimpses were small and empty. In the corners of my eyes, magic danced, pulling at me. I longed to zoom across space again. Closing my eyes, going back there, would make me magic's child forever. And my own child would be magic's too.

To prevent that, I had to remember everything my mother had taught me. How to run, how to escape, the importance of reason.

It didn't matter how calm it was, how beautiful. Magic had consumed my family, generation after generation. I had to stop it.

I was human. Or, at least, I wanted to be again.

And yet to win my freedom I had to close my eyes one more time, and if I did that, I didn't know if I could resist Cansino's world.

I slowly brought my eyelids down, seeing their faces through my eyelashes just briefly, lit in the colours of the setting sun. Their voices shut off, as did the smell of flying fox, of the fig tree, of jasmine. I clung to the memory of those senses. No sunset-lit faces, no squeak and flap, no sticky smells, no wood underneath my fingertips.

Here they all seemed so unnecessary, threadbare. Cansino's world was vast, beautiful. Space opening up onto space. A giant ocean of magic stars. It called to me. I wanted to follow all the patterns, the twisting spirals of Fibonaccis, perfect numbers, primes.

I forced myself to narrow my gaze, to turn away from the spreading universe of lights and into myself. My own magic. The numbers within.

I could see my Fibonaccis; I could see the Cansino magic inside me threaded through each one. I could see how to destroy it.

So I did.

Piece by piece, I turned it off. I saw lights wink out one after another. I watched Cansino space recede. First galaxies gone, then stars, then darkness, just the backs of my own eyelids.

I opened them and fell. Hard.

Sarafina and Esmeralda were already on their knees. Something shattered in the next room. A rank smell filled my nostrils, and little explosions went off all over the house.

"What?" Esmeralda asked.

"It's going," Sarafina said. "Gone."

"Centuries . . . wasted," Jason Blake said. He moaned, as if Danny had hit him again. But Danny was just standing there, confused.

My magic was gone and now theirs too. I hadn't just turned off mine; I'd switched off all the Cansino magic. I'd freed my mother, my grandmother, my grandfather, and the hundreds of magic objects throughout the house.

I had become magic, after all, been the Cansino pattern itself. And now that pattern—unlike primes, or Fibs, or perfect numbers—had reached the end.

"Huh," I said.

In front of me Jay-Tee and Tom were holding each other so close there was no space between them. I had a sudden horrible thought. They weren't together, were they?

Ewwww.

The doorbell rang.

I stood up, feeling shaky and incredibly hungry. Hungry! And not for power or magic or knowledge. Just for *food*. I looked at the fruit bowl, but I'd already eaten all the rambutans. Didn't matter. I was pretty sure that everything would taste good now.

"I'll get it," Jay-Tee said, but she didn't let go of Tom.

"No," I said. Somewhere in my mind—my newly restored *human* mind—I had the feeling it was important.

I walked to the door as steadily as I could, feeling the wooden floor beneath my feet, noticing that it was hot. I hadn't been aware of the temperature since Raul Cansino had changed me. Summer felt wonderful. My skin started to glisten with sweat. Esmeralda and Sarafina followed.

I blinked and saw only the backs of my eyelids, and shivered. This was what it felt like to be free of Cansino's magic. I slipped my hand into my pocket and felt for my ammonite. It felt like a smooth stone. Nothing uncoiled from it. Numbers did not cascade through me.

I didn't need any of that. I didn't *need* magic. My chest felt hollow.

The bell rang again.

Esmeralda put her hand gently on my shoulder, stepping ahead of me to open the door. A woman was standing there. She looked at me, and I recognized the sadness in her smile. "All ready for your test, Reason? I said I'd come to pick you up."

"Um," Esmeralda started. "I don't think I—"

"Jennifer Ishii," the social worker said, holding her hand out to Esmeralda. "And you are?"

35
God's Children

After Reason left to take her test—with an entourage of mother, grandmother, and social worker—Jay-Tee decided it was time for her and Tom to talk.

She walked back to the kitchen, readying herself for what she had to say.

Tom was watching as Danny raided the freezer. "What are you doing with all that ice?"

Danny winced. "Little-known fact: you punch someone, it wrecks your hand."

"Oh," Tom said. "So that's why boxers wear those big gloves? I always thought it was to make sure they didn't mess up each other's faces too much."

Danny wrapped the ice in a towel and then around his hand, and gave Tom a look that would have made Jay-Tee laugh if she wasn't so upset.

"Is it weird that I'm really hungry?" Tom asked.

"You're always hungry," Jay-Tee said. "It's not weird at all. Tom, I really think—"

"So, Danny," Tom said. "How long you think you'll be staying?"

So Tom *knew* he was in trouble and was trying to avoid talking about his decision.

"Man," Danny said. "I have no idea. Right now I need to find a bed before I keel over. Jet lag is a bitch."

"You can sleep in my room," Jay-Tee said. "Top of the stairs. Turn around and it's the first door on your left."

Danny hugged his sister and kissed the top of her head. "You take care. It's been a very long day."

After Danny left, Jay-Tee didn't know what to say first. She felt wobbly. Not body wobbly, brain wobbly. "Let's go outside, sit on the porch."

"Okay," Tom said nervously.

As she opened the door, Tom let out a gasp.

"What?"

"It's not . . . There's not . . . New York City's gone."

He stuck his head out. "Wow. It's just the backyard. Reason really did wipe out all the Cansino magic." He shivered.

Jay-Tee knew exactly how he felt. "Welcome to my world," she said, "where a door is just a door."

"Right," Tom said. They sat down together on the third-to-last porch step, with their feet just above the soggy backyard. He picked up a dried old leaf from amongst the smatterings of leaves and twigs on the porch behind them and tore it into tiny little pieces.

Jay-Tee tried to speak, but her throat was clogged. How could Tom have chosen magic? Maybe life without it wasn't as good as life with, but being alive was *much* better than being dead.

Tom picked up another leaf and set about destroying it. And then another. If he didn't say something about his crazy choice soon, she was going to scream.

"My brain is going to explode," she said at last.

Tom turned to her and smiled. He had a really cute smile: it was kind of uneven, and always made his left eyebrow go up slightly.

"You and me both," he said.

"I can't believe . . . " She trailed off. She really didn't want to fight with him. "Wanna make out?" she asked instead, though for the first time since they'd started kissing, she didn't feel like it. But at least it would give her something else to think about.

"Nah."

"Me neither."

"It's too big." Tom held his arms out, and a rain of little broken leaves fell on the yard. "Everything is too big. I keep trying to understand, but I can't."

"Yeah," Jay-Tee said. "And thinking hurts."

"Yup."

Jay-Tee wondered if they'd ever want to kiss again. Maybe they'd already broken up but just didn't know it yet. How long would Tom want to be her boyfriend now that he was permanently-and-forever magic and she was permanently-and-forever not? He'd start thinking she was lame 'cause she couldn't do anything special anymore. She *felt* lame. She felt angry too.

"I'll probably have to go back to New York, you know."

"That's what your brother wants, isn't it? Crap! Now the door's buggered, how'll I come visit you?"

"I believe they're called aer-o-planes."

"Very funny. How am I going to afford to be on a plane once a week?"

"You won't want to come once a week."

"How else am I going to see you as often as I want?"

"Doof." Jay-Tee punched him lightly. "You don't have to worry about the money, though. I'll pay. Danny says my dad made us rich. Or Mere. She's got piles of money."

"Can you wait to go back until it's warmer there? The weather's horrible right now."

"Sure," she said, though she had no idea how she was getting back. Could she get a passport so far from home? Could she pretend that she'd lost one? Would they know that she'd never had one? If they did know, she'd get into trouble, wouldn't she? Maybe she could stow away on a boat and get home that way. She hoped Mere would be able to figure something out.

Tom was ripping yet another leaf apart.

"Don't get mad at me, Tom, but why? Why did you tell Reason no?"

"I'm not, Jay-Tee," he said, brushing her cheek with his hand. "But I had to keep my magic. I *love* my magic."

"I loved it too. Yours and mine. I miss mine. It's like I'm suddenly color-blind. Like . . . But I'm not afraid anymore. Not of Jason Blake or my father—"

"I've never been afraid of my parents. Not like that anyway,"

Tom said. "They're not magic, remember? My mum's like you now."

"But there are other magic-wielders out there who are just like Jason Blake. If you'd given up your magic, you wouldn't have to worry all the time about—"

"You've said all that," Tom said. "I made my decision, okay?"

"No, it's not okay."

"I'm sorry, but it's done. I wasn't *saaaved*." He dragged the last word out and then paused like he was about to say something. Then he shook his head.

"What?" Jay-Tee asked.

"Nothing."

"There was something. It's all over your face."

He shrugged and then cleared his throat, tearing at another leaf. "It's a bit weird."

"I don't mind."

"You won't laugh?"

Jay-Tee shook her head, smiled at him.

"Okay. When Reason was all changed like that—so changed she was hardly human anymore—well, then how could she still have been one of God's children? I mean, don't you believe that we're made in God's image? That's in the Bible, isn't it?"

"Huh?" Jay-Tee asked. It wasn't exactly what she'd been expecting him to say, and she didn't want to confess that she wasn't that strong on the Bible. She'd looked at bits. Well, sort of. The bits they read in church. But she was kind of foggy on most of it.

"Doesn't that mean she was turning into a devil or something?" he continued. "I mean, you said that magic being real means that God is too, but doesn't that also mean that devils are real? Don't you think that's what the strange old man was? And what Reason almost became?"

"I thought you didn't believe in God," Jay-Tee said, stalling. She *had* thought that Raul Cansino might be a devil, but not Reason.

"I don't. I'm just trying to figure out how you think about it. Isn't magic what witches and devils use? Don't you think a magic-wielder is automatically one of the bad guys?"

"No," Jay-Tee said, but it wasn't true. When she was little, she'd worried that she was going to hell because of the magic, despite what her dad told her. "Okay, maybe. I used to think I was cursed, that my family was. That we were a demon family. Don't laugh!"

"I'm not laughing."

"Better not. Anyway, Dad said that was crazy, that being magic made us closer to God, not further away."

"Then why did you want me to give up my magic?"

"Because . . . " Jay-Tee paused, trying to figure it out. He was right. If it made her closer to God and now she'd lost her magic . . . She felt different since her magic had gone, not just because the world was dimmer, but because her thoughts and feelings had changed. But she didn't feel further away from God.

The idea of it, of the change, had been at the edge of her brain, but it was hard making the thoughts come together. Not having magic made her feel less . . . She didn't have a word for it. Since changing, she was thinking about herself less and about Tom and Danny and Reason and Mere more.

"Reason kept saying magic was evil. You heard her, right?" Tom asked.

Jay-Tee nodded. "I'm not sure *evil* is the right word."

"What is, then?"

"Um." Jay-Tee tried to figure it out. The magic going away had made her less selfish. But Tom wasn't selfish. Maybe it wasn't just the magic being gone. All the stuff that had happened since she first met Reason . . . Maybe all of that had made her—she hated to think it, 'cause it was the kind of thing her dad would have said before he became so horrible—but she was a bit more grown-up, more considerate or something. "I think not having magic makes you . . . kinder."

"Kinder?"

"It's probably the wrong word. I don't really know what I mean. Magic changes us. Makes us less, well, *good*? No, that's not it. Whatever it is, it gets worse as you get older. I think my dad was maybe wrong. Magic might bring you closer to God. But only if you use it right. And most people don't. It makes them less good. It's like . . . it's like if you get rich. Money makes lots of people not good people. They get greedy and worry about losing their money and how to make more and they go all evil. I think magic's like that.

"And I don't want that happening to you. I hate the idea of you dying young, but it would be even worse to see you turning into someone like Jason Blake."

"I would never!"

Jay-Tee didn't say anything. But she could imagine it. When he was a bit older and his dying closer. Mere had said she'd give anything for a few more weeks, a few days . . . even if it meant stealing magic from someone else. One day Tom might be like that too.

"Does this mean you don't want to be my girlfriend anymore?" he asked.

Jay-Tee laughed. "Hell, no! I just have to make sure you see the light and don't stray into the path of evil."

Tom laughed, but Jay-Tee was deadly serious. She wasn't going to let him go over to the dark side.

"Shall we start by cleaning up the mess downstairs?" Tom asked.

Jay-Tee rolled her eyes. "Doofus, I was talking big evil! Not lame housework."

It wasn't too bad. They mostly just picked up all the broken magic stuff and threw it into garbage bags. The Cansinos sure had collected a lot of it over the years: antiques and pieces of wood—even the stones were all in pieces now.

Their magic was over. Finished. Done.

It made Jay-Tee feel less bad about her own missing magic. She bet the magic schoolhouse next door looked like a bomb had hit it.

The house was almost spotless before Jay-Tee realized what the other thing bugging her was.

"Where did Jason Blake go?"

"Oh, yeah," Tom said. "Good ol' Jason Blake. I bet he did a runner. You didn't want him to hang around, did you?"

"Are you kidding?" Jay-Tee would live happy if she never saw him again for the rest of her life.

"Do you reckon anything valuable's missing?" Tom asked.

Jay-Tee looked at the full garbage bags. "How would we tell?"

"Too true."

Jay-Tee wasn't sure how she felt. "I wish he'd been punished."

"Did you see that black eye Danny gave him?"

"That's not enough."

"Jay-Tee, he *was* punished," Tom said. "He's got no magic."

"That means *I'm* punished too."

"No," Tom said. "You were *saved*, remember?"

"Very funny." But she was starting to believe that she had been saved. She certainly didn't *feel* punished. Running and dancing weren't the same, but she had the feeling she'd get to like the non-magic version of them too. She was a whole new person. A kinder, less selfish one. But maybe that had already started back when Reason stumbled through the door into a New York blizzard.

One thing was certain: Jay-Tee was starting to like this new person. She was looking forward to seeing how she was going to turn out.

"It must be worse for him," Jay-Tee said, thinking it through out loud. "Magic was all he ever cared about. He didn't love anyone. The only thing for him was magic and now it's gone. I've got lots of things to live for. My life isn't over. Not even close."

"Course not," Tom said. "We're pretty much finished, right? Time to make out?"

Jay-Tee laughed and kissed him.

36
Reason Cansino

I passed the exam. Well, not exactly passed. I got a hundred per cent for the maths, and a strong suggestion that I might get a history and English tutor before I started year ten.

Truth was, I barely made it through the exam. Only the maths problems kept me going. Once the magic had gone, all my emotions came rushing back. I was knocked sideways by love, anger, jealousy, hurt. It was all I could do to concentrate.

I sobbed for ten solid minutes after I put my pencil down.

After that, there was no getting out of seeing a counsellor once a week. Isabella Sanditon said to tell her everything. Hah! But I did tell her about the baby and how scared I am to be fifteen and almost a mother. Especially when I don't know how I feel about my own mother and how she brought me up, knowing so much about mathematics and science and almost nothing about anything else. How she lied to me.

Omission, we decided—the counsellor and me—is as bad as a lie.

Sarafina apologised, explained. And I didn't forgive her, and then I did, and then I didn't again, and we screamed and fought. Knowing that she was right, had always been right, in a way, helps a lot. She always knew that magic was evil.

And really, if she hadn't kept me away from Mere, would I have been able to save us? For that alone I forgive her. Today anyway.

Mere forgave me for taking the magic away. Sometimes I'm not entirely sure if I forgive myself. I can't help wondering what it would have been like: me and my baby floating in Cansino's world together—no pain ever.

What mother doesn't imagine giving *that* to her child?

Sarafina and Mere have been locked in plenty of their own fights. Hardly a day goes by that Sarafina doesn't threaten to scarper back out bush, out the window, down the drainpipe, and away. But mostly they just scream at each other.

School starting in February turned out to be a relief.

It's school for both me and Sarafina; she's trying to finish the education she barely started. I'm pretty sure she won't run away again till she's all educated.

My grandfather Alexander/Jason Blake disappeared some time between me closing my eyes to turn the magic off and Jennifer Ishii coming to the door. None of us miss him. Jay-Tee hopes he was left destitute, with no credit cards in his pocket and no explanation to the authorities as to how he wound up in Australia without his passport.

But then a package arrived for Tom. It contained three keys and four addresses, in Bangkok, Auckland, Dallas, and New York. So I suspect that my magicless grandfather is doing okay. Though why he cares about Tom I don't know, unless he just didn't want his precious doors to go to waste.

I was right about Jay-Tee and Tom. While I'd almost been swallowed whole by my great-great-great-etc.-grandfather's magic, they'd been off kissing! Unbelievable. And to top it off, they kept disappearing together, leaving me alone with my guilty, angry, loving mother and grandmother. More than enough to make *me* want to run away.

If I could have, I would have.

And no boyfriend for me. Danny hadn't ever been anything more than a magic-induced crush (well, *partly* magic-induced). When Raul had started to unravel, the Cansino magic wanted a baby, and Danny was conveniently there to be the father. I was grateful that he was decent about it. He wants to help with raising the baby, and not just with money. He wants the baby to know him, to have a father, even if he lives such a long way away.

There's so much to cope with. The coming baby and Sarafina. They both need me.

And Jay-Tee too. She couldn't stay in Sydney with Tom like she wanted. She had to go home with Danny, and while the adults sorted out her passport problems, and when she wasn't off with Tom, she spent her time crying about not getting to stay and worrying about Tom using too much of his magic.

All of which barely affected him. He didn't regret his decision. Not for a second. I don't think he believes he'll die. Who really believes that until it's too late? And once a week he makes one of us something excellent to wear. Mostly Jay-Tee, of course, but he never entirely neglects the rest of us. Tom reckons everything is roses: he has a girlfriend he loves, he's had the mother he hardly knew returned to him, and there are no more secrets or lies in his family.

I did my best to persuade him. But I don't think anything would have changed his mind. Tom doesn't believe he's anything without magic. And sometimes, when the Fibonaccis aren't cascading through my head like they should, sometimes I think he might be right.

Life was easier before I knew magic was real. Before Sarafina went mad. But I'm not sorry it changed. My life with Sarafina hadn't been the way I'd always told myself it was. Sarafina did wrong by me, keeping me from making friends, from knowing the truth. And even if that's how I ultimately saved my family from magic, it still wasn't right.

I have friends now, a family of more than just me and Sarafina. And though they all drive me insane, I wouldn't give them up.

I can't count the way I used to. The numbers don't unfurl in my head, but I'm still better at maths than most people. I've got a good shot at going to university and becoming a mathematician. Jay-Tee still runs faster than most and dances like a dervish. Sarafina can still tell direction by the stars. Mere is still one of the top actuaries in the state.

My baby's due in October. Danny's going to fly back for it, even though that's right after he starts university and joins his fancy university basketball team. Jay-Tee will be here too.

We're calling the baby Magic Galeano Cansino. And she'll be as magic-free as I am. I think she'll be the luckiest baby in the world.

Epilogue

The first time Tom ever held a baby in his arms was when Mere handed him Magic. She was less than a day old.

He'd already pointed out that it was a stupid name. Aside from the obvious objections, what was her nickname going to be? Maggi? Like she was a soup mix or something? And Maggie and Mags weren't much better.

But Danny was all, *Are you crazy?* Magic (Some-surname-Tom-forgot) was the greatest basketballer (or, sorry, *basketball player*—Tom never got it right) of all time! It's an honour to have such a name, blah, blah, blah. And Reason said she liked it and that besides, it was a nice reminder of the family secret.

Tom kind of thought him being around and still being magic would be reminder enough. But apparently not.

So they ignored him about the name and now they were ignoring him about not wanting to hold her.

He *really* didn't want to hold Magic. Babies grossed him out. Tom didn't understand how anyone could think they were pretty. Yet there were Mere, Sarafina, and Jay-Tee leaning over the hospital bed, pretty much ignoring Reason, who was lying there knackered, cooing over her baby with its squished-up little face like a monkey's. Even Danny was grinning and saying how gorgeous she was.

Gorgeous! Her skin was a weird colour somewhere between blue and khaki, which might work for a coat or a pair of jeans but was a bit of a disaster as a skin tone. And she had *way* too much hair on her head. It looked like a badly made wig.

"Do I *have* to hold her?" he asked. "Babies make me nervous."

"Tom! You're practically her uncle," Jay-Tee said. "Of course you have to hold her. Plus wait till you smell her." Jay-Tee put her nose to the baby's too-hairy head and breathed in deep. "She smells soooo gooooood!"

Eww.

Danny grinned. "She does smell good, doesn't she?"

Reason nodded.

"Fine," Tom said, "but if I drop her I want it noted that you were all warned and it's not my fault."

"You won't drop her," Mere said, coming around the bed with the tiny little hairy monkey-child. "Just make sure you're supporting her head and neck."

"She doesn't *have* a neck."

"Her head, then. Make sure your hand is under her head."

"What if she shits on me?"

"Tom!" Jay-Tee and Danny said at once. Reason just smiled.

"She's wearing a nappy, Tom," Mere said. "Nothing will get on you."

"Fine." Tom tried to arrange himself the way Mere was demonstrating. Then, before he was ready, she eased Magic into his arms, making sure his right hand was under her microscopic head.

Tom didn't notice the way she smelt. He was too distracted by the tingling that had started up in his arms. He sat down in the one armchair, clutching the baby tight. His eyes narrowed until they were filled with hexagons.

"What's wrong, Tom?"

"Nothing . . ." he said, because nothing *was* wrong. Reason and Danny's baby was right as rain. It was just that they'd been spot-on with the baby's name. She lived up to it completely.

But she didn't have the weird, golem-y, Cansino kind of magic; she had the old-fashioned kind, just like him. Tom wondered why it hadn't occurred to any of them that even after turning the Cansino magic off, Magic would still have the normal kind.

Oh well. Too late now.

He looked up at them: Jay-Tee, Reason, Mere, Sarafina, and Danny. Not one of them had the tiniest skerrick of magic. Dead spots. They were looking back in his direction, but not at him: at Magic, full of happiness because of the new baby. How was he going to tell them?

"She's heavier than I thought," Tom said. "Doesn't smell *too* bad, I s'pose. If you like that kind of thing."

Later, Tom decided. He'd tell them that there was another magic-wielder in the Cansino line *later*.

THE END

Glossary

bitumen: it can mean both a paved (sealed) road and the black substance (usually asphalt) used to pave (seal) the road

a bit thing: particular. If someone is a bit thing about how they dress it means they are particular about their attire.

blue heeler: an Australian cattle dog

bugger: damn. The thing you say when you stub your toe and don't want to be *too* rude.

chunder: vomit

croc: short for *crocodile*

daggy: a dag is someone lacking in social graces, someone who is eccentric and doesn't fit in. The closest U.S. approximation is *nerd*, but a dag doesn't necessarily know a thing about computers or mathematics or science. *Daggy* is the adjectival form.

dog's breakfast: a mess, a disaster. To make a dog's breakfast out of something is to really mess it up.

four-wheel drive: SUV

grouse: excellent, wonderful. However, it can also be a verb meaning *to complain*, as in, "I wish you'd stop grousing about everything."

knackered: very tired, exhausted

Libs: abbreviation of the Liberal Party of Australia, which despite the name, is the conservative party.

lift: elevator

mad: in Australia it means *crazy;* in the United States, *angry*

poxy: unpleasant, crappy, or annoying

skerrick: a very small amount

slab: a case of two dozen cans or bottles of beer

unco: short for *unco-ordinated*. Someone who's unco isn't much chop at sports or juggling. For some unco types, even standing can be a challenge. Your humble author has been known to be unco, though only since infancy.

wanker: poseur

Acknowledgments

Way back in late 2003, Eloise Flood took a chance on me and bought this trilogy on the basis of a proposal. I'd never sold a novel before, and there she was, buying three unwritten ones. I still can't get over it. Without Eloise I doubt these books would exist, and if they did, they wouldn't be nearly as good. Thank you. You've been the best publisher, editor, and friend possible. And extra thanks for bringing in Liesa Abrams as my other editor. There isn't a better team in the business.

And thank you, Scott Westerfeld, for being my first and last reader, meanest critic, sternest taskmaster, and for convincing me to become a full-time novelist before I'd sold a word. Gulp!

The Razorbill team of Eloise, Liesa, Andy Ball, and Margaret Wright is extraordinary. Wow. It's been a privilege working with you all. Thank you for everything.

Marc J. Cohen provided three beautiful covers, Christopher Grassi made the innards look lovely, Annie McDonnell did a great job proofing, and Polly Watson is the bestest copy editor eva.

Thanks to everyone else at Penguin who worked hard on this trilogy, from sales to marketing to publicity to all the other departments. Extra-special thanks to Sharyn November for giving the paperback editions of the trilogy such a wonderful home at Firebird.

My foreign rights agent, Whitney Lee, is the greatest and so far has found a home for the *Magic or Madness* trilogy in Brazil, France, Germany, Italy, Taiwan, and Thailand. Thank you for all your hard work.

Some of the very best critiquers read and dissected *Magic's Child*. Without Holly Black, Cassandra Clare, Karen Joy Fowler, Pamela Freeman, Margo Lanagan, and Scott Westerfeld, it would've been the worst dog's breakfast imaginable. I owe you all big-time. Especially you, Karen, for being excellently annoying and inexcusable and saving this novel.

Thank you Holly Black, Libba Bray, Cassandra Clare, Diana Peterfreund, and John Scalzi for being my lifeline when we were all struggling with books due around the same time. Don't know what I'd've done without you lot to compare notes with and whinge to.

Thanks to the fabulous New Bitches: we all rule!

David Levithan and everyone at the YA drinks nights in NYC are wondrous beyond words. I don't make many of the meetings, but the ones I get to are golden.

Thanks to Luz Barrón for removing all hassles from my life while I wrote most of the first draft in San Miguel de Allende in Mexico.

Denise Lynch and Tony Vinson, respectively, answered my questions about social-work services and education in NSW. Any mistakes are mine, all mine.

Since the first volume in this trilogy was published, many advocates—librarians, teachers, and booksellers—have gotten behind my books in ways I never imagined. Thank you to Agnes Nieuwenhuizen, Mike Shuttleworth, and Lili Wilkinson of the Centre for Youth Literature, in Melbourne, Victoria; Katheleen Hornig, Merri Lindgren, Hollis Rudiger, and Megan Schliesman of the Cooperative Children's Book Center in Madison, Wisconsin; and also to Sara Couri, Megan Honing, John Klima, Jack Martin, Kimberly Paone, Sandra Payne, and Karyn Silverman. Ron Serdiuk of Pulp Fiction books in Brisbane has been a one-man promotion machine. Everyone at Galaxy and Gleebooks in Sydney has been awesome, as has Justin Ackroyd of Slow Glass Books in Melbourne. Not to mention Dreamhaven in Minneapolis and Borderlands in San Francisco, as well as Jennifer Laughran of Books Inc. in San Francisco and everyone at Peter Glassman's glorious Books of Wonder in NYC.

Another unexpected boon of being a published writer is all the wonderful folks who've written to me about the trilogy. It makes a huge difference to know that these books are being read and enjoyed.

Lastly, my family: Niki Bern, John Bern, Jan Larbalestier, and Scott Westerfeld. Thank you for the security of knowing that, whatever happens, you four have got my back.